"Your little revelation last night was unexpected," said Marcus. "I never expected you to say such a thing."

His eyes locked with hers, and he took a step back. And then another, his eyes burning her as he slowly walked backward. She stood, as if mesmerized, and followed him as he skirted around the chairs without even looking behind him. Abruptly he reached out and tugged her into an alcove. Shivers streaked through her.

He touched a curl that lolled along her shoulder blade. "What would you have me say, Bella?"

You are the most beautiful woman I've ever known or *Let's retire from this ballroom to pursue a more wicked pastime* or *I've loved you forever.*

Yes, the last one.

"You don't have to say anything, Marcus. Forgive me for a late night's rambles."

He fingered the curl. "So you didn't mean it?"

Her eyes tried desperately to close, but his gold gaze pinned her. Standing here, in front of him, in a silent alcove, the portraits on the wall leaning closer to hear, and having to choose whether to bare part of her soul or to play safely and laugh it off.

To be left with a decision, a declaration or not. That whatever she said would determine the course of future events.

"I meant every word."

What Isabella Desires

Anne Mallory

AVON

An Imprint of HarperCollinsPublishers

This is a work of fiction. Names, characters, places, and incidents are products of the author's imagination or are used fictitiously and are not to be construed as real. Any resemblance to actual events, locales, organizations, or persons, living or dead, is entirely coincidental.

AVON BOOKS
An Imprint of HarperCollins*Publishers*
10 East 53rd Street
New York, New York 10022-5299

First Avon Books paperback printing: August 2007

Avon Trademark Reg. U.S. Pat. Off. and in Other Countries,
Marca Registrada, Hecho en U.S.A.
HarperCollins® is a registered trademark of HarperCollins Publishers.

Printed in the U.S.A.

10 9 8 7 6 5 4 3 2 1

To Mom, for everything once again.

To all of the lovely readers who read Masquerading the Marquess *or* Daring the Duke, *and wrote to ask for Roth's story. I hope you enjoy the tale.*

To Esther—

I hope you enjoy the book. :) Hugs to you!

Anne Mallory

Special thanks to May, Paige, and Pam.

What
Isabella
Desires

Chapter 1

She watched as he moved through the crowd, his tall, languid grace at odds with the look in his golden eyes, alert and predatory.

Women whispered that Marcus Stewart, Lord Roth, was a fallen angel. With his dark hair and whiskey eyes, his lush lips and artistic hands, she had never believed otherwise.

He nodded politely to one of the friendlier couples of the ton; the other man standing taller, the woman growing more animated as the conversation continued. Even from her vantage point across the room, she could see a small smile curve Marcus's beautiful mouth and a warmer light enter his usually cold and distant eyes.

She swallowed, her throat suddenly dry in the moist late spring air. She had been privy to his real smile, the one that reached all the way to his eyes and lit up his face, the one that caused her to forget her own name and her body to lean closer to his. Silk felt smoother and chocolate tasted better when he unleashed that smile. And she was selfish and wicked enough to want it all to herself, to taste him as his mouth curled, to feel his long, lean fingers curve around her waist and into her hair as he drew her forth.

She saw him moving on into the crush of people and watched full lips thin into a dangerous smirk as he said something cutting to a man she knew he disliked. That was the danger with fallen angels, she had always thought—they could show you all the delights of heaven or easily deliver you into the fires of hell. Most women found the dichotomy all the more exciting, and though she might scoff aloud, in the darkness of her bedroom, ensconced beneath her covers, left to her dreams, her mind agreed.

He finally stopped his forward momentum at a foursome of the fashionable and notorious. As he joined their conversation, his shoulders relaxed infinitesimally; unnoticeable to anyone else, but she hadn't spent years observing him for naught. The Angelfords and Marstons were his closest friends. Friends with whom he could relax and dispense with the facade that society demanded; friends who generated more than their own share of gossip.

That his two best friends were now happily married had society poised for Marcus's capitulation as well. But he was not the least bit interested in marriage, and although the reasons for his feelings were secret, the actual matter of his opinion was not.

That had not stopped every matchmaking mama with daughters of a marriageable age from throwing their daughters in his path. Oh, no. The Roth title was distinguished and enduring, more so than many of the dukedoms. Marcus had power, lots of it.

That, coupled with his looks and brooding nature, made for no shortage of young misses, or married women, ready to fall at his feet. All of them wishing to be the one to tame him.

He carried a darkness that only dissolved when he unleashed one of "those" smiles. And perhaps, more desirous than the feeling of the smiles turning her to goo, she longed to see the shadows behind his eyes banished and his inner light relit.

She wanted to be more than just his chess partner and friend. She wanted—

Pain crashed through her foot, causing her to jerk upright and look to the side. Her mother, her handsome features highlighted by her upswept hair, continued to look straight ahead at the stuttering young man conversing with them, acting as if she hadn't just deliberately crushed her daughter's toes to dust.

Isabella, Lady Willoughby, quickly contained her mortification at being caught staring. Not that it mattered overly, since she wasn't one on whom the ton kept close tabs. She was just nice, plain Isabella Willoughby, widow of an equally nice and plain member of society. And like the pretty but unremarkable paper that covered the walls of the ballroom—she belonged in the scene but was eminently forgettable.

No one expected much from her besides pleasant conversation and a convenient way to introduce their daughters into society. Her spotless reputation and the fact that she genuinely liked to make outings easier for the young debutantes in their first seasons had ensured the ton matrons' continued benevolence in the ten years since Isabella's own debut.

Of course, a single whiff of scandal would grind all past benevolence to dust. Thus spoke society.

The man talking to her mother excused himself, allowing her mother to pin her with a knowing gaze. Isabella tried to look contrite, but her mother shook her head in exasperation. Polite exasperation, of course. After all, they were still in the public eye.

"Isabella, you need to stop *woolgathering*. One day someone other than your mother is going to catch you staring."

Isabella cringed. Sometimes her mother could

still make her feel fourteen. "I know, I know. I'm sorry, Mama."

Charlotte Herringfield tapped her fan and sighed. "Don't apologize, dear. I still don't know if your father and I did the right thing by pushing you into marriage with a man that wasn't . . ." She waved her fan in Marcus's general direction.

Isabella swallowed. "You didn't force me to marry George. And it was the right decision. George was a . . . was a good friend," she finished softly.

"But you didn't love him." Her mother's shrewd eyes missed little.

"No, I loved him, you know I did." And she truly had, even though she had never been *in* love with him. He had been a good companion and friend. They had been comfortable. Her stomach had never clenched and the sheer thrill of life had never occurred in his presence, but then those were not necessarily the things on which to base a marriage. Still, she had never experienced that extra spark with George, and had always felt that she'd somehow slighted *him*. That she was the one who had denied him love. He had scoffed lightly at her confession on the day he had asked for her hand, instead joking and making her laugh.

"Not the type of love we are talking about." Her mother's look was slightly censorious. They had beaten around the topic many times since his death.

"George always said that we shared something better," she explained. "Friendship. Respect. The gardens." She laughed, but it was slightly strained. "He was just so ill much of the time, especially there at the end . . . "

Her mother had a faraway look in her eyes. "Oh, Isabella. I just wanted you to be happy." She sighed and looked toward Marcus, who ironically was now chatting amiably with Isabella's father. "I still do, of course."

"I was, Mama. I am."

"Hmmm . . . "

Isabella narrowed her eyes. "Don't hmmm me, Mama. I'm no longer in leading strings."

Her mother patted her arm, somewhat sadly. "No, indeed you are not." She straightened. "Will you be coming with us to Devonshire?"

The season was nearly over, and her parents were always eager to return to the country. Her gaze shifted back to Marcus and her father. "Perhaps in a few weeks."

"Mmmm . . . "

"You are losing your vocabulary, Mama. Need I be worried?"

Her mother swatted her with her fan. "When I'm old and infirm, I will still be able to match wits with you, my dear."

Isabella briefly rested her head on her mother's shorter shoulder, breaking a rule of etiquette and for once not caring. "I know you will."

Her mother harrumphed, but looked pleased all the same. Her father was making his way toward them through the crowd and Isabella blinked, realizing that she had lost sight of Marcus. Perhaps that was for the best.

"Francis is on his way over, so I'm sure we will be leaving for home soon. Dreadful crush, and we don't want to be stuck with thirty carriages in front of us and nothing to do about it. We'll call on you before we leave town, of course." She paused, as if wrestling with something. "And perhaps it is time you pull one of your dreams into reality, dearest. A woman in your position is accorded more freedom than you had when you were eighteen or even twenty-one. Just don't do anything too far beyond the pale."

She grimaced, and Isabella grinned. Her mother was very straitlaced about certain things, so for her to suggest something daring like that nearly defied imagination.

"Why, Mother, you wound me."

"I will wound you if you get into trouble," she muttered. "Don't make me regret this."

Isabella gave her a squeeze, and her father winked as he joined them. "Did I miss something?"

It was on the tip of her tongue to repeat what her mother had said—her mother's glare only a minor deterrent. "Mother is just worried about what you two will do inside a carriage for an hour while you wait in the queue to leave. Shall I find you a deck of cards?"

"I'm sure we can find something to occupy the time." Her father waggled his dark brows and her mother's face tinged pink.

Charlotte Herringfield gave a sniff, pressed her empty cup into Isabella's hand and turned to walk away, but Isabella noticed that she stayed close to her father's body as they left.

Her parents' marriage was a love match by any standard. She wondered if that aspect of life would have been different if she had been reared by parents who were distant and cold. Would she still pine for love and all it entailed?

She tucked an errant strand of hair behind her ear—as usual, her too heavy hair strained to be free.

Turning back to the crowd, she nodded as one of the more timid debutantes passed by and smiled. No, she was not unhappy with her lot in life, no matter what the pitter patter in her heart said when she brushed Marcus's hand while playing chess or cards. At least she was still able to be near the one she loved.

The dance floor had grown even more crowded,

the young bucks and maidens eager to catch their final dances. She watched a risqué widow capture the attention of the men on the edges of the floor as she expertly whirled in her partner's arms, the train of her rose-lavender dress swirling about as she arched her back to expose more of her décolletage. Isabella had to keep from arching a brow as the men salivated. They would assuredly vie for the widow's hand in the next dance.

Isabella looked down at her own demure ball gown. A bright blue, not the perfect shade for her skin, but adequate and within the fashion dictates of the season, which edged into the brighter colors. It was unfortunate that the bold, deeper colors she looked best in were not currently in fashion. Oh, every color could be *made* fashionable, but the character she played in society would never be dressed in something daring or risqué.

She bit her lip. And yet, there was a tiny part of her—all right, more than a tiny part—that wanted to whirl and twirl and transform into a butterfly instead of a passable moth.

She compared the dresses of the other married and widowed ladies in the crowd to her own gown. Yes, she was definitely one of the more modest ladies in attendance. Being on the edge of fashion had never been one of her aims. Just being in fashion was enough. She'd much rather be tending her garden, or playing chess, or speaking with Marcus, than worrying about what to wear. However, if she wanted to be seen as more than just a friendly face, she knew she would have to rearrange her priorities.

She sighed. She had fallen in love with him ten years ago, and even now, at twenty-eight and a respectable distance from widow's weeds, she still found him the most entrancing man she'd ever met.

He, of course, had never returned the sentiment.

She continued to survey the ballroom and nearly dropped her mother's cup. Marcus was looking straight at her, his whiskey and gold eyes connecting with hers. He smiled, but there was no heat in his gaze, no glint of passion. She swallowed heavily and smiled warmly in return. She was well-practiced by now at keeping her real emotions hidden. She looked away, pretending interest in a raucous group near the corner.

She was a coward. A complete and utter milksop. What if she showed her interest and his eyes turned cold or disappointed? She had seen that expression on his face for others. She didn't know if she could bear it being turned on her.

And if that wasn't a cowardly thought. . .

Yes, it was definitely time to take her courage in hand. She just couldn't take this any longer.

She would make a few changes and see what happened. She just wanted to—

A warm whisper of wind caressed her ear, and she knew who it was before his husky, sinful voice formed words. "Good evening, Bella."

Chapter 2

The first thing most people noticed about Isabella Willoughby was her hair. Thick, lustrous and coal black, it evoked images of harem veils and moonlight bouncing off the dark wavy sea.

To most people it was her one outstanding feature, usually constrained to a bun or upswept in a style that inhibited it from tumbling around her shoulders in the lazy haze it deserved. Marcus had often thought she should allow the riotous mass to have its way.

As he leaned forward to whisper in her ear, a curl brushed his cheek and the fine edges of the tendrils slid across his upper lip.

"Good evening, Bella."

She stiffened before turning. He greeted her with a lazy grin and watched her expression ease into a welcoming smile. Others might never look past her glorious hair, but the thing that he liked best about Isabella was the way the edges of her lips curled upward, spreading to the tiny crinkles at the edges of her eyes. Her smile transcended mere lips or eyes and showed something much deeper.

"Good evening, Mar—Lord Roth."

His lips curved again. "You can call me Marcus in public, Bella. I'm surely not going to start calling you Lady Willoughby."

He had never liked her married name.

She raised a brow. "Lord Roth, I see that you are in pleasant spirits tonight," she said somewhat tartly, but the sparkle in her eyes spoke otherwise. "A rousing discussion of the weather with Miss Cross?"

"Were you watching me, Bella?" he said in a low, seductive voice, amused when her lips tightened. "Trying to make sure the ladies under your wing don't come to harm?"

"But of course," she said airily. "The infamous Lord Roth, despoiler of innocents, is on the prowl tonight, didn't you know?"

The light scent of wildflowers, uniquely Isabella's, drifted up to him. "Sounds like a man who knows how to have a good time. Do introduce us, won't you?"

She waved a hand in dismissal, her fan clacking at her wrist. "He isn't that exciting. Likes to bury his nose in a book when he could be out in the garden or enjoying the sunset. You are aware of the type, I'm sure."

"The scholarly type, you mean? Not the brutish, slightly addled type like our dear friend Lord Marston?"

"Brutish, whatever *do* you mean?" Her tone was questioning, but he could see the amusement in her blue eyes for his poke at Stephen.

"Men who can't do a thing with their brains and must resort to constantly moving things about with their hands."

"I think most women appreciate a man who knows what to do with his hands."

The undercurrent of the conversation rippled through him. Her face held only innocent interest, but even as a staid and proper lady, she was far too intelligent not to recognize a double entendre when it passed her lips.

One of her fingers tapped the bottom of an empty cup, and he saw the bottom of her blue dress sway slightly to hide a definite fidget beneath.

He considered Isabella a friend, and would never have entertained thoughts of a less savory nature about her, but his lips suddenly disconnected from that part of his brain.

"No woman has ever had cause for concern with me in that area, I assure you."

She nodded, and her wide eyes narrowed in

thought as she examined him. "You *are* an exceptional pianist. I suppose there's that. You certainly have the fingers to play."

The disconnect in his brain seemed to have encompassed more than just the route to his mouth. It seemed his ears had been affected as well. Either that or Isabella Willoughby had secretly sprouted horns.

A flash of movement from the dance floor made her head turn, but he continued to watch her face, trying to decipher what the devil was going on. An expression of longing, of deep desire, passed over her face. He turned to see what had captured her attention.

A woman was dancing particularly close to her partner, her dress swirling around her. He looked back to see the expression wiped clean from Isabella's face, her eyes riveted back on him, patiently awaiting his response. What did she long for—the dance, the closeness of the couple, or the man? Fenton Ellerby was a scoundrel, and there was something about the man that always put him off, but Ellerby's handsome features and devil-may-care attitude inspired blushes and swoons wherever he went. More than one young lady had been shuffled off to the country after a rumored liaison with him.

Did Isabella carry a tendre for Ellerby? That could only end badly. Women like her, gentle, caring and unerringly polite, would always be sought by the well-meaning men of the ton. But the rogues preferred prettier, curvier, richer meat.

He would know.

He opened his mouth to say something, but her expression suddenly shifted again. Longing? Disappointment? Resolve?

"Goodness, Miss Cross is waving me over. I do hope she hasn't gotten herself into a pickle with Mr. Sethy. I must be off." She gave him a brilliant smile and pressed something into his hand.

"Be a dear and dispose of this, would you, Lord Roth?" Her fingers lightly brushed across his, leaving behind her empty lemonade cup. "Oh, and Knight to C6. I believe that is check, my lord." She sauntered away with her usual stately grace.

Well, damn.

He looked at the empty cup in his hand, his mind still processing what had just transpired. His eyes tracked her movements. Was she leaving to move closer to Ellerby, who had just insinuated himself in a group near Miss Cross?

And damn it all, he had completely expected her to move her rook, as that had been consistent with her previous strategies.

He could easily remove his king from check. The move she had just made was an obvious one, but not at all her style. All of a sudden she was changing her game? It was going to take him well into the night to figure out a countermove to whatever her new strategy was.

"You look as if that cup has done you immeasurable harm."

Marcus looked up to see James Trenton, Marquess of Angelford, staring at him in amusement.

"I believe it may well have."

"And how is Lady Willoughby tonight? I haven't had the chance to greet her. Scared her off again, have you?"

He gave James a dark look. "She moved her knight."

"Ah."

Marcus dragged a hand through his hair. "Never mind." He scanned the crowd, looking for the rest of their close-knit group. "Where is Lady Angelford?"

"Socializing. Calliope knew I wanted to speak to you alone."

Marcus immediately looked back at James. "Something's gone wrong again, I take it?"

James's expression darkened. "Yes, we need to speak outside."

Stephen Chalmers, Duke of Marston, appeared at their sides as they walked through the thinning crush of bodies and the gilded terrace doors.

"I take it I'm the last to know this time," Marcus said, casting a look at Stephen.

"You've lost some of your touch, old boy. Always with your finger on the rhythm of the world. But lately taken to the ladies more than usual. You've been through what, four of them in the last two months?"

Marcus made a rude gesture, which he covered from a passing couple by pretending to cough.

"Not a ton record, by any means," Stephen continued, blithely ignoring the gesture as they found a spot on the terrace where they could observe others without being overheard. "But rather gadabout of you. None of them up to your standard? Or are you trying to escape from something?"

The last comment hit a little too close. Marcus scowled.

"I don't know what you found wrong with the last one. Mrs. Cavenwell, was it? Seemed a good enough sort for a mistress."

Marcus gave him a withering look. "I'll make sure to inform your wife."

But Stephen just smiled. "Audrey also thinks Mrs. Cavenwell would make you a good mistress."

She would. Audrey wasn't the usual society wife. "I don't want or need a mistress."

Sometimes he wondered if he wanted friends either, with ones like these.

Stephen clapped Marcus on the back and

looked at James. "Calliope will be most pleased, won't she, James? She has her eye on a few marital prospects for you and has just been waiting for you to come around."

Marcus resisted the urge to find a quill and jab it through his temple.

While Stephen chattered, James watched Marcus silently. "You've changed over the past few years," he said. "We've all noticed."

Stephen shed his carefree facade and he too looked up at Marcus through shrewd eyes. They had been dancing around this subject for weeks.

Marcus waved them off in dismissal. "Stress over the past years' happenings. It's not as if the two of you have been in any position to judge. I remember you both muttering and wailing until your wives whipped you into form."

"We're worried about you. All of us."

Marcus looked at Stephen. Of the three of them, Stephen had been the one able and willing to express his feelings. Marcus envied him that, even as he cringed at the banality. With his free upbringing and carefree attitude, Stephen had never expected to inherit the title that had been thrust upon him a year ago. In contrast, he and James had known since infancy that they were to carry the family mantles—the pride, arrogance, and responsibility. It predisposed one to a more stoic mien. And now Stephen outranked them both, though he tended to eschew the political and power manipulating that Marcus loved and James tolerated.

Upon gaining the inheritance, Stephen had promptly pitched his title's inherent power and his House seat into Marcus's hands. It had been a mutually beneficial arrangement.

Marcus had already wielded enough power to select who sat in any office in the government, his power more than the other two men's, no matter that they were a duke and marquess, and he a mere baron. After gaining Stephen's block, he had wielded more power than anyone in the House. Perhaps more than anyone in the country who was not of royal blood.

Political intrigue was one of his loves. The love that would be the first to fall.

Cold swept through him. He was getting quite used to the feelings of dread these days.

"Don't be ridiculous, Stephen. There is nothing to worry about."

"You're grooming St. John to take your place. Why? You love all that bloody trite and boring mess in the House. Even for the Foreign Office, I've seen you mentoring him. Right scary, it is."

Marcus knew his face showed nothing. He had been playing power games for far too long to reveal anything. And he had an edge over the other two in years. Not by much, but he'd been playing politics and shadowing the underground longer. Whereas James and Stephen were good, excellent in fact, at what they both did, he was better. It was his life's work. His goal. His ambition. And it allowed him to forget, to escape, if only for the length of a job. And then he would find another job, another task, another political intrigue on which to focus.

He didn't fidget, didn't brush his sleeve—telling signs that might give him away.

"Sinjun is a good sort. Young, though. Loves the ladies a bit too much. Better tell Audrey to watch her sister with him."

A half smile played around Stephen's mouth. "I know. But you are changing the subject."

"Sinjun is growing and realizes he needs to take over more. You are well past that stage." He looked down his nose. "You need to start sitting more regularly in the House."

Stephen waved a hand dismissively. "But you love it. Better to keep me out of the way. I'm like a puppy, and you wouldn't want drool on the House floor, would you?"

Marcus smiled despite himself. "It would be right in line with types like Ainsworth and Yarnley, who piss all over it."

"So why are you grooming Sinjun, and pushing me, all of a sudden?"

Marcus cocked a brow. Stephen had made too many trips to the lemonade bowl if he thought that tactic would work. "It's not all of a sudden. Now, are you going to tell me the real reason we're out here?"

They were his friends. Real friends. And he didn't have many of those in his type of work, so he valued their opinions greatly. But he wouldn't talk about his personal life. Not even with them.

Stephen looked like he might argue, so Marcus turned to James. "Angelford. You have always been the more sensible one. Out with it."

James raised a brow. "Fletcher's missing. One of the officers informed me about twenty minutes past. The grab had the stamp of the Crosby gang."

Marcus swore, his bones growing cold as he instantly calculated what this would cost them and where new men would need to be deployed. He wasn't set to meet with his men tonight, something he'd have to rectify.

"Is there any other information?"

"No."

"Third abduction this week," Stephen added.

Marcus gripped Isabella's cup in his palm. "We obviously didn't get the right Crosby member."

"No."

"These one word answers aren't endearing you to me, Angelford."

"Shall I pretend to move my rook instead?"

"Ha, bloody ha."

Three men missing or dead. And the key players still unknown. Marcus clutched the cup. He hated making mistakes. And this mistake was costing his men their lives.

"Have you talked to Hildebrand?"

"No, but the officer said Hildebrand wanted us to report in early tomorrow," James said.

"He must be going spare," Stephen said. "Been a bit tetchy of late."

Hildebrand was fairly new to the position, after the death of their last leader. Best not to think about that, though, Marcus told himself. Another mistake in a long list of them. Marcus had been asked to lead the office, and had seriously considered taking the position, but in the end chose to remain in the field.

He might not be able to express his emotions as freely as Stephen, but he didn't want to end up as one of the wax museum figures from burning the desk work at both ends—politics and intrigue. He wouldn't be able to do either for much longer anyway.

"Yes, Hildebrand would be a bit tetchy."

Stephen looked past him, toward the terrace doors. "It's getting late. Audrey and Calliope are waiting for us by the doors."

"Off with you two," Marcus said. "Go back to your doting wives."

James cocked his head, and Marcus felt the stirrings of a headache. Not this again. Why did every bloody, happily married person feel the need to interfere in the lives of others?

He held up a hand to forestall the meddling. "Angelford, I'll have your head on a platter if you say one more word about my private life."

Stephen's green eyes twinkled, but James must have seen something in Marcus's face beyond the warning because he gave him a mock salute and pushed Stephen toward the doors.

Marcus felt the stirrings of a more severe headache as a wave of nausea broke over him. He swallowed and inhaled deeply. *Damn*. He looked around the terrace, pretending an interest in the foliage. Mentally he counted the steps to the doors just in case. The layout of the ballroom was clearly impressed in his mind, but the shifting bodies on and around the dance floor always presented a challenge.

His vision dimmed around the edges as he strode inside. It was past time for him to leave.

He deftly maneuvered around the dancers and headed for the door, hoping to get to the blessed darkness of his carriage before he became physically ill. Perhaps it was time to leave London for good. Finish up this last case and retire to the country.

Away from pushy, well-meaning friends, the work he loved, and all the things he preferred not to think about.

Chapter 3

I sabella dropped her cushion on the grass and sank onto it.

"My lady, one moment."

Her maid tugged her bonnet forward and Isabella glared from beneath the laced fringe. "Bertie, my bonnet is just fine. Pull your own forth, if you must. I have nary a freckle, more's the pity."

Her maid gasped.

"It would serve you right if I did," Isabella muttered, and picked up her spade. "You're gasping as if London were ablaze."

"It would be!"

"Lady Angelford has a few freckles, and I daresay they look quite attractive on her."

Bertie started muttering to herself about difficult charges and placed the rest of Isabella's gardening tools near her. Bertie might be a pain about some things, but was tireless in helping her when she needed it.

"Hand me the first of the white lilies, will you, Bertie?"

Her maid dutifully handed one over from the basket and started weeding some of the creepers near the left edge of the plot, using her own hand awl. The plot had doubled in size last year, and Isabella was grateful the man who managed the land, a somewhat cantankerous old codger, had finally allowed her to have more space. She didn't know what finally convinced him to relinquish more ground. His disdain for flowers was evident. Perhaps Stephen had said something after she'd bemoaned it one night. The caretaker had been somewhat obsequious ever since.

They worked in silence until Isabella finished planting the patch of lilies. She brushed an arm across her eyes.

"The orange pansies now, I think. And then I'll stake the delphiniums. No matter that lilies are appropriate, I don't want the delphs flopping."

Bertie's pinched, concentrated expression softened a notch. "The delphiniums are beautiful, as are the others. We'll be in the country soon. Your parents were talking about extending the gardens. Think of the possibilities."

Isabella stared at the stone marker and the small memorial plot, then focused on the rows of crosses and markers extending over the grounds. Some with flowers, some decrepit from age and neglect. Since she could never get to them all, she planted a single flower on a different spot each visit, and tended her little plot near the middle of the cemetery—a place where she could come to remember everyone she had lost and feel them in the soil. No matter that most of her friends and loved ones were buried elsewhere. To her it wasn't where the body lay. It was the spirit of the matter.

The cemetery was a resting place for working-class men and women. People who could afford a stone, cross, or other marker, but didn't have the wherewithal for extravagant monoliths or tombs. She liked its simplicity, and its location in a bright section of town containing plenty of small wildlife—squirrels, songbirds and butterflies.

Two women in fading muslin gowns walked past and exchanged greetings with her. There were some places where station had no bearing, and never should. She attended and enjoyed the ton parties, but there was something simple and calming about her weekly routine here. It invigorated her and at the same time let her keep peace with her own demons. Usually.

Movement near the entrance caused her eyes to stray that way. A small procession came through. Pallbearers carried an unremarkable coffin toward the newly dug grave by the fountain of Demeter. She had thought to plant a flower on a grave near the fountain before seeing the freshly piled dirt. She still hadn't chosen where her single white lily, already in bloom, would be planted. Maybe near the rolling hill graves by the cemetery cross-roads.

An indrawn breath made her focus back on her maid.

Bertie was looking toward the procession, a strange look upon her face. "Isn't that Lord Marston's sister-in-law?"

Isabella turned and saw a woman in black. It was indeed Faye Kendrick, Audrey's sister. Faye was a beautiful woman, with untamed red hair and sherry eyes. Her eyes were a different shade from Marcus's, but both had the power to—

The spade slid from her grip and plunked into the dirt.

Marcus was walking beside Faye. Her hand was wrapped into the crook of his arm and he leaned down to hear something she was saying. Their heads, his dark and hers a bright flame, mixed together. They made a beautiful pair.

Isabella looked down at her dirty work gloves and soiled hem. Her lip slid between her teeth. Not even at her best could she compare to Faye. Still, it was silly of her to think such thoughts. She knew the two of them were just friends. If there had been any connection beyond friend-ship between Marcus and Faye, she would have observed it long ago at one of the smaller, more intimate gatherings. She reclaimed her spade and tapped it against a rock she had uprooted.

Just friends—much like Marcus and herself, she thought, chagrined. It was a poor position she was currently in, especially without the beauty or outrageousness that might garner a second glance.

The service started, though she was far enough away to overhear only the loudest of the pastor's words. Bertie tried to gain her attention, but Isabella just patted her hand and kept watching.

She watched Marcus. Heads were bowed around him, eyes looking toward the uneven grass. But Marcus looked straight ahead. His lips pressed together and she could imagine the tight lines around his mouth. He looked straight forward as the prayer was read. Straight forward as a woman gave a tearful speech. Straight forward as the coffin was lowered into the ground.

She wondered who had died. She knew of no one who had passed. Viscount St. John, Stephen, and James were there as well, so it must have been someone in the government. Why Faye would be there too, she was unsure.

The service ended and most of the mourners left, Stephen, James, and Faye among them. St. John said something to Marcus, who shook his head in response and made a cutting motion with his hand.

"My lady?"

All of a sudden Marcus's eyes fixed on her, pinning her to the spot where she knelt.

Isabella lifted the large white lily she had brought to plant on one of the grave sites, never looking away from Marcus.

"My lady?" Bertie said again.

"No worrying, Bertie. I'll be back in a thrice."

She stood, carrying the flower and her spade. She rolled her head and shoulders to get the immediate cricks out, then walked toward the crossroads. Marcus and Viscount St. John stood silently watching her.

"Good afternoon, my lords."

"Lady Willoughby."

"Isabella."

St. John tipped his hat and walked through the exit she had seen Faye take.

Isabella looked at Marcus. "I'm sorry you are here."

He raised a brow.

"Were you close?" She pointed to the grave that was now being filled.

Marcus lowered his voice. "Not close. But close enough."

"I see."

She didn't see at all.

"Planting again?"

"I come every week."

"I know you do."

She started. "And how is that?"

A half smile worked its way across his mouth. "My, my, I should ply you with wine more often while we play. You told me last month. Besides, I heard you talking with Stephen about it last year."

She blinked. "Oh."

"You are almost as daft as he when it comes to crawling vines."

Her spaded hand moved to her hip. "I see."

He smiled. The kind of smile that made her heart flip. "Do you?"

Her breath caught, but she managed to shake her spade at him. "Don't think I don't remember who trampled through my first garden."

He raised a brow. "You can hardly blame me. That monster dog was trying to bite me."

A vision rose of the dignified boy he had been, poised on the verge of manhood, chasing through the grass with an Afghan hound nipping at his heels.

"He was not. Bartholemew did not bite," she said witheringly.

"Bartholemew, my foot. That dog's name was Cerberus."

"You dare!" she gasped. The darkness lifted from

his eyes for a moment, and she forgot to breathe.

He smirked. "How old were you, six? You barely knew what a rose was."

"I was seven and a half," she said primly. "And you trampled my sainfoin conicals. Someday I will have my revenge."

His eyes turned shadowy. "You'll have to wait your turn, Bella."

"Pardon me?" She didn't like the darkness beneath his tone. She wished she could take back her words, though how was she to know? In some ways she knew him so well, and in others not at all.

"I wonder what flower you will plant for me in your memorial plot," he said.

"That's a little morbid, don't you think?"

"And your visits here aren't?"

She stiffened. "Not in the least."

He fingered a petal on the lily in her hand. "George again?"

She looked at him sharply, trying to discern his meaning. But there was only curiosity and a deep weariness in his gaze. "'Tis not only George for whom I visit."

He looked off to the distance. "Yes."

"Are you unwell, Marcus?" She scrutinized him.

He turned back to her and smiled blithely. "I'm as well as can be."

"I see. I'm not sure I believe you."

"It is at once as hard to believe as it is to disbelieve."

"That makes as little sense to me now as it did when you spouted it at the Pettigrews' house party."

"A house party where you should never have stepped foot. He looked down his attractive nose.

"I was mature enough to have chosen to attend." She lifted her chin.

"Were you?" He looked amused.

"Yes. And as I told you then, there was—there *is*—no need to nag after me like a wayward child."

"Little Isabella, sprouted up and charging the breeze, instead of the other way around."

He patted her shoulder. She didn't know whether to growl or groan.

"I'll see you at the Capley tea, little warrior. I hope you find a nice home for that flowery sprig. Don't stay too long in the morbid midday sun."

He tweaked a petal and strode away. His jacket snapped and swayed around him in a feral caress.

It couldn't have been worse if he had patted her on the head.

Blast. It was time to do something drastic.

Chapter 4

Isabella handed her card to the Angelford butler as she walked into the grand house on St. James. She spared a glance for the magnificent ceiling, painted to reflect the heavens, while the butler took her embroidered pelisse.

"Lady Angelford told me to direct you to the back salon when you arrived. She will be with you in a moment, Lady Willoughby."

"Thank you, Templeton." She followed the severely dressed man through the hall to a cozy room overlooking the rear gardens.

Calliope breezed in a few minutes later wearing a bright green muslin dress that set off her stylish blond hair. "Isabella! We didn't get a chance to speak at the Ferdot crush. How have you been?"

Isabella smiled and accepted a cup of tea from the embellished silver service Templeton had placed before her. "Very well, Calliope. My parents are leaving for the country soon, but I'm not sure when I'm going to join them." She blew gently across the top of her cup.

"Excellent. We aren't retiring for another two weeks. James has some things he needs to take care of at the Office."

The *office* was another term for the Foreign Office, where James, Stephen, and Marcus helped the government. They contended that their work consisted of mostly diplomatic matters. But she had heard whispers of missions and secrets, and shared looks that bespoke of something more than finding out whether the emperor from one country liked cheese or if the ambassador from another had a proclivity for less reputable social pursuits.

"How are the twins?" Isabella asked and looked around, hoping to see a small mop of hair peeking around one of the chairs.

"Still growing like weeds. Deirdre took them to the theater for the day. Said she needed more time with her niece and nephew. And believe me, as much as I love the termagants, I take every chance offered to share them with someone else for an hour or two 'adventure.' In the house it is different, of course. Even with the nanny, I don't want them to feel pushed to the side."

Calliope spread her hands down the fine weave of her dress skirt and then picked up her tea. Isabella knew enough of Calliope's history to know where those feelings had been spawned.

"And, of course, I have to save the nanny," she said. "She's already on a two glass a day gin ration in response to their antics. I can only imagine what it will be like in a few years. Someday I may take you up on your offer."

Isabella smiled into her cup. She loved the twins and had threatened to steal them away in the night. A strong wave of longing broke over her, but she resolutely pushed it away.

She gathered her courage for a different line of questioning. "You will be here for another two weeks? Then you plan to attend the after season parties?"

A twinkle appeared in Calliope's eyes. "Why, Isabella—" She put a hand to her chest. "—certainly you aren't saying what it is I think you are saying?"

Suddenly, Isabella was assailed with doubts. This was not her brightest idea. She had never stayed for the racier parties that occurred on the cusp of the season—the last bit of wildness that allowed members of the ton to indulge before rusticating in the peaceful countryside for several months, months in the country that afforded them an opportunity to live down any spawned rumors.

But those parties were for the most daring of the fashionable. A group of which she was not a part. And she could only imagine the reaction she would receive were she to attend, the orchestra pulling to a screeching halt as she pushed through the doors and tried to act as if she belonged.

"Well—"

Calliope put a hand out to cover hers, which was grasping the china cup more tightly than necessary. "I'm merely having a bit of fun. I think it would be wonderful if you joined the madness. A proper blossoming into the ranks of the questionable and notorious."

Isabella smiled at her sardonic tone. The Angelfords were known to attend some of the racier parties, but while there, they only had eyes for each other.

Calliope clapped her hands together. "Now, then. The Grenstridge masquerade is in two days. It's the perfect opportunity to introduce you, then the invitations will start pouring in." She cast a critical eye over Isabella's high white and gray chintz gown. "We'll need to pay a visit to Madame Giselle's, however."

Isabella smiled wryly. She knew she had made a good decision in coming to Calliope. She'd barely said two sentences and her friend had taken them and run. "I know. I scheduled a consultation with her this afternoon."

"You did?" Calliope perked up. "Do you mind if I come with you? Deirdre and the twins won't be back for another few hours."

"Of course. I was hoping you might."

"Excellent. You finish your tea while I grab a few sketches I've been meaning to drop off at the modiste."

Isabella smiled and sipped her tea as Calliope practically skipped from the room. If she knew her friend, Calliope would bring multiple designs for Madame Giselle to go through in order to create something marvelous to keep her husband's eyes glued to her all night. Not that his eyes ever strayed from her regardless of what she wore.

Soon enough they were in the Angelford carriage heading toward the shopping district.

Madame Giselle welcomed them, after giving Calliope a strict reprimand for not scheduling an appointment.

"Oh, I'm here for Lady Willoughby. I have brought some designs that might suit her."

Madame Giselle's brow smoothed.

"And one small one for me too, if you get the chance."

The seamstress sniffed as she ushered the women into a spectacular sitting room. She studied the designs, instructed Isabella to undress, then evaluated her from all angles. "Deep blue, I should think. And perhaps dark mauve."

The seamstress went to work. After several hours of pokes and tucks from her girls, and comments from Calliope, four dresses were chosen. An already created gown and day dress that needed few alterations, and two new designs from Calliope's stack.

Calliope seemed pleased and ordered a dress for herself.

Madame might sniff, Isabella mused, but the Angelfords were one of her best customers, and no matter how busy she might be, she would no doubt always make time for Calliope. By association, she had been taken under Madame's wing, but had always shied away from the smarter styles of her friend, sticking instead to the strictly fashionable but ordinary forms.

"I am glad to see the lady has finally decided to try more flair," the seamstress said as she made some last minute adjustments.

"I thought that perhaps it was time for a small change."

"Indeed, Lady Willoughby. With these new dresses you will make a splash. Enough to catch the interest of the gentlemen."

Isabella felt a blush rise. "Oh, no, I'm not trying to catch the interest of the gentlemen."

Madame tutted. "You are too young to waste away against the walls. I'm sure many nice gentlemen would be glad to peel you away."

Madame Giselle always had a way with words.

"Or just that one special gentleman," a soft voice said.

Isabella met Calliope's eyes in the mirror. They were gentle and understanding. Isabella's breath caught. Isabella wondered how long she'd known.

"Well, yes, of course that special one," Madame said, glaring at Calliope. "What do you take me for, Lady Angelford? A wicked woman trying to pawn off my ways?"

Isabella was glad to have Calliope's attention diverted as the two exchanged barbs. Soon it was Calliope's turn on the stool, and Isabella happily trailed over to the window and drew back the curtain to peer outside. The street was bustling with activity. Carriages and peddlers clogged the road and shoppers ducked in and out of the storefronts.

A herd of children moved in time with a nanny and housemaid, alternately fanning out and closing together like a flock of birds in flight. A man argued with a street vendor and barely missed hitting a woman with his flailing arms. The woman hustled past, pushing her two children, a girl and boy, so that they were on the inside of her as they walked along the pavement.

Isabella watched the little girl, her eyes wide as she took in her surroundings, her dark curls bobbing as she swung her head from side to side. Just as the threesome reached the shop window, the little girl stumbled and fell to her knees, her curls bouncing as she caught herself on her hands.

The girl's lower lip trembled as she raised her head, and their eyes met. The glass was slick against Isabella's palm as her hand slid down the pane. The wide blue eyes shimmered with tears, an entreaty in their depths.

Isabella's hand dropped from the window. She stepped back, prepared to run outside and comfort the little girl, but paused when the mother turned and knelt beside her fallen child.

The mother's movement broke their connection, and the girl wobbly nodded at whatever her mother was saying. Then the woman's arms wrapped around her daughter, the little girl leaning into her.

Eyes aching, the scene blurred, and Isabella put a hand on the rough wall next to the thick glass. She leaned her forehead against the cold, hard surface and blinked. The scene sharpened into focus. The woman was saying something to her daughter, and the son was awkwardly patting the little girl on the shoulder.

The woman tugged the children back into motion. The girl turned, and Isabella's last thought was of blue eyes replaced with warm brown eyes tinged with gold.

"Isabella?"

She took a breath before turning. "My apologies, Calliope." She swallowed. "I seem to have wandered."

Calliope didn't look convinced, but if she had borne witness, she was kind enough to say nothing.

They thanked Madame Giselle, gathered the two modified dresses for Isabella, and called for the carriage.

Golden eyes haunted her. Eyes that were. Eyes that could be.

On the way home, Isabella worked up the nerve to ask Calliope, "How long have you known?"

"That you were in love with Roth? Since we met at the Pettigrews' house party."

Her heart tightened and she found it difficult to breathe. That had been two years ago. "Does Lord Angelford know?"

Calliope shrugged lightly, as if they were merely discussing the weather instead of the world-rocking event that Isabella felt. "James is very observant, as are Stephen and Audrey. I would be surprised if any of them are unaware."

She swallowed, her mouth gone dry. "And Marcus?" Her voice caught.

Calliope's eyes were sympathetic and then thoughtful. "I don't know what Roth thinks even a quarter of the time. He's very perceptive, but he holds his cards close to his chest."

So foolish. Had she been pining so obviously? Had he been feeling sorry for her all this time?

"Don't look that way, Isabella. Roth would

never use your feelings against you. He can be harsh and judgmental, but he cares for you."

"As a friend," she whispered.

Calliope didn't argue. "Yes. It is up to you whether you will take the chance on more. From the looks of this trip, I would hasten to say you have decided to?"

Isabella nodded, and Calliope's hopeful look curved into satisfaction. They turned onto her street.

"Excellent." She patted her hand and smiled. "And, Isabella, if anyone can pierce Roth's shell, I think it will be you. I can share some general tips and experiences, if you'd like to drop by tomorrow."

Mortification turned easily into nervous excitement. But could she pull it off? Could she turn Marcus's friendly interest into the romantic? Could she capture a man who had slipped past every other woman—the beautiful and witty alike? "Yes. Please."

Calliope smiled reassuringly. "I'll see you tomorrow, then. Call around two?"

Isabella nodded and accepted a hand from the servant who opened the door. She moistened her lips, threw back her shoulders and readied herself for a foray that might well turn into a siege.

Chapter 5

◦◦◦◦◦

It had been an exhausting day of sessions. He felt like a cat denied a nap for three days. Both Houses of Parliament had been especially fraught with tension. Marcus knew he would have to keep a stricter eye on some of the warring factions in the Lords and the Commons. They were too obviously creating strife between them, indicating that something was happening behind the scenes. Someone was manipulating the players.

"Roth!"

Marcus gripped his walking stick fractionally tighter, but maintained his pace beside James as they walked past St. Margaret's Church through the gray haze that had dropped over the city. The last thing he wanted to do was chat with Ainsworth.

"Roth!"

He could see James looking at him from the corner of his eye.

"No," he said tersely, answering James's unspoken question of whether he was going to stop for Ainsworth.

"Roth!"

Ainsworth was one more on the list of incompetent, greedy landowners who were trying to strangle the country by strangling the people. It seemed as if Ainsworth hadn't paid attention in his history lessons, for these things always bit back after awhile. Besides, healthy workers made for better production. If the owners weren't so incredibly shortsighted and intent on increasing their own pleasures, and if they spent half a second giving back, they would reap more in return.

And wasn't that the point in the first place?

"What's the matter, Roth?" said a loud, strident voice. "Not going to dignify Ainsworth's presence either? A bit too high on the instep these days? Anyone would think you were a prince, not a baron."

Marcus considered which action would be more satisfying. Crushing Blakely with his walking stick or walking blithely past the man. He knew which one would be worse for Blakely. And it was definitely the latter. He hated being ignored. Blakely was an earl who was strict about the social order. It chafed him raw that he, a baron, held more power.

Of course, if Blakely weren't such an obnoxious toad, he could have been a great politician.

The man was cunning and smart, but he let his stunted emotions rule everything. And since his brother's suicide, Blakely had had it in for him.

Blakely's brother had been weak. Just like . . . no, best to keep those thoughts firmly hidden. Neither was his fault, and he wouldn't let them be.

Marcus walked past him, looking straight ahead, and withheld a smirk as Blakely growled. He had to take pleasure in the little things these days.

"Roth! I need to speak to you!"

He saw a group of men watching intently—among them Charles Ellerby, Fenton Ellerby's younger brother, though they looked nothing alike. Charles was a mere baby in the House of Commons, but had been causing undue strife in sessions, alternating between obsequiousness and superiority. He was going to be in for a major shock when someone put him in his place soon.

Ainsworth caught up to them as they passed Charles Ellerby and his cronies. James looked bored, and he knew the same expression was reflected on his own face.

"Roth." Ainsworth wheezed a bit. "What the deuce were you trying to do back there?"

Marcus raised a brow. "To what do you refer, Ainsworth?"

"The bill! You struck it down! I know it was you."

"Thank you for attributing the credit to me, Ainsworth, but you are less aware than I thought if you believe I alone voted against your measure."

Ainsworth's face purpled. "It was a good bill! My district needed it."

"Why?"

Ainsworth waved him off. "We need the subsidy! The bill was a good one. Whose side are you on?"

Marcus watched him coldly. "Pray tell why your district needed a subsidy. You don't farm. You don't mine. You don't graze. It's a complete mystery what you do there other than make your dependents more miserable."

"That's what the subsidy is for! We need to get things back in motion."

Had Marcus not thought such things crude, he would have rolled his eyes. "Things? Motion? Try being a little more specific, Ainsworth. Your lack of clarity and planning is the reason why you don't have the bill in your pocket. That and the fact that you are not interested in the welfare of your dependents. That money was going straight in your pocket."

Ainsworth shook his head, his jowls flopping. "No, the people would have benefited. Everyone knows a happy landowner is a good landowner."

"What a terribly interesting insight, Ainsworth."

Ainsworth pointed a finger. "The people will

suffer now, and the blame will be on your head. It's because of you and your machinations."

"Again, thank you for the credit. But really, your lack of foresight or any grasp on intelligence shine far brighter as reasons. I feel sorry for your dependents, regardless of your reasons. What type of gentleman are you?"

It was hard to believe Ainsworth could turn a darker shade of purple, yet somehow he managed it. "How was this bill any different from the motion you introduced to help *your* dependents? This is what landowners do."

Had the man never learned to read? The answer to that question was once again in doubt. "That I need to explain it to you at all answers any lingering questions regarding your intelligence."

Marcus checked his pocket watch. The action had the desired effect.

"Am I not worth your time, Roth?"

"No."

"No, I'm not worth your time?"

Marcus started walking again.

"Roth! I'm not done talking to you."

Marcus thought that presenting his back and walking away basically said everything needed. James paced alongside him.

Charles Ellerby joined them a second later. "You should look back to see old Ainsworth's face."

Marcus didn't need to turn around to see Ainsworth's face. He knew exactly what the man's expression would be.

"You sure put him in his place."

Marcus felt the ever-present headache he sported these days bloom. If he recalled correctly, Ellerby had been toadying to Ainsworth just yesterday. Probably would be toadying again tomorrow as well.

"I wanted to talk to you about the Corn Laws and how we can increase their effectiveness."

There were so many brilliant people in both Houses, why did there also have to be such bad ones? Though to be fair to Charles Ellerby, he was still wet behind the ears. Fresh from Cambridge with ideas, plans, and dreams. Most of them half-fledged and extremely flawed, but one had to begin somewhere.

"Why are you talking to me, Mr. Ellerby?" He didn't feel like being fair at the moment. The younger man irritated him.

"I've been watching at sessions. I know which way the wind blows. I want in."

Marcus counted to five. "You want in to what? The secret counsel?"

"Yes," he responded eagerly. Marcus almost felt sorry for him. Almost.

"There is no secret counsel, Ellerby." It was true. There wasn't one—there were many, many secret counsels. "You have to earn your place. And you need to know to whom you are speaking."

"Why, I can't speak to you?"

Marcus looked straight ahead. He didn't need to see Ellerby to know what his reactions would be. There were a hundred Ellerbys out there. "Why would you approach me on the Corn Laws when I've never shown a scrap of support for the topic?"

"You work behind the scenes. Besides, you are a landowner. Of course you support it."

"Your powers of observation thus, you will never earn a place in the secret counsel. Good day, Ellerby."

"What? Wait, you said there wasn't a secret counsel." He hurried to keep pace with them, his shorter legs eating up less distance.

"Not for you there isn't."

From the corner of his eye Marcus noticed the darkening expression on Charles Ellerby's face.

"You shouldn't get on the wrong side of me, Lord Roth. I'm going to be a very dangerous player soon."

"I'll keep that in mind. For now, though, you are embarrassing yourself. Run along."

Ellerby stopped dead, while Marcus and James continued on.

James whistled. "Two down in nearly as many minutes. Color me impressed. Haven't seen some-one so red since you took down Yarnley. You definitely need to find a mistress. Relieve some of that angry tension."

"Angelford . . . " he said in warning.

"Roth," he mocked. "Seriously, though, what has you in a twist today?"

"They are both idiots. All three, really. Tell me that you don't agree."

"You know I agree. But you are just as apt to stare coldly as to verbally shred. Especially in the midst of a flux in the Houses."

Marcus spared James a look, tapping his stick as they walked. "Staring coldly is a time-honored tradition."

"Why did you feel the need to break from it today?"

"You think I ruined my charitable reputation by being too hard on them?"

"'Charitable' reputation? No. But you have been more verbal and blunt these past few weeks. Pushing forward rather than staying in the background."

It was a last foray. Things were more important all of a sudden. More intense. He couldn't explain it to James, though. He didn't want anyone to know about his headaches and blackouts. His dark family history. His cloudy future. Least of all friends who cared and would worry.

"Just trying to stir the murky waters and keep things interesting."

"It worked." They walked a few more paces. "Did you want to stop by for tea? Calliope and Lady Willoughby are probably back from shopping."

"Shopping for new frocks?"

"I suppose. Calliope was awfully excited about something."

Marcus felt a twinge. He wondered what Isabella might have gotten herself into this time. "That sounds dire."

"Very well could be."

"I'll pass."

Hearing about a surreptitious shopping trip and all it entailed was not his idea of fun. Besides, he had a niggling feeling that he wasn't going to like something about it. Calliope with a plan was always a scary proposition. And involving Isabella . . .

Wildflowers whispered in the breeze. "I have to run by Peel's to see what to do, if anything, about Ainsworth." He tapped his stick twice in annoyance. "The man doesn't do revenge well. He really is an idiot."

"Charles Ellerby and Blakely?"

He shrugged. "Add a few more to the barrel. Nothing like a few enemies to keep things interesting. Besides, Blakely's been after me for years."

"His brother still?"

"Of course."

He hadn't given Blakely's brother the gun, nor shown him how to use it. He *had* pointed out that his brother's social and monetary credit was extremely poor on the House floor—but it was only the truth and relevant in the proceedings. That Blakely had balked at giving his own brother more money was entirely his own affair, Marcus thought, not his.

That Blakely's brother was weak and had chosen the easy way out of the whole matter irritated him. Someone who was healthy and whole and had their whole life ahead of him had instead chosen to waste it. Considering his own circumstance, it was hard for him to feel sympathetic.

"Let me know if you need help," James said.

Marcus nodded and they separated at their respective carriages.

His head pounded. He hadn't been eating well. Gray mist hovered in the air. Something further was coming, and he knew he wasn't going to like it. It was a good thing that he eschewed sympathy for himself.

Chapter 6

Two days later, in a new dress and armed with the knowledge of how to use it to her advantage, Isabella watched the parade of carriages edge up the drive toward the masquerade. Two days of practicing new moves with her fan, mask, and dress in the mirror hadn't made her feel one whit less nervous. In fact, she thought she was more nervous now than when she had birthed this idea.

Calliope's silk-gloved hand touched her bare arm. "Everything will be fine. Breathe in deeply and remember why you are doing this."

Oh, she hadn't forgotten. She just wondered if she was going to regret this as much as her last attempt at pushing herself forward. Somehow, her presence at the Pettigrews' house party had been hushed up by attendees too willing to believe that Isabella Willoughby had inadvertently attended the wrong party. If she decided to make a real stride in this new direction, her position in society would dramatically change.

"Thank you, Calliope. For everything."

Calliope patted her arm, blue eyes sparkling behind her mask. "I think you will do wonderfully. And it will be excellent to have someone else to talk to at these things. James can be a dreadful bore when he's feeling stuffy."

Her handsome but at times severe husband lifted an eyebrow, then made a motion with his hand that Isabella didn't understand. However, the blush on Calliope's face seemed to indicate that she did, and she pulled a less than steady hand through her top locks, in a parody of straightening them. "Well, yes, then."

Isabella held back a surge of friendly envy and instead focused on the footman who was approaching their slowing coach.

Would Marcus be here? Would he recognize her behind the mask? Would the expression on his face show something other than polite friendliness? And if it didn't . . .

The carriage door opened and she surged out to stare at the large light stone town house flanked by two brick houses. It shone between the darker buildings as if the moon held it in special regard.

It wasn't until she noticed the amused faces of both the Angelfords that she realized she had alighted without help from either the footman or James.

"Oh." She blushed, but Calliope shook her head in amusement and gently pushed her toward the door.

"You go in ahead of us to stay anonymous. We will meet later. Remember what I told you about holding yourself and using your accessories differently."

Isabella nodded and quickly set forth, slowing when she was joined by another group of people making their way up the steps. She merged with their group as they slipped through the corridors, upstairs and into the ballroom. She paused on the threshold and held herself there for a moment as she took in the sight. Gaily dressed people danced and talked and flirted, the atmosphere jovial and alive. She quickly caught sight of her prey and moved in his direction, but not directly to him.

Despite the new dress and lessons she had practiced, she didn't *feel* any more confident in her ability to fish for beaux. She was a novice among the skilled hunters of the ton. She strolled to a threesome who looked more nervous than she and smiled.

By the time she felt the warm breath close to her neck, she was having a genuinely good time with her new companions. It seemed social situations were the same no matter the level of raciness. Make other people feel better and soon she'd be feeling better too.

The breath of air tickled, but she knew instinctively that the person behind her was not Marcus.

"I couldn't help but overhear your delightful laugh, and I had to find the lovely creature possessed of such a voice."

She turned to see Fenton Ellerby, with his charming smile and hawklike nose, holding out a glass of champagne. She accepted it with a smile and took a sip.

"You flatter me, sir."

"No, it is you who flatter us with your beauty."

Ah, yes, she remembered now why she had avoided this type of gathering. Useless compliments and excessive flattery, all with one goal in mind.

Of course, she had to concede that if the man uttering them had been dark-haired and golden-eyed, she would have been swooning in girlish glee.

"Please, I must beg you to allow me this dance."

Isabella saw the new set forming. Calliope had warned her of the increased number of waltzes and the more vibrant nature of some of the other dances.

She also saw two pairs of blue eyes and one pair of golden watching her. Calliope and James were standing alongside Marcus. A woman clung to Marcus's arm, trying to gain his attention.

She looked back at her new companion. Ellerby was a notorious rake and one of Marcus's least favorite people.

"I would be delighted," she heard herself say.

He led her onto the floor and the first strains of a violin caressed the air. He twirled her and she forced herself to relax. She loved to dance, but usually felt as if she were on stage. Closing her eyes, she pretended she was in Marcus's arms.

Marcus and she had danced together before, but she was always too constrained by propriety and too nervous at holding onto his broad shoulders and firm arms, so different from her own soft ones. Ellerby's arms didn't feel as strong, and he didn't smell of spicy cinnamon and piano keys, but she imagined that it was Marcus's fingers caressing her waist and claiming her hand. That it was he who wanted to dance with her and flirt with her and teach her all the naughty things he knew.

Her head dropped back and she allowed her skirt to flare out. She felt free.

She heard Ellerby's breath catch, and a surge of triumph soared through her. Perhaps Marcus—

A hand slipped to her rear, and her eyes

snapped open. Fighting the urge to smack the man, she forced a smile and pulled his arm back into position. She might be here on a mission to snag Marcus, but she sure as Mary wasn't here to fish for anyone else.

"Lud, sir. Don't you know that a lady likes to be romanced first?"

A flash of surprise passed his features, and he suddenly looked more interested. "Like a bit of a game, do you? Excellent. I love a challenge."

His voice was low and meant to be sexy, and she had to admit that it probably would be to ninety percent of women—Ellerby didn't have his reputation for naught.

"I don't know if my heart could take it."

"I'll take good care of it."

She held back a snort.

The final notes of the song tapered to a close, and she caught Marcus still looking in their direction. She wondered if he had watched them dance the entire time.

She hoped so.

She cocked a brow toward the refreshment area. Ellerby laughed lightly and placed a hand on her waist to lead her forward. They had barely reached the table when she felt *his* presence at her side. The side unoccupied by Ellerby. She felt her body instinctively lean toward the warmth on her right.

"Ellerby."

Ellerby stiffened. "Roth."

"And is this lovely creature with you?"

She couldn't stop her fan's movement as she felt the heat start from her cheeks and spread through her body. A lovely tingle that had her eyes at half mast. Yes, she had been right. All it took were the right words issuing forth from the man of her dreams and she puddled at his feet.

Ellerby looked irritated. "I don't think—"

"Marie." She held out her hand, cutting off Ellerby and causing a slow smile to curve Marcus's lips. A predatory smile. She shivered. She'd seen it before, of course, but it had never been focused in her direction.

He placed a soft kiss against her knuckles and she caught her breath. "My pleasure entirely, Marie."

She could sense Ellerby's agitation at her side, but couldn't bring herself to care. Marcus was staring at her as if she were a ripe dessert. She wanted to make sure he got every last bite.

"Would you care to dance, Marie?"

Isabella hesitated, a bit of sense returning. Marcus was the most perceptive person she knew. What if she did something stupid?

Then again, what had she come here for, if not to take the chance?

"I would love to."

He smiled and led her onto the floor and away from Ellerby's darkening face.

She tried to steady her nerves as they took their places and he took her hand.

"Are you enjoying the masquerade, Lord Roth?"

Their gloves slid against each other, satin against silk. "I am enjoying it now."

The warmth of his hand seeped into hers. "Do you attend these parties often?"

She heard the pull of a bow across strings as his body moved against hers.

"Often enough." His hand held her protectively as he twirled her around. "You, on the other hand, do not attend these parties."

Her breath caught, and a wisp of hair dislodged from behind her mask and blew across her cheek.

"Oh, but I may."

"How the silver lie slips from your tongue, Marie."

"This is a masquerade. How would you know if I had attended one like this before?"

"I assure you it would have been memorable."

"Nonsense," she said, but her breath came a little faster. "You could have seen me a dozen times over. Perhaps this is only the first time you've paid attention."

His eyes caressed her mask. "Mmmm . . . "

He pulled her closer and twirled her so that her skirts flared and her breath quickened—and she didn't have to imagine a thing this time, because it was better than all her fantasies. She held onto him, her eyes never leaving his. They whirled and danced and their movements sung together. Like two liquids in a glass merging into one.

It wasn't until the last sighs from the strings that she felt him tense. Following his eyes, she saw Ellerby watching them. Watching her.

Marcus picked up her hand and brought it to his lips. "Allow me to escort you out for some fresh air?"

Isabella's heart beat a rapid staccato in her chest. "Of course."

He tucked her hand into his arm and led the way through the mass of dancers. She could see Ellerby trying to reach them, but Marcus maneuvered through the throng as if trying to put as many obstacles between them as possible. Ellerby was soon lost in the crowd.

But what was important was that Marcus was taking her outside. To get a breath of fresh air. Which everyone, even a proper girl like her, knew was synonymous for an assignation.

An assignation. Outside. With Marcus.

The balcony doors loomed ahead and her breath caught. Ten more steps. Nine. Eight. Seven.

And suddenly they were walking down a narrow hall that she hadn't even noticed in her Marcus induced haze. And he was pushing open a door and urging her inside.

Bookshelves lined the walls. Books as far as she could see.

Isabella could barely think straight. Had he bypassed a few stolen kisses on the balcony to consummation in a library? And how did she feel about this? Yes, she wanted him. She loved him. But this was moving a little too fast for her.

He thought she was someone else. At the beginning of the evening that hadn't quite mattered in the way it did now. "What are we doing?" she said, unable to keep the nervousness from her voice.

"I'm going to seduce you on the settee." He pointed to the plush green velvet bench in the middle of the ornate room.

She stared at him for a moment, unable to do anything other than blink. She registered the inane action, but there was nothing she could do about it, as that function of her brain seemed to have come to a complete halt.

"For the love of . . . I'm not going to seduce you on the settee, Isabella."

"Oh, well, that's . . . er, Isabella? Whatever do you mean?"

His fingers touched her mask and nimbly removed it from her face before she even registered his hand's movement.

"I seem to have lost my dancing partner, Marie," he said sardonically.

Her heartbeat increased. "Oh, well, I'm terribly sorry about that. Had I known what would cause you to know it was I—"

"You twit. I knew it was you from the moment I first saw you."

That threw her for a pause. He had flirted with her. *Her*, not some random unidentified woman. As if he were actually attracted to her, not simply exchanging their friendly parries of normal.

"Then why—" She looked him in the eye. "—why did you act as if I were someone else?"

His eyes looked tired. She had the distinct impression that he was looking at her as if she were a wayward little sister. "Bella—"

"Don't call me that." She suddenly hated that name. It was a name for someone beautiful, and no matter what style of dress or makeup or hairstyle she wore, she knew she would never be more than an average sort of pretty. A trait that someone would find acceptable in a little sister.

"Bella," he said more determinedly, "this *is* a masquerade."

She lowered her head so he couldn't see the film over her eyes. Dear Lord, she was becoming pathetic.

"Bella, what are you doing here?" His voice was still low and dark, but there was an underlying gentleness beneath the words. She looked up.

"I'm attending this lovely masquerade, same as you."

His eyes burned and his voice grew darker. "This is not a lovely masquerade. This is a debaucherous party where men take advantage of lonely widows."

She bristled, outrage overcoming self-pity. "I'm not lonely."

She just wanted *him*, damn the man.

"Seeking adventure, then," he said, as if the matter was resolved in his mind.

She wanted to say she was seeking him, but that wouldn't be too smart, given the way the current conversation was going. She'd seen enough women throw themselves at him to know how he'd react to the ones he didn't want. Her courage didn't extend as far as losing him as a friend too.

She smoothed her navy skirts, the satin cooling her fingers. "So what if I am? I'm old enough to fend for myself."

Sowing her wild oats, as it were—the perfect excuse.

"Bella, you are a lamb in the midst of wolves."

Her jaw dropped. "Calliope is here!"

"Calliope can take care of herself."

She crossed her arms. "And so can I."

"Some rogue will attempt to toss up your skirts the moment you step into a darkly lit corridor," he said rather bluntly.

Is that an offer? The less restrained side of her wanted to ask. Instead she said, "Well, you would know."

"What?" The man looked positively delicious even when tinged an angry red. She wondered what color his skin turned in passion. Would it be a darker tone to heighten his golden eyes and black hair, or a reddish hue to make his full lips stand out?

"You've tossed plenty of skirts at these functions, or so I've heard."

His knuckles turned white around the high back of a chair. "Lady Willoughby, I'm taking you home. And then I may have a talk with your mother."

She winced at his use of her address. He never called her anything other than her first name, or a variation of such.

"I was invited to this party and I'm staying. If you need to retire, then please feel free. And my mother will quite understand, I assure you." Well, she would. Mostly.

"No she will not. She'd be appalled at you being here."

Frustration beat its wings. "Why is it acceptable for you to be here, then?"

"I'm a man." As if it were the most obvious thing—which it unfortunately was.

"What about Calliope? I don't see you haranguing her."

"She has James to pester her. And don't try to change the subject. Calliope attended these functions long before she got shackled to James. She knows exactly what to do. Besides, no one would touch her. James would kill them."

That was true. But beside the point. "I can handle myself fine. I would never let some rake take advantage of me."

"Like Ellerby? His hands were all over you. You wouldn't have lasted a minute with him down in the gardens."

"Do you think I'd just roll over for the sod? That I'm so weak-willed I'd succumb to him the minute he made an overture?"

"He'd make more than an overture," Marcus said darkly.

"I'm not weak!"

"Everyone has a weakness. Some succumb to it, others remove the temptation."

She couldn't help it. She rolled her eyes.

He abruptly moved forward and captured her chin with his long, smooth fingers; freezing her in place and making her forget the thread of the conversation.

"This is a different sort of weakness, Bella."

His fingers caressed her chin and slid back to the nape of her neck. He leaned down and brushed his cheek, just roughening from the long day, along hers, his breath tickling her ear.

"If he promised you pleasure and untold delights . . . would you say no?"

She stood stunned, with her cheek pressed against his and his low voice murmuring in her ear. *No* wasn't even in her lexicon right now.

"If he pulled you into his arms and made passionate declarations . . . would you believe him?"

Her body pulled against his, and his free hand slid around her waist. She felt dizzy and drugged.

"Using all the skill he built from doing the same thing to countless women, would you feel you were the special one? The one who could change him?"

He began to slowly rock their bodies in a sensual parody of a waltz. She could hear music, faintly, the violins shimmering around the edges of her consciousness. A consciousness that was solely centered on Marcus.

"If he pulled off your gloves because he said it was too warm in the summer air, would you let him?"

Somehow her hands had risen to his chest, and the hand that had been caressing her neck slid down to capture one of hers. He pulled the glove away from her first finger, slowly, and then the second and third, and soon his hand was sliding up her wrist and arm, to the edge of her glove and slowly, so slowly, pulling it down. And when it bunched, his long artistic fingers slid back down over hers and began tugging again, smoothing the glove down over her digits and pulling it free.

"And if he then took your hand in his and proclaimed himself so overcome with emotion that he had to lay a kiss there . . ."

He brought her hand slowly—everything felt so tortuously slow—to his lips and pressed them to her knuckles.

" . . . and if you made no mention of impropriety, would you let him proclaim his undying affection by kissing it again?"

He gently turned her wrist, and his lips grazed her pulse point, which was beating hot and heavy.

Her eyes followed his lips as the tremors scuttled through her, and when he lifted his head, she locked eyes with him.

"And if you leaned into him, your breathing shallow, your eyes glazed, with that sultry look that begs for him to throw you on or up against the nearest surface . . ."

He leaned forward, eyes still locked with hers, the intense gaze that never dimmed heightened by sexual awareness, his lips a hairbreadth from hers. Her eyes slid shut and she felt the barest touch of his lips sliding across hers.

" . . . would you let him?"

Oh, yes. She leaned forward to press her lips against his, but he leaned back at the same time. The music had stopped. The room was silent save for harsh breathing, which she realized was emanating from her. His whiskey eyes were dark and shuttered.

Oh.

Oh.

She felt color flood her cheeks. Silence filled the air, and it was only with the strictest will that she kept herself from filling it with stutters and stammers.

He leaned forward again, and the spell relit, not quite shattered as yet. He trailed her freed glove across her chin.

"Weakness, Bella. Stamping out the temptation is kinder in the long run. Stay away from these parties. Stay away from dresses like that. And most definitely stay away from the rakes."

Then he turned on his heel and walked through the door.

Chapter 7

Isabella's heart pumped as the many layers of silk, satin, and lace dripped through her fingers.

She should be in bed. It was well past sleeping time, and well into waking time. Alas, she was knee deep in clothing, not in the least drowsy after the night she'd had. The feel of him was still imprinted on her ... Marcus leaning so close, holding her, nearly kissing her. . .

She closed her eyes and took a deep, dreamy breath.

"You know, my lady, it would be much easier if you'd just tell me what you wanted changed?" She cracked an eye to see Bertie standing with her hands on her hips near the wardrobe.

Bertie was a bit sterner than most ladies' maids, but her heart was always in the right place, and her loyalty was unquestionable.

They had waded through a massive pile of

dresses, Isabella tossing each one as soon as it entered her hand. None of them were right for her plans.

"I need something a little more daring. The hemline raised, or the bodice dropped, or, I don't know, *something*. Something with more verve than what I wore tonight."

Unfortunately, Bertie's tired eyes were the only thing raised in the room. "What has gotten into you? That dress you wore had plenty of skin on display."

Isabella fiddled with a pin. "But I can't wear it again so soon. And the other new gown I have from the shop is a day dress. Madame Giselle will not have the others until the day *after* tomorrow. I need something for tomorrow."

She heard Bertie mutter something that sounded like, "Tomorrow—you mean today," and chose to ignore her.

She looked at her clothing pile in disgust. She hadn't thought there was anything wrong with her wardrobe two weeks ago, but now . . . "Something obviously modified from what I have."

Especially after Marcus's comment. *Stay away from dresses like that.* If that wasn't an odd reprimand thrown in the midst of his little seduction tirade, she didn't know what was.

Bertie tutted. "Don't know why you need a dress with more 'something,' whatever that includes. What's wrong with this?" She held up a mignonette-green gown, pretty and staid. "You look lovely in this. And it doesn't show off anything unseemly."

"Why is everyone so worried about my dignity these days? Haven't I proven to be the epitome of the retiring and invisible lady? Why is it that when I show a hint—a *hint*—of wanting to have a little more fun, then everyone is up in arms?"

Bertie just looked at her. "It's because you *are* such a retiring type, my lady. You aren't a flash. And pardon me for saying so, but I think you do very well as you are. People like you. You have plenty of gentlemen interested in taking tea with you or riding through the park."

Isabella gripped the pin in her hand. "In order to find out what I think their chances are with other women. In order to have a pleasant conversation as a 'respite' in the middle of their courting schedule."

"Plenty of nice gentlemen are here because of you alone, and you know it," Bertie admonished.

Isabella wilted. "Oh, I don't mean to be a brat. But those gentlemen aren't here because of me. Not the real me." She walked to the window and pulled back the draperies on the dawn. "They just find me unobjectionable and *solid*." She grimaced. "I can't tell you how it stings to be told you are a good sort, not too giddy, and well grounded."

"There are worse things."

"Of course there are," she murmured, watching an early morning wanderer walk by in the fledgling gray light. "But it's nothing to make a heart flutter. And neither are the men who profess interest in me."

"And you are set on finding something to get the flutter going, I suppose. Perhaps with a dark-haired someone?"

Isabella dropped the drapery and sat down on the bed, putting the pin on the bed stand and smoothing the linen of her chemise. "Isn't every woman interested in something that makes her heart flutter?"

"Usually the fluttering leads down a dark path. Or a baby eight months after the wedding. Sometimes it's better to stay out of temptation's grasp."

"So I've been told," she muttered.

Bertie crouched on the floor. "None of us wants to see you hurt, is all. The man you fancy included."

She looked at Bertie and couldn't stop the sadness from showing. "I know. I never said he didn't consider himself a friend or some sort of strange protector. I wasn't alone two minutes in that room before Calliope came running in, looking confused and asking what trouble I was in—Marcus had to have immediately sent for her after leaving."

"As well he should have," her maid said in her upright voice. "Widowed or not, you shouldn't be alone with strange men."

"I wasn't alone with any strange men!"

"You might have been, had Lord Roth not rescued you. I've heard tales of Ellerby from other maids. Not to be trusted, that one."

"Oh, for goodness sakes, I don't have a tendre for Ellerby. And I've been married, in case it escaped your attention all those years. I'm not a green goose. I know you care for me, but stop acting as if you need to protect me from the world. It's appreciated in gesture, but not especially in actuality. I am twenty-eight years old. Quite old enough to handle myself."

Bertie looked chagrined, and Isabella couldn't resist patting her hand to take the sting out.

"I know my behavior has been a little addled these past few days. It's just ... I feel as if I'm letting something pass me by. I know it's easier to stay calmly on course, but it's as if I'll lose something entirely too precious if I don't take the chance," she finished in a whisper, and looked at the lines on her palms, rubbing one thumb over the longest furrow.

Bertie stayed silent for a long moment, then patted her knee, a serious look in her eye. "Then let's fix you something to wear. It's not as if you have to *change*. We'll merely *stretch* you until he can't do anything but be too tempted to grasp you in return."

A slow smile overtook Isabella's face and she clasped Bertie's hand between hers.

"But don't do anything too outrageous." Bertie grimaced. "Or God have mercy, your mother'll have my hide."

Marcus pushed through the doors and out to the terrace of the fourth gathering he'd been to that night. They had gone successively downhill. Not that much could have topped the Grenstridge masquerade three parties back for the sheer toll on his nerves. He had been trying to work out his pique ever since. Unfortunately, none of his regular haunts had done any good.

There were few people out at this point. It was either too late in the night, or too early in the morning—the faint light of dawn peeking over the London houses. Only the true carousers were still up and moving.

Isabella had assuredly been tucked safely into bed, covers drawn up to her chin, hours ago.

He still couldn't believe she had shown up at the Grenstridge masquerade. What had Calliope been thinking? He'd nearly wrung her neck when she'd given him a smug glance in answer to that question. Stephen and James had merely looked amused.

Isabella didn't belong at parties like that. Was he the only sane one in the bunch?

Though with the way she had reacted to him in the library, all supple limbs and husky voice, one would never have known that she didn't belong. He'd cursed himself blue afterward for what he had done to *himself* when trying to warn her away. Having her warm, curvy body pressed to his as he attempted to scare her had done nothing for his libido. It had taken a good thirty minutes, after a curt word to Calliope and a quick escape, before he had been able to enter polite society once more. Good thing the party had barely approached polite.

He felt somewhat horrified to have thought of her in a sexual way. She was sweet, innocent Isabella. Not innocent is some ways, she had been married, of course—and she could be downright surly sometimes—but overall, she radiated a sort of pure goodness that he liked to bask in, like a cat in a sunny spot. She maintained a positive outlook on the world that he refused to taint.

He flipped his pocket watch as he neared the gardens. A sturdy hedge separated them from the yard beyond. He reached his destination and whistled a low tune to announce his presence.

He felt the person on the other side of the hedge before he spoke. "Evenin', Lord Roth, or morning, as it were."

"Good morning, Kurp." He scanned the gardens, but the few stragglers outside weren't close enough to hear. "Your report?"

Meeting with underground contacts visibly during the day was stupid, and Marcus didn't consider himself a stupid man. No one expected him to meet his men during social functions, which made them perfect. This meeting was closer to daylight hours than usually planned, but the bleary eyes of the guests would compensate.

"Not good," Kurp replied. "Crosby gang got Fletcher, and we ain't heard from Fysh in a sennight. The lads try not to show it, but they're gettin' nervous."

Marcus clutched his watch. "Yes. It's understandable."

"This was left."

Marcus lifted the heavy paper that was passed under the hedge.

You are running out of background players, Lord Roth. On whom will I satisfy my vengeance when the last is gone? Perhaps bigger game? Your compatriots at the top? Your friends? I'll have my due. This I promise.

The paper crunched between his fingers.

"Do you recognize the handwriting, my lord?" Kurp's voice was expectant, hopeful.

Marcus relaxed his grip and examined the looping *l*'s and *t*'s and the scrawl of the base letters in the faint light. "No. He is too smart for that. He'll have had someone else write the letters. Still, I'll run it by Stephen."

Marcus sensed the disappointment through the hedge, and felt its echo. They all wanted answers. They were all relying on him.

"Send a purse to Fletcher's wife and tell her about the place in Dover. What about Kramer?"

"Had a pint with him a few hours ago."

Relief washed through him. Relief that at least a few of his men still survived. "Good. He's holding on, then?"

"He said he wasn't worried. Y' know how Kramer is. Would take someone cuttin' out his bleedin' heart before he showed fear."

Marcus watched a guest stumble toward the gardens, before another man grabbed him and steered him back to the terrace. "Will you see him again this week?"

"Should."

"Tell him to stay low instead of doing his routine at the docks next weekend."

Silence greeted that announcement. They had never pulled back before, and it would grate on the boys to show fear of what was happening.

Marcus turned his pocket watch end over end in his palm, closing his eyes briefly. "I know,

Kurp. It's not what I like either, but I want to get a handle on this before going forward. Things have gotten out of control since the shake-up."

"Yes." Kurp sounded resigned, then determined: "We will find this bastard and give him his collar day."

Marcus gave a mirthless grin. He had the feeling that the man responsible wasn't going to make it to a formal execution. If nothing else, one of the men would probably "slip" while transporting him. He could just imagine it. "Sorry sir," they'd say to him, "My knife slipped from my hands. Right between his ribs. Right queer it was."

It wasn't a question of whether he and his men would find the man responsible. They would. They always did. And after murdering two of their number already, and with another missing, blood lust and resolve had taken hold.

"Yes we will, Kurp. You have my schedule for the next week?"

"Aye."

"Good. Send someone tomorrow night around one. I'll have some papers."

"Aye."

Marcus felt Kurp slip away, though the man was silent as usual. He looked at the terrace doors and saw a pair of dancers twirling inside, though music no longer played, the musicians having long since retired. The woman was blond, but his vision overlaid dark hair caressing a revealing navy dress that was more seductive than he was used to seeing against such dark hair and light skin. His grip on his watch tightened and he slipped it back into his pocket.

He felt old all of a sudden. Barely thirty-six, and old already. As if life was passing more rapidly then he could grasp.

At this age his father had already . . . well, best not to think of that.

He carefully placed the threatening note inside his jacket. He hoped they could find something there, but held little belief that they would. The man doing this was desperate, but clever. A dangerous combination. And he couldn't discount the possibility that more than one person was involved.

On the other hand, if someone else had truly written the note—that person was a liability. If they could capture the note writer . . .

He smiled grimly.

Two men dead, and a third body most likely waiting to be found. He had too many enemies to list, but no one before had taken such systematic measures in eradicating his network of informants.

There were at least two bills in the House that could be the cause, and any number of actions on the streets or overseas—they all blended together at this point. He had ruined three men in the last year, all deserving of it, but all with justifiable reasons for revenge.

And now others were paying the consequences. People who counted on him. People with families that counted on him.

He loosened his fists as he strode back inside the nearly empty ballroom. At this point he would do anything to find the man responsible and make sure he was destroyed. And he would use anyone and anything in his path to make it happen.

Chapter 8

The Hennings' rout was a mix somewhere between acceptable and slightly scandalous. One could argue either way, depending on the level of one's propriety.

Marcus watched with growing vexation as Isabella changed one partner for another on the dance floor. She was wearing some light blue gown that he had seen before but couldn't remember being quite so low. He resisted the urge to walk over and tug the bodice up, and turned to James, who was watching him in amusement.

"Something on your mind, Angelford?"

"I can't figure out whether you resemble a jealous husband or an irate father."

"What the devil are you on about?"

"Every time Lady Willoughby comes within your sight, you get this sort of green-tinged, puckered expression on your face. It's quite amusing."

"I'm delighted for you."

"So which is it?"

He flicked a piece of lint from his sleeve. "Which is what?"

"You know very well what I'm asking."

"Whether I'm green-tinged or puckered? Neither is very appealing."

Unfortunately, James didn't seem put off in the least. "Are you a jealous husband or an irate father?"

Marcus watched Isabella twirl. "Last I recall, I was neither married nor a father to some poor bastard."

"I think you're jealous."

"That is your prerogative, of course."

James whistled. "Damn, but you are a close-mouthed bastard."

"I couldn't agree more," a voice chimed in from the side. The Duke of Wellington stepped into view. "What is Roth being a bastard about now?"

Marcus didn't move, but his eyes tried to encase James in ice.

"We were discussing the vote last month," James said smoothly.

Marcus decided his friend could live another day.

"Ah, yes. Bit of a mangy beast that."

"Always said you were a mangy beast, Wellington," Sir Robert Peel piped in from the other side, insinuating himself in the group as well.

Wellington sent an unimpressed look Peel's way. The two were often combatants, sometimes friends, occasionally collaborators, frequently allies. This looked like an evening for the former.

"Still on about the police force, Peel? I thought we had reached the end of that discussion."

"We'll never reach the end of that discussion, Wellington. What about you, Roth, how goes it backstage maneuvering the Corn Laws'?"

Marcus turned his back to the dance floor to keep focus. "A mess at the moment. Can't get Rogers and Cartwright to stop fighting in chambers. They actually took to boxing the other day."

"Boxing? Each other? Oh ho! I bet that is a right treat to see."

Marcus smiled. "Yes. And if you ever have need to brush up on your cant, all you need do is lurk in the vicinity—Rogers must be hanging around the docks these days."

"Tell me it at least makes them more productive?"

"Yes. I expect them to settle themselves into a full partnership soon."

Peel nodded, satisfied, as Marcus knew he would be. He'd gotten the implicit message that they had formed some solid outer party ties that would help them repeal the Corn Laws in the years to come.

"I don't understand why you deign to be involved, Roth," Wellington muttered, nudging a fallen ribbon with his dark boot.

"You never know when finding allies in one place will help you with another."

And he thought the Corn Laws were wretched, but he didn't verbally espouse his beliefs often. He much preferred staying behind the scenes to manipulate the players. Much like playing a game of chess.

However, it could be excruciating to wait for all the players to get in place and for the game to begin. It was fortunate that patience was one of his better qualities. He had enough bad ones as it was.

On the flip side, sometimes things took too long and the players withered, or crumbled where they stood. It was all part of the risk of the overall game.

"That is true," Wellington said. "Allies are sometimes hard to find. And are sometimes blinded by their pet projects." He gazed pointedly at Peel.

"All it takes is a vote for my police force," Peel replied. "We can compromise. London for now, the country later. We'll have you in the prime minister's chair in no time, Welly."

"Peel, do we need to meet at dawn?"

"I wouldn't dream of it. Have a new mistress now, didn't I tell you? Still going strong in the dawn hours. Much better use of my time." Peel waggled his brows.

Wellington pointedly ignored him, turning to Marcus instead. It actually took a lot to impress the man these days. But he was still a fair man. And more importantly, he still listened to Marcus.

"Roth, I will see you in the morning. Angelford."

Marcus inclined his head and James did the same, while Peel just smirked.

James excused himself to dance with his wife, and Marcus gave Peel a look as they were left to themselves, on the edges of the crowd. "Amusing yourself?" Marcus asked.

"Wellington can be as starchy as a twelve inch cravat."

Marcus tried not to be amused. Peel could be just as starchy. They were both good men. Friends of his, after a fashion, but too involved in politics and the like to dig more deeply into a real friendship. They both made excellent tools. And he knew they used him as well. While they played the public faces, he was the one with the contacts—with the network that stretched across London, through areas like Mayfair and the east end equally.

Not every bill or act that became law was to his taste, but that was unfortunately the way things worked. He wasn't sure when that had ceased to be depressing. He wondered if he was already well past jaded.

He also wondered if Isabella would be appalled if she knew. She could be pretty rigid on what she deemed right and wrong. Politics didn't allow for a lot of that.

Not that it would matter much longer.

"Are you working on the new bill?" Peel asked.

"I'm working on Sanderson. He'll work on the bill."

Isabella swirled around the floor in Ellerby's arms. *Damn the man.*

"Ah yes." Peel smiled wryly. "How could I think otherwise?"

He turned to Peel. "Does that bother you?"

Now why on earth had he asked that?

"Why on earth would you ask me that? Has it ever bothered me in the past?" He shot Marcus a queer expression. "I know where things stand. I know where you stand. Usually. That is enough for me. I trust you at the heart of it."

Marcus kept the surprise from his face, merely nodding and accepting the compliment. He had never cared about how someone else might see his background machinations before. Why would he suddenly care now? He knew *Peel* didn't care. Maybe he had gone past jaded and landed in soft.

Peel turned back to watching the crowd. "I'm going to try and find Rogers. See if his cant really is up to par. I'll see you tomorrow afternoon. Too many damn loose ends to tie up before everyone leaves London."

Marcus nodded, but didn't watch as Peel slipped back into the crowd. He watched a light blue dress instead.

Isabella twirled around the floor. She was having a marvelous time dancing. Ellerby had taken to her side, doting on her and making sure she was always in motion. He was an excellent dancer, and she could see now how his partners had always shown so well on the floor.

She had never danced with him before the masquerade, having been far beneath his notice. But tonight he had noticed her right away. She supposed it was hard to miss. Most of the people were regular attendees. It didn't take much of a stretch to put together that she had been the person at the masquerade. Ellerby's face had shown surprise before a slow smile had wound its way across his face. She wondered if she should be worried.

"Lady Willoughby, have I told you how marvelous you look tonight?"

"I don't think ladies ever get tired of hearing such things, Mr. Ellerby."

"Fenton. Please call me Fenton."

"Oh, I think I'll stick with Mr. Ellerby for the time being. I wouldn't want to be too hasty."

Same girl, different dress. Blossoming was tougher than it seemed.

"Haste is the very nature of such gatherings," he replied with a smile.

Isabella looked around. This wasn't such a racy gathering. Perhaps not as staid as the ones she normally attended, but the masquerade had been more wild, and the party tomorrow was rumored to be a scorcher. All in all, other than the freer dancing, it was pretty average.

"Mr. Ellerby, are you sure?"

It was meant to be a teasing challenge, but instead it emerged as an outright challenge. Flirting was just not her strength.

His fingers traveled along the back edge of her dress, but she barely noticed. It had all the effect of a maid fixing her collar. His fingers grazed the skin, but no pleasant shivers accompanied the action, no flutters to make her heart skip. If anything, she was nervous about how terrible she was at flirting. How was she going to flirt with Marcus if she couldn't flirt with Ellerby?

"All you are seeing now is the main area of the house. How many couples have slipped away to the back or into rooms? Have you missed seeing anyone on the floor? Anyone you notice that has slipped away?"

Marcus was the only one she was keeping an eye on. She could care less about the others. She had felt her reputation pretty safe ever since stepping foot inside the Hennings' ballroom.

"Like how you and Roth slipped into a closed room for nearly twenty minutes at the masquerade. Twenty minutes is a long time, Isabella."

She tensed, focusing on Ellerby's smirk. Perhaps she had better rethink the status of her reputation. But she could stand to lose a few notches if she gained Marcus.

"We were talking, is all. And I didn't give you leave to call me Isabella. We were hardly gone any time at all."

"You thought it went unnoticed, didn't you?" His voice was amused as he ignored her previous statements.

"I don't see why anyone would notice. It was a masquerade."

And that was as false a statement as she had ever uttered. She lived and breathed the rules of the ton.

"I can't decide if you really are this innocent or if it is all a delicious act."

She wasn't innocent. She was just sometimes caught up in her dreams, not that she was going to let Ellerby in on that thought.

The dance thankfully ended. "It was a delight, Mr. Ellerby." Well, it had been a delight until they had started talking. "Thank you for the dance."

But instead of bowing and letting her go, he

grasped her hand. "Oh, no. I mustn't let an innocent morsel such as yourself go unattended. Please, allow me to escort you to the refreshment table. A glass of champagne, or some punch perhaps?"

She nodded. Politeness dredged up automatically, even though she'd rather be somewhere else.

Ellerby filled two glasses and switched back to being the inveterate flirt, straying only to safe topics. She relaxed and sipped the tart punch.

She watched Marcus as he talked to the other guests. He seemed to detach himself quickly from the females and collude with the more powerful members of the House.

That he didn't stay with any of the females trying to gain his attention pleased her. The light shone off his dark hair in a mockery of a halo, and his whiskey eyes caught hers.

The air buzzed around her. Her breath caught. Was there a flicker of interest there? A flicker that hadn't been present a few days ago?

He broke contact and turned to the man next to him.

She bit her lip and took another sip. It was a dangerous game she wanted to play. Marcus wasn't the type of man who sought her out. Oh, they were friends and enjoyed an odd camaraderie over their love of chess. But she had never pierced his internal shield. She used to think she could see beyond it back when they were young, but something had happened to him at school or home. When his parents had retired to their estates, disappearing from public view, Marcus had gone too. He hadn't returned the same boy. Hadn't returned a boy at all.

He was a dark and capable man who ruthlessly took what he wanted, and she had learned that there was little that ever stood in his way. No, beyond friendship, he was not attracted to her type—the calm, friendly sort who issued few passionate vibrations or sexual intentions.

She took another sip, Ellerby's voice droning in the background. She was completely fooling herself if she thought there was interest there. Marcus showed the interest of a big brother. One who had never had a little sister, and had adopted her instead. An overly protective friend.

Trembles ran through her chest as she stared at the parquet floor. Golden eyes that would never be.

The maudlin thought had her lifting her glass again. She paused as the ballroom tilted. Strange. Ballrooms rarely tilted. And she rarely got so down in spirit. She looked at the glass in her hand. What number was this? Her third?

A moment of clarity pierced her maudlin veil— the tart taste of the punch. It had probably been drenched in alcohol. She didn't usually drink much, but between watching Marcus and absently nodding to Ellerby, she had been lifting her glass. And Ellerby had kept giving her new ones. It was an old trick. One she castigated herself that she should know better to watch for. She internally mouthed an unladylike swear word, followed by an uncharacteristic giggle.

She focused on Ellerby.

". . . and that is why when a stallion mates with—"

"Mr. Ellerby," she interrupted. "Are you trying to get me drunk?"

A disconcerted expression flitted across his face, before the normally charming one appeared. "Of course not, Isabella. Are you not feeling well?"

"I feel fine, Mr. Ellerby." And indeed she did. All of a sudden she had switched from feeling maudlin to feeling *quite* fine, blissful in fact. Which is why she needed to find Calliope and leave the party. Though the party was so lovely. And hadn't the lights just dimmed to such a wonderful shade?

She needed to leave.

She plopped the nearly empty glass into Ellerby's hand and rose. "Good night, Ellerby."

Isabella headed off in the direction she had last seen Calliope. Someone hit her as she veered left. Now that she was standing and moving, the ballroom was tilting a bit more. Very unstable floors.

She stopped for a moment and narrowed her eyes as the expanse of room filled with bodies before her. She needed to get to that pillar over there near the plant. A potted fern? She squinted. No, a philodendron. If she headed straight for it, she could pause there and then figure out her next course of action.

She held her head up and walked breezily through the crowd. Perhaps *marched* through the crowd was a bit more descriptive, but she couldn't be too choosy at the moment. She just needed to make it to the pillar, lean smartly against it and find Calliope. No problem.

She was almost there, having seen fit to avoid a few other people who perhaps found the ballroom as tippy as she did, when something blocked her way.

She stared at a gold button before tilting her head back and looking up at a most welcome sight.

"And where are you off to in such a hurry?"

She couldn't think of any better place than right here. She smoothed her hands down the front of her modified peacock blue dress, and saw his eyes follow the movement. She drew a hand back up and played with the rosette at the center of her bodice—all of Calliope's advice suddenly seemed natural. Having Bertie modify this dress had been a stroke of brilliance.

"I can't recall." Her voice rode on top of the heavy beat of her heart—as if she were out of breath.

His eyes darkened to a molten gold. "You can't recall?"

She waved him forward, absorbed in watching the light move across his face as he leaned toward her. "You are looking quite handsome tonight. Delicious, really."

A dark brow drew up and she watched it in fascination.

"Like chocolate and caramel. A dessert to savor."

The brow rose further. She put a hand on his chest, just over the button at eye level. The gold accessory was nothing compared to the color reflected above.

"The caramel is for your eyes, of course. I don't know of any eyes quite as golden as yours. Not that I want to eat them or lick them. The color just reminds me of something delicious."

Her fingers curled against the pleasantly smooth yet rough texture of his jacket. Something told her that this wasn't a conversation she wished to be having.

She withdrew her hand. "Have you seen Calliope? I believe it's time to leave."

The angel finally spoke. "It's been time to leave since the moment you stepped in the door."

"Oh, how lovely." She smiled brilliantly, something euphoric coursing through her veins. He held a tendre for her too.

"You shouldn't have been here in the first place."

His voice was dark. Like he wished she wasn't there. Well, obviously. If he had just kept her at home with him . . .

"I know. The fishing was rather scarce there for a while."

Marcus's brows drew together violently. "Fishing?"

She waved. "Fishing. You use a pole." She giggled, and couldn't help glancing down. "No, a rod." She giggled some more. She met his eyes again—for some reason he didn't look amused. She motioned with her hands. "Fish. You reel them in."

"Reel them in?"

"Only the ones you want to keep, of course. You have to toss all the others that grab your line."

"And you are looking for a certain type of fish?"

"Oh, yes," she said dreamily.

"And what does this fish look like?"

"He's tall and handsome. And brave. And handsome. His eyes—so lovely. And his brows slash together just so."

She poked a finger between his brows. He

grabbed it and pulled her hand between them so that the side rested against his jacket. He was holding her hand. It was lovely and warm.

"Isabella, are you looking for a lover?"

His voice was dark and deep. She had always thought it sounded so low and mysterious. She'd like to swim in the river of its . . . of its . . . something.

"Oh, yes." How did he ever guess? It must have been the punch.

"And why have you suddenly decided you need a lover?" She saw him look around. He tugged her behind the pillar. The leaves of the philo-fern-thing—blast, she could tell every variety of plant at a dozen paces, but she wouldn't be able to sort a rose bush from an oak at the moment—the leafy green thing brushed the bare skin of her arm.

"Is it not normal to seek companionship?"

"Yes. It's called marriage."

She scoffed and her hand flew out, ruffling the leaves. "As if that has ever stopped you. What about that last woman of yours—Mrs. Cavenwell? Did you seek marriage with her for wont of companionship?"

"Of course not. How do you even know about that?"

"What, you think me a simpleton?" She glared.

"No, I think you're foxed."

She crossed her arms. "I will seek companionship if I please."

She looked to the dance floor and saw Ellerby dancing with a woman in green. She couldn't see much from her vantage point, and everything had gone a little wavy.

"I see." His voice was remote. She didn't like that at all. "Don't tell me you are after Ellerby."

His fingers traveled along the back edge of her dress. She felt each touch, each area of skin his fingers skimmed. Shivers raced through her.

She reached up and touched his firm jaw. "Don't be silly, Marcus. I'm after you."

Chapter 9

*D*on't be silly, Marcus. I'm after you.

Isabella stuffed her head into her pillow and groaned. She lifted her head and groaned again.

Stupid, stupid, stupid. She pounded her pillow.

And *that* was why she didn't drink much alcohol. That was why she told the new debutantes to watch their consumption levels, not that the watered down concoctions usually found at the more sedate gatherings contained much alcohol.

What had been mixed in the punch? An entire bottle of brandy?

She vaguely recalled Calliope mentioning something about taking care at the refreshment table, but she had been too busy watching Marcus to pay much attention to the warning. Well, she would be busy watching him from now on, because he assuredly wasn't going to be talking to her.

"Wake up, my lady."

Isabella groaned again as her maid crashed through the door. "Bertie, let me sleep."

"Now none of that. You're deserving of a little pain this morning."

"Excellent. Your support warms my heart."

"You shouldn't have drunk so much."

"Undoubtedly. I made a right fool of myself last night."

Bertie frowned. "What did you do? You barely talked to me last night when you returned."

"I told Lord Roth that I wanted to have an affair with him."

Bertie flopped into a chair, her mouth gaping like a beached fish. "I don't believe you did so."

Isabella grimaced and sat up, pushing her thick mane of hair away from her face. "I did. He will probably never speak to me again."

Her maid said nothing, simply sat there in shocked silence.

"Oh, why are you looking at me like that?" she snapped, the pounding in her head making her waspish. "Of course he will speak to me again. But it will be quite uncomfortable. Worse than after the Pettigrew party, I should think."

Bertie reached over and patted her hand sympathetically.

It wasn't until noon and several home remedies later that Isabella began feeling better, at least physically, and decided to work in the garden.

She was still morose about Marcus's reaction. She could clearly remember his shuttered features in response to her declaration. He had hustled her to his carriage, bundled her in, and sent the driver on his way. He hadn't uttered a word to her in response, though she remembered that she had waxed on about him taking charge and all sorts of nonsense as he had dragged her outside.

She savagely pulled weeds in her garden, while deciding whether to book passage on a ship to France today or tomorrow.

Her housekeeper appeared at the door to the gardens. "My lady, the packages from Madame Giselle's have just been delivered."

Glory be. Now she had two new dresses with which to tempt absolutely no one.

"Bertie has taken them to your chambers. Is there anything you'd like, my lady? Water, tea?"

She'd like someone to erase last night from her existence.

"I'd love a glass of water, Velma. Thank you."

Velma bobbed and Isabella returned to attacking the interlopers in her garden. By necessity of space, this garden was tiny compared to those at her parents' country estate, or, she thought wistfully, to her beautiful gardens in Oxfordshire. When George had died, the property and baronetcy had passed to a cousin, and with it her well-loved gardens.

Tending the gardens had kept her sane through George's long illness. Planting the seeds. Nurturing the tiny blooms. Watching the sprouts grow.

It had been a wrench to leave them behind.

George had loved those gardens as well, though he had been unable to tend them after his chest cough had steadily progressed into chills, fevers, and violent fits that had wracked his body. But he had held on for two years, and she had stayed either at his side or working in the gardens that they both loved. Their chambers had faced the rear gardens, and George had enjoyed watching her work in them on the days he couldn't make it out of bed.

It had been a shared passion, gardening; tending new life and watching it grow. They had wanted a family. They had achieved a beautiful garden instead.

Isabella swallowed and extracted the root of another weed. She hadn't deserved George when she married him, loving another as she did, but she liked to think that they had worked things out between them in the end.

The loneliness, though, had been hard to banish, especially at the end of George's illness. She had argued with Marcus that she wasn't lonely. She desperately wanted to believe it.

George's illness had been a horrible strain on everyone. But even with the supportive family members who had passed through regularly, no one knew, truly knew, what it had been like to sit there day after day watching him waste away. For she *had* loved him. Not a mad, passionate love, but a loyal, gentle, caring love all the same. The illness had taken a terrible toll, and by the end it was nearly a relief when he had succumbed.

She winced as she whacked her gloved finger with the edge of her spade. She would rot forever for that thought.

Was she the only one horrible enough to have experienced those cursed thoughts? To feel that wretched relief? She was too much of a coward to ask anyone—even her own mother. She couldn't bear to see the look of disgust. The look that would reflect her own feelings.

She ripped another weed from between her roses, her thoughts morbid and sad. She would make sure never to touch a glass of punch again.

"My lady?"

She looked up to see Bertie standing before her, wringing her hands.

"Is there a problem, Bertie?"

"The new dresses arrived."

"Yes, Velma informed me." And because curiosity always got the best of her . . . "How do they look?"

"Well, that's what I'm here to talk to you about. They are quite . . . original."

Which was Bertie's term for scandalous.

Isabella sighed. She pushed off the ground and removed her work gloves and apron. "I'll be in shortly. Have Velma deliver the water upstairs, will you?"

Bertie nodded and rushed inside. For a woman getting on in her years, Bertie could be quite spry. Isabella pushed back some of the escaped tendrils from her hair bun. She had found three gray hairs today, without even attempting to look for them, so maybe she should refrain from comments about age.

Stepping out of her shoes, she walked into the house in her stockings and climbed the stairs. Her first impression upon entering the room was Bertie's frown, then her eyes drifted to the magnificent dress on the hanger.

Isabella sucked in a breath. It overpowered everything else in the room. She cautiously approached the gown and touched the sarcenet fabric, letting the thin silk slide through her fingers.

The dress was bold, the color of the scarlet vivid and deep, with veins of indigo sliding behind. A border of flowers and leaves in dark satin graced the hem and crept upward. Pearls were sewn within each bloom. Small sleeves with delicate ornamentation completed the work. The dress was designed to look as if it would slip from her shoulders at any moment. A modest front with a low-cut back. A teasing dress. It would be un-expected on her. She imagined a strand of pearls woven through her locks, a large golden comb nestled into her plaited hair.

"My lady?"

"It's wonderful," she said softly, still entranced with the fabric, design, and cut. This was a dress not to be ignored. She would have admired it greatly on Calliope. But on her?

"My lady . . . red?" Bertie's voice was agitated.

Isabella turned to her. "I never asked for red, though I can't say I'm displeased. Turkey red has been fashionable for years, though I've never worked up the courage to suggest nor order it. And scarlet? No. Calliope must have changed the order, the minx."

"But surely you can't go out dressed in—"

"I want to try it on, Bertie."

Her maid pulled a face, but took the dress down and helped her change. Isabella watched her reflection in the mirror as Bertie sashed it up. She looked like a different person. Her hair was still plastered about her face from working in the garden, but the deeply veined scarlet lit her skin and highlighted the color in her cheeks. She had always dreamed of wearing red, but had never worked up the nerve to stand out in the crowd.

"My lady?"

This was her dress. This was the dress that represented everything she had been thinking and dreaming. Taking a chance. Gathering the courage. Putting forth her desires.

"I'm wearing it tonight, Bertie."

"But, my lady! I thought you weren't going out this evening, because of the business with Lord Roth and what you said earlier. You said you were going to cancel. And this dress!"

Isabella pivoted to take a peek at the back. "Is fabulous, I know."

"No! It's outrageous!"

"Hush, Bertie. Help me out of it. I need to wash up and take a nap or I'll continue to be out of sorts tonight."

Her mind was overflowing. She was going to the Pudgenets' party, and she was wearing this dress. The earlier alarm and worries of seeing Marcus dulled to a tiny murmur in the back of her head. She looked at the gown. Something shifted into place, and she knew she had to go. To not give up before the battle had begun.

The dress was not one of defeat, but a full stop declaration of war.

Marcus prowled the edges of the ballroom.

Two of his most ardent political supporters had been trying to get his attention for the past twenty minutes. He had been given the crushing news that yet another of his men was missing, a headache hovered over the edges of his vision . . .

. . . and the only thing he could think about was *what* she was doing in that damned dress.

And damned it was, colored a bright scarlet with darker trimmings. It moved, no, *slid*, around her like a serpent undulating in water. Mesmerizing.

If he hadn't already correctly guessed what her motivation was for attending these parties, he'd know now without a doubt.

In fact every widow hunter in *London* knew now.

Calliope looked as smug as a cat that had lapped a pantry full of cream. She was attired in a dark gown, not quite black, but an iridescent shade between navy and pitch. When they stood next to each other, Calliope's dress set off the trim and undercurrent of Isabella's gown, and Marcus was under no delusion that Calliope hadn't done it on purpose. Devious woman.

Men were fluttering around them as if they were the only women in the room. Calliope turned any attention directed to her onto Isabella, then watched with a pleased expression.

Isabella seemed to be soaking up the attention just fine. Tonight her natural graciousness seemed much too intimate for his taste. She was going to pick up a lover in no time.

If he could just persuade her to return to the former friendly, *proper* Isabella, then he wouldn't have to cause bodily injury to the men around her.

He saw James standing nearby and made a beeline for him.

"Angelford."

"Roth."

"What is your wife doing?"

James gazed over at the crowd, a look of feigned boredom on his face. "Chatting."

"She is not chatting."

"That is true. She is making everyone chat with Lady Willoughby."

Marcus clenched his teeth and forced himself to relax. "Why?"

James shrugged, his lack of concern irritating. "She looks beautiful tonight, doesn't she? Didn't know she had it in her."

"You think her unappealing usually?" Marcus asked, though if he were truthful, he'd admit it came out in something of a snarl.

James smiled. "No. Actually, I think her prettier every time I see her. But she does not have the type of looks that usually attract this kind of attention."

Marcus watched the swarm of men. "I never thought her an attention seeker." It was not something he found attractive. It made his blood boil.

"She's not. Don't let jealousy cloud your judgment and make you stupid."

"Jealousy? You've lost your wits. She's in over her head." He pointed to the crowd. "Anyone with half a thought can see."

"She looks as if she's enjoying herself."

"And you think she's going to be having fun nine months from now?"

"Are you insinuating that Lady Willoughby can't handle herself?" James continued to look amused.

"I think that she is too green in these matters. Your wife is behind this."

"Is she? She hasn't confessed her diabolical plan to me yet."

"Isabella suddenly has all these peculiar notions that she didn't have before."

"I see."

"Why am I still talking to you?"

"I don't rightly know. Perhaps you should venture over to the crowd and preach to Lady Willoughby."

"I find I suddenly dislike you, Angelford."

"Yes, that does tend to happen. I myself disliked Stephen quite a bit when he pointed out how my jealousy was impeding my good sense."

"How can it impede something you do not possess?"

His ex-friend merely smiled. "I now owe Stephen a bottle of that brandy he likes so much. Dratted man always manages to win, even when he bets on you. Carry on being dense."

Marcus whirled away from James, not caring that his behavior might be noticed and commented on by others. At the moment he couldn't have cared less.

Which was stronger: his desire to see Isabella happy, or his desire to see no one else make her light up the way—

"Roth."

He didn't stop. The last person he wanted to talk to was Stephen. Cheery bastard. Probably wanted to express his thoughts about Isabella, and gloat too. Perhaps he could slip past him. He'd hate to be the one to kill Stephen after so many failed attempts by others.

"Marcus."

He pushed through the crowd to the terrace doors, happy that the ballroom was on ground level.

"Damn it, stop walking."

Marcus didn't want to talk. He had a meeting with his contact in ten minutes, and he wanted to focus on the matters at hand.

"You know, you are acting more emotional than my wife. And she has the excuse of being pregnant."

Marcus stopped next to a large potted fern and

tapped a foot. "What do you want, Stephen? I don't have time to dillydally."

"Obviously, if your flight from the ballroom was any indication. Should get Calliope to caricature it. 'Flight from a ballroom' is a great title."

He looked down his nose at his friend. "I'm going to kill you slowly. Without using my hands, so as not to dirty them."

Stephen held up a hand and smiled. "Fine. I'll stop baiting you. But I have information on the note you gave me."

Marcus discharged his general irritation, automatically reaching for his center to calm himself. He succeeded only partially. "What did you find?"

"The man who wrote the note is in printing. There are dustings of printer's ink on its back."

Marcus nodded slowly. "Fletcher's body was found near Ackermann's. Have you talked to anyone there?"

"Actually, I thought I'd take Calliope with me. Do you mind?"

Calliope had many contacts there, having sold her caricatures almost exclusively to the print shop. "No. Just make sure James knows. He'll kill you before he kills her."

Stephen smiled. "I know." He hesitated. "Marcus, about the other, maybe—"

"No."

Stephen looked disgruntled. "How do you know what I was going to say?"

"That sentence was going to end with something nauseating like, 'We need to speak' or 'You should heed your emotions' or 'You should take a wife.'"

"Er."

"Probably the former. Does Audrey ever get tired of wearing the breeches between the two of you?"

Stephen winked slyly. "I never get tired of her wearing them."

"Please never say something like that to me again. Have a good night, Stephen."

His friend laughed and strolled inside. The lights from the ballroom winked, the yellow and white and gold blending in a soft glow.

A soft glow that grew ever dimmer.

Marcus's headache returned full force. Or he at least let himself remember it.

The red of a rose, the blue of a pair of fine eyes. Would he still remember the brilliance and hue when he could no longer view them?

The layout of the gardens shifted before him.

Fifteen steps to the edge of the terrace, two potted plants and a garden table to avoid, ten steps to the ballroom door. From there it would be a crush of bodies, but he had the inside layout firmly implanted already.

He despised this weakness. Despised the eventual end it would bring. Despised what it would cause him to lose—and what he could never hope to gain.

"My lord?"

He spun around. Kurp was a shadow against the garden wall, partially hidden behind a short pine. He had been completely wrapped within himself, a sure way to die or get someone else hurt.

"Kurp."

"Finley's missing."

"I know." Another funeral to attend. Another family to console. He felt old, so old, all of a sudden. He retrieved a sheaf of papers. "Here are your instructions. Set up a meeting at the usual place for the day after tomorrow. Hopefully we will have more to go on at that time and can start planning."

Kurp took the documents and nodded, bravery etched in the lines of his face.

"Be careful tonight, Kurp."

He looked up sharply, and Marcus grimaced. It seemed his newly discovered odd behavior was once again reasserting itself.

"I'm fine, Kurp. We've all had a rough week. That is all. Good night."

Kurp slipped back into the shadows as Marcus carried his shadows inside. A glimpse of color lit his vision, and he stopped a moment, watching, weighing. There was only one way to deal with this.

He strode toward shimmering scarlet crowned by black.

Chapter 10

Isabella executed a turn and met her enthusiastic partner again in step. She had never danced with him before, and although a bit over-eager, he wasn't a bad partner. She knew the spate of attention was not so much for her charms as for what her dressing in this manner represented. Her attire was a clear indication she was looking for companionship.

If only the man she was wishing for wasn't ignoring her so completely . . .

So here she was, hours later dancing the night away with one gentleman after another. Some the more mundane type of widow hunter, and some more surprising. Men who had previously been interested in friendly chatter suddenly had a different gleam in their eyes.

She chastised herself. How many times had she told a debutante—look like you are interested and having fun and others will want to have fun with you? When had she forgotten to apply this to herself? Had marriage changed her so much?

George had been gone for three years, but she had immersed herself in too many projects to take a good look at herself.

Some men, just like women, were looking for a friend. Some were looking for a companion. Some were looking for—

"Lady Willoughby, you are well turned out tonight," her partner said.

"What a handsome compliment." It could use some work.

"Your dress makes me think of the fires of hell." He stepped on her foot in his need to move closer.

"Why thank you, Mr. Burns."

"Do you think I might taste that hell tonight?"

—some were looking for something a little *quicker* than companionship.

The music, thank Mary, stopped and she forced a cracking smile onto her face. "I think not, Mr. Burns. Thank you for the dance."

He executed a neat bow and took himself off to see if the next woman was more willing. At least he made no pretense about what he was interested in—and didn't seek to pester her when she wasn't.

If only—

"Is this next dance taken?"

She licked suddenly dry lips at the smooth voice. "No, it isn't."

He came into her view, all sinful dark hair and caramel eyes. "May I have it, then?"

She tilted her head. Her heart started beating faster as his eyes traveled down her neck. "You may."

His hand curved around her waist as the first violin began to play. A soft heat spread from where his palm rested and his fingers curled. She put her hand in his and a tingle shot up her arm. They held that position for a few beats as the other couples started whirling around them. And then the lights and colors rushed by as he began twirling her too.

"You have been absent much of tonight," she said.

This was the first time they had spoken to one another since he had packed her into a carriage, inebriated and delivering all sorts of embarrassing— and true—confessions.

"Have I? I feel as if I've been haunting the edges of the ballroom all night."

She swallowed. Watching her? "Is that so?"

He looked above her head. "Yes, there are some important matters happening in the government."

Crushing disappointment hit her and she tried to rein it in. "Oh."

His eyes tightened and she wondered at what he was looking. "You haven't been haunting the edges of the ballroom, though. I've rarely seen you off the dance floor."

"Oh?" Her heart picked up again.

He focused on her. "That dress is . . . interesting."

"Your compliment brings me to my knees, my lord."

He didn't smile. "Do you suddenly desire to give the male half of the town visions in the night?"

She swallowed. "That one was much better."

"I aim to please."

"Do you?"

His arm tightened around her. His expression didn't change, but his voice was light. "Only on Tuesdays."

The short piece ended and he bowed to her, his fingers slipping under hers, the pads trailing as he let her go and melted into the crowd.

The confusion continued. Dance after dance she would catch sight of him, only to lose him in the crowd. There was something darker and more dangerous about him tonight. He was like a hunter prowling on the edges of the forest floor.

Her nerves were screaming by the tenth set. The dancers moved apart for a moment and she caught sight of Marcus lounging next to the terrace doors. He was talking to Giles Pepper, a man of considerable political influence. However, his hooded, brooding golden eyes were trained on her.

Her breath caught, but the dancers took a step forward and she lost sight of him.

"Lady Willoughby, you look smashing tonight."

She refocused on the man who had just joined her and smiled, trying to still her racing heart. "Thank you, Mr. Sethy."

"I was wondering if you could help me catch Miss Cross's attention?"

Her smile grew and she regained a semblance of sanity. It seemed some things would never change, no matter how she dressed. "Of course. Why don't we talk over there?" She pointed to a few unoccupied chairs set apart from the others but still in full view of the entire room.

He sported a relieved grin, somewhat crooked in shape, and escorted her over. Though really escorted was a pleasant way for saying hustled. Thirty minutes later Mr. Sethy stood and skipped off to draw up a list of unusual romantic notions, as she'd suggested—something beyond flowers and poetry. She wondered, not for the first time, what a young man like Mr. Sethy was doing at a party like this.

She patted her hair and discreetly checked the ballroom for Marcus, who was once again nowhere in sight. Unfortunately, Ellerby was, and he was headed toward her, determination set in every line of his face. She withheld a sigh. It would take him a few minutes to reach her, and she wondered if perhaps she shouldn't just slip out of the room first. She didn't know what Ellerby's agenda was, other than the obvious, but he unnerved her with his bold advances.

She prepared herself for a bout of playing off his words and discouraging his roaming hands, as she'd been doing prior to Mr. Sethy asking her to dance and chat—bless him. She didn't know if dealing with Ellerby was worth watching Marcus vacillate between ignoring her and staring broodingly at her while he stalked the edges of the floor like a feral beast.

A shadow fell across her. Her breath caught.

She felt him, felt his presence behind her, and knew he was mere inches away—she could feel him breathing.

"Giving the honorable Mr. Sethy nightly visions?"

She tensed but stared straight ahead. "Just some friendly advice."

"Must have been quite some advice. He seemed most caught up in whatever it was you were telling him."

"It would be most poor of me to give away his secrets, would it not?"

"And what are your secrets, Isabella? What dark mysteries lurk behind those clear blue eyes?" His voice was low and deep.

Marcus stepped closer. The hairs on the back of her neck stood as displaced air moved between them. So close.

"Nothing so sordid, I assure you. My thoughts are of a most mundane variety."

But her breath was coming out in short bursts. Her voice higher than usual. Her thoughts anything but mundane.

He was here. With her.

"Silver lies again, Marie?"

His fingers grazed the nape of her neck.

"It's my middle name."

"I know. I know everything about you."

She turned to face him. His eyes were a dark gold beneath slashing brows, his expression serious. "Not everything."

His eyes traced her face. "No." He paused, as if unsure of himself for once. "Your little revelation last night was unexpected. I never expected you to say such a thing."

Her heart beat more quickly. Acknowledgment. Where would they go from here?

Something tugged at her awareness. There had been a nearly imperceptible hesitation in his voice. "You didn't expect me to say such a thing?"

His eyes tightened. "No."

"You didn't expect me to say such a thing, but you knew, didn't you?" she asked, a hitch to her voice.

He looked over her shoulder toward the dance floor. Something passed across his face that she couldn't read.

"Marcus, did you know?"

His eyes locked with hers and he took a step back. And then another, his gold gaze burning into her as he slowly walked backward. She felt an invisible hook in her center as more ground opened between them. He walked too slowly to be leaving her completely, his eyes pulling her forward. She felt the tug, like a rope tautly stretched and seeking a return to a comfortable state. She stood then, as if mesmerized, and followed him as he skirted around the chairs without even looking behind him.

As if he had their layout memorized. Which was a ridiculous notion, of course.

The tug didn't dull her wits completely. The one question on her mind—the question that might change everything—still lingered in the air.

"Were you aware?" she asked again, her tone more persistent as they performed some strange parody of a dance without touching, but with him leading her forward.

His eyes stayed with hers, and she watched the gold darken further. She followed his path, step for step, eyes locked together until she found herself in a hallway with him. Abruptly, he reached out and tugged her into an alcove.

Shivers streaked through her.

"Did you already comprehend—" she started again, as if asking a thousand different ways would somehow produce an answer.

He touched a curl that lolled along her shoulder blade.

"What would you have me say, Bella?"

You are the most beautiful woman I've ever known or *Let's retire from this ballroom to pursue a more wicked pastime* or *I've loved you forever.*

Yes, that last one.

"The truth."

She looked into his eyes and saw scrutiny, anger, and the fond look he always reserved for her. The one given to a dear *friend* or *little sister.*

She moved back a step. "No. You don't need to say anything, Marcus. Forgive me for a drunkard's ramblings."

He fingered the curl and something shifted in his eyes—disappointment or relief? "So you didn't mean it?" he asked.

Her eyes tried desperately to close, but his gold gaze pinned her. Standing here, in front of him, in a silent alcove, the portraits on the wall leaning closer to hear, and having to choose whether to bare part of her soul or to play safely and laugh it off.

"What would you have me say, Marcus?"

A dark brow lifted above a golden eye. "The truth."

To be left with a decision, a declaration or not. That whatever she said would determine the course of future events. That he would either continue to look at her as a friend, safe and secure. Or that something else might happen. That his eyes might show relief for her confession to be true, instead of relief for it to be false.

She took a deep breath.

"I meant every word."

Chapter 11

He studied her for long moments, playing with the lock of hair in his fingers. She couldn't read anything on his face.

He hadn't always been so skilled at hiding his emotions. He had gone into seclusion with his parents for two years until their deaths. She hadn't seen him again for six years. When they had been reintroduced at one of her pre-debut outings, he had been a virtual stranger—though a very polite one. He had always made sure to dance with her. To bring her into conversations with the pinnacle of the fashionable, who had begun to court him as he gained power and grew more handsome every year. To help her bloom into a confident young member of society.

It hadn't taken long for her to become besotted with him.

"Every word?"

"Yes."

She had lingered for three seasons, hoping he would declare. Her infatuation had turned into love, but her girlish mind had matured as well. She had seen his unrelenting courtesy for what it was; a fondness for her—as a friend. And as one season turned to two and two into three, she had steadily realized that it wasn't to be.

He released the curl from his fingers. "You are looking for a lover."

She paused for a moment to recall her drunken words.

"Yes."

"And you've decided on me for the moment."

For the last decade, really, though she'd never say it aloud. "You seem the best choice."

"Do I?" Amusement warred with something darker.

"The choicest cut, as it were."

"Mmmm . . ."

"You were my favorite exploring partner when we were young."

"This is hardly the pond in the back woods. And this isn't a minnow you are trying to catch."

"A minnow would not suit my purposes."

He raised a brow. She raised one in return.

"There are half a dozen men in that ballroom that would be a better choice for a lover, for some-one to *explore* with, than me."

But she didn't love any of the men inside. Why

would she want to choose someone else? And there was also the teensy matter that she wasn't really "exploring," but it wouldn't hurt to keep that to herself for the moment.

"I don't trust any of them. I trust you."

Something dark passed over his face, but it was gone too quickly.

"And what if you become too attached and get hurt?"

His saying that hurt, but she smiled instead. "I'm a mature woman, Marcus. I keep telling you that you should stop worrying. We are friends, are we not? I know what I'm getting into."

Silver lies. Delivered with a friendly smile.

He looked away from her to a portrait on the left. The woman inside seemed to be leaning forward in her frame, but Marcus's eyes were unfocused.

"You will just go on this foolish mission with someone else," he said, mostly to himself. "Just like when you were eight."

One time when she was angry with him, she had gone off with a group of children she didn't know. It happened *one time*. But if she could use it . . .

"There is that."

Time ticked. She rocked on her heels but didn't look away. Let him take the bait . . .

He sighed. She had never heard him sigh before. "Very well."

Overwhelming joy and relief crashed through

her, before his words and tone caught up— It was as if she had just asked him to stave off death. She crossed her arms automatically. "Well you don't have to sound so disgruntled about it."

His eyes met hers once more, and she was relieved to see amusement overlaying the darkness. "Not very well done of me, was it?"

"No."

She waited for him to properly rephrase his response. He reached out and ran a finger along her exposed shoulder blade instead. She stood rooted to the spot. He dipped a finger around the curl still lying there and brought the strands to his lips. "You always smell of flowers—wild and free. But that dress . . . you are wild and free tonight, Bella."

She couldn't have looked away if the building caught fire. Her heart raced, but all of a sudden the thoughts running through her head were languid and slow.

He leaned forward and the curl slipped from his fingers. Those long fingers, graceful and sure, ghosted across her cheek. The touch almost reverent. They slipped to the nape of her neck and drew her forward, slowly, gently.

"You are going to regret this," he said softly.

"No, I won't."

His eyes never left hers. His lips, soft but strong, touched hers. Just a touch. Heat flamed through her and she was caught in a heady feeling of exhilaration.

He was going to kiss her.

"Yes you will," he murmured.

And because he was moving too slowly, being too wrenchingly cautious, she kissed him instead. Just a press of her lips to his.

The texture was unbearably smooth. He pulled her closer, his lips stroking hers, opening her mouth beneath. His hand gently pressed her neck, the other softly touching her cheek in a reverent manner, as if she were delicate and beautiful and desired.

He tasted like cinnamon, deep and spicy. She was kissing Marcus, pressed against him, and nothing had ever felt so good.

He pulled her closer still and her dress flowed around his legs, as if a breeze were caressing an elm.

Cinnamon enveloped her. His hand trailed down her arm.

He pulled back slightly and traced her features. "What am I going to do with you?" he whispered. "I should let you go, but I can't stand to see you looking at another man the way . . . "

. . . *the way you look at me*—She finished his sentence in her mind. Left unsaid as if it was his darkest secret.

That he would want to be with her thrilled her so much that her heart echoed a stampede. Everything should be perfect. Yet . . . his reserve, his obvious reluctance . . . shouldn't he be happier? Shouldn't that desire be a good thing?

She pushed the thoughts gently to the side to examine later. "I won't."

And if that wasn't putting her cards on the table . . .

"You should. If you get involved with me, there are a few things you have to recognize."

She pushed the pain away and touched his face. "I know."

And she did. She knew all arrangements with Marcus were temporary. She knew that Marcus had no interest in marriage, for some reason. She also knew she wouldn't be a standard bird in his aviary.

What that made her, she didn't know. But she could work with it.

She'd have to work with it.

And if it made it harder to let him go in the end, she would just have to work with that too. She had already cast her lot. She had already decided exactly what she wanted. What she wanted could change in the future; that she wanted Marcus would not.

"You shouldn't know anything of the sort, Bella. You should run as far from me as you can manage."

"Why would I do that?" she said lightly. "You've always been faster."

His face was still far too serious, and it worried her more than slightly.

"Marcus, I don't believe you have graciously accepted this offer or presented one in return."

He regarded her for a long moment before bowing over her hand. His lips connected with her gloved knuckles, but she could feel the heat as if he'd stripped them bare.

"Pardon me, Lady Willoughby." His eyes locked with hers. "Would you do me the honor of becoming my companion for the unspecified near future?"

The "near future" part hurt, but the roguish look in his eyes warmed her.

"I gladly accept, Lord Roth," she said pertly. "Now where are you going to ravish me? I seem to recall you have an aversion for settees?"

The mischievousness on his face didn't diminish, but she caught sight of the drifting shadows.

"No settees tonight. Return to Calliope and James. I will see you tomorrow."

"But—"

He stroked her cheek, and she cut off abruptly to lean into the gesture. "Not here. Not like this. Not with you. We'll talk tomorrow."

She nodded slowly, half afraid if she left now, it would all turn out to be some dream from which she would awaken.

His face was growing more closed, as usual. But she had enough to hope.

"Off with you, Bella, before a demon swoops down to gobble you up in that delicious dress."

She watched his eyes; amusement and just a trace of ferocity present.

That look would haunt her dreams all night.

Marcus watched her go and leaned against the wall. No one had interrupted them, much to his surprise.

Much to his regret?

No, right now, with the feel of her smooth skin and lips embedded in his mind, in his fingertips, he didn't regret. In the future he knew he most definitely would.

How was he going to disentangle himself from this mess? A mess partially of his own making.

He wanted her. It wasn't an admission he was comfortable with acknowledging yet. He had spent too long denying emotional entanglements, staying away from anyone with the ability to get close, merely taking relief as needed. But finding relief had been harder and harder, thus the string of women Stephen had annoyingly pointed out. One unsatisfying pair of legs after another.

None of the legs had been bad on their own . . . but he had the vaguely terrifying notion that they had just not been attached to the right woman.

Either Stephen was finally rubbing off on him or something about this current situation was subtly changing him. He didn't know which was worse.

He pushed away from the wall. No, the latter was a hundred times worse. No matter what happened in the next few weeks, the outcome would not change.

He had promised Isabella a short-term relationship to deal with her quest—her panicky female situation. Widows tended to get restless around her age, he'd seen it before, he just had hoped it would never happen to her. It would have been kinder to let her go off with some other bloke. Someone who could take care of her and convert an affair into marriage.

He strode down the hall, boots clacking on the marble.

But he had promised her, and he never broke his promises. Not even to himself.

And that could only end badly.

Chapter 12

Isabella moved her bishop one space to finish the game they had been playing in the ballrooms for the last few weeks. "Draw."

Marcus had been covertly watching her all night. She was extremely nervous.

He lifted his head and reached over to refill her glass with the delicate wine he always kept on hand for her. When she had first realized he was stocking it for her a year ago, Bertie had barely been able to grab her before she had floated off into the starry night.

He preferred darker, headier wines, while the other members of their party drank their own favorites—scotch, brandy, Madeira. Fruit juice for Audrey, who had become attached to oranges somewhere in the first few months of her pregnancy and had drunk little else since. He'd ribbed Stephen about the constant shipments of citrus for months now.

Tonight's gathering was a small affair. His affairs always were. James, Calliope, Stephen, Audrey, Calliope's sister, Audrey's sister, Viscount St. John, Robert Cruikshank, Peel, and a few of their cronies wandered around the game room, gabbed, and took a stab at some of the more interesting games that Marcus liked to collect.

"Still playing that mind-numbing game, you two?" Stephen chirped.

"We were just at a draw."

"Excellent. Come away from there. We are going to play a few hands of whist."

More than a few people chimed their interest.

"Looks like you have plenty for two separate games," Marcus called out, then looked at her, his gold eyes challenging. "Shall we continue?"

For some reason the other guests waited for her response as well.

"Yes. I'll dispatch you in a quick game, and then we'll rotate in with cards."

"Well said, Lady Willoughby," Stephen murmured with a laugh.

Bodies shifted to the other end of the room, away from the two high-backed leather chairs and small checkered table near the fireplace.

"A quick game, Bella? So eager for defeat?"

"I'm always eager for your defeat, Lord Roth."

Marcus smirked and leaned forward to put his black pieces back into order. Long fingers clasped the head of a pawn, tapped the body of a knight, seated a bishop. It wasn't until he was settling his queen on the board that she realized she had been staring. She hastily moved her white pieces into position.

There was something in the air. Something that wasn't usually present during their matches. Or at least was usually only present on her side.

He watched her from beneath hooded eyes. His forefinger absently traced a pattern in the arm of his chair.

He appeared unsure how to proceed.

She couldn't stop a relieved smile.

He lifted an eyebrow and stopped tracing. "Yes, Bella?"

Mischievousness shot through her. "I was just thinking of what boon to ask when I win."

A slow smile spread across his face. It started at his eyes, then cheeks, to his full lips, as the corners tipped upward.

"A challenge? For our intrepid adventurer? Fine, then, what shall it be? Or would you rather keep it secret?"

Sometimes he made things so easy for her. At other times . . . "A secret, I should think."

"I figured as much."

"And you?"

He leaned forward and his fingers brushed hers. "A kiss, I should think."

Her breath caught, and he lifted her hand from the board. She leaned toward him without thought . . . and he abruptly turned the tabletop so the black pieces stopped in front of her.

She blinked at them for a second as he released her hand.

"And just to make it proper . . . it is my turn to make an offer, is it not, Bella?"

He moved her, *his*, white pawn to the opening of the king's gambit, traditionally her favorite opening of the game.

"It would be quite unladylike of me not to accept, Roth."

She moved the black pawn, unfamiliar in her hand, to e5 and accepted the gambit.

"To titles, is it, Bella? A game to determine the winner?"

They always played to win, but this time the stakes were for something greater.

He moved another pawn to f4, and she used her gambit piece to take it.

"Taking material so soon, Bella? How uncivilized. Your bloodthirstiness knows no bounds."

"What can I say? I love having your pieces in my control."

From where had that come?

"But it remains to be seen if you can stand to have your pieces in *my* control. Every last one of them."

A shiver wracked her. "Mmmm . . . so it does. Let us then hope, for my sake, that I stay on top of the game."

He moved his bishop and she took an early check position with her queen. But he easily moved his king out of harm's way, and she pushed another pawn forward. His bishop took her pawn.

"Tut tut, Marcus. Taking material so early? How trite."

"But now I have something to do with my fingers. Small, yet perfect to play with."

He pulled the pawn through the fingers of one hand, the tips caressing the pebbled head on top.

The material of her dress, of her chemise, grew coarser.

They spent the next five turns shuffling pieces and getting into position with no further material loss or gain.

When her pawn took his kingside bishop, he smirked and tapped her already captured pawn against his lips.

They played three more turns until his queenside bishop grabbed her pawn. Up until now, the game had been one of shuffling, edging, and testing. Each feeling out new strategies by the other. Trying to see where the other stood and what they intended.

She attacked, pressing her queen up to b2 and taking a pawn.

And then he moved his bishop to d6. D6? Both rooks completely open for the taking, which would leave his king alone in the back, the queen in an unstable position to defend.

What was he thinking? She examined the board, rotating the table a bit to observe from other angles, and still . . . he was leaving the way wide open to her better position.

Marcus was devious. The best player she knew. But he made mistakes too, whether he cared to admit them or not. She had won her fair share of times, helped every so often by controlling white.

She toyed with the white bishop she had captured, rolling the pointy top between her fingertips. She could capture either rook—one with her bishop, the other with her queen.

"I thought you said you wanted a quick game, Bella?"

"So eager for defeat?"

She picked up her bishop and moved it a space over from his king, plucking his kingside rook from the board.

"It depends on whether it would really be defeat. I have yet to learn your boon."

He moved a pawn to e5.

She hummed. "It could be something terrible, of course."

She took his queenside rook with her queen,

creating check, though her nerves were screaming. She was on the attack, but he wasn't defending at all. "Check."

"Then I should make sure to win. So sweet a reward on my side."

He moved his king from check. Even if she laid chase to his king with her queen, he had plenty of board to maneuver, and her bishop would be rendered useless for hemming.

While she looked back to her own pieces, she tried to think of a way to verbally bait him.

She did a double take. Oh. No. Oh, no.

She looked up at him and saw that same half-mocking smile that he wore when he pulled one over on her. But the warm glow in his eyes caused her to think about forgiving him this time.

Someday.

He winked—one slow drag of long sensual eyelashes over his cheek and back up.

Forgiveness could be had in the near future, at the very least.

His next two moves saw her in check both times, and it was only with the dogged determination of the damned that she continued moving her pieces—the actual game long since over—she had gone from offensive to completely defensive in the span of a couple moves.

In one of his last moves, he left his queen open on purpose, damn man, and in a fit of doomed pique she took it before he could checkmate her. Marcus rarely if ever sacrificed his queen.

He'd lost nearly half his pieces, including both rooks and his queen, and had still destroyed her, hemmed in by his lone bishop and two knights.

"Are you two finished yet?" Stephen called from across the room.

Isabella nodded and rose. She was warm from the look in Marcus's eyes as he surveyed her somewhat smugly, and warm from embarrassment. He was going to be smug about this win for weeks.

"I need to get my bag from the carriage," she called out.

"Running away, Bella?" Marcus asked, dragging her queen along his lips.

She watched the piece slide across his full lower lip. "Of course not," she said sourly, though it lacked the full tartness it would otherwise contain after such a monumental defeat. "I have our winner's trophy in the carriage. I'll return in a moment."

She retreated into the hallway and leaned her forehead against the wall. A semblance of sense returned, but really, no one liked losing. And so badly!

Sure, she could be a *mite* competitive. Perhaps even a disgruntled loser every *once* in a very *great* while . . .

"Are you going to speak to me after this, Bella?" Marcus's voice was amused.

She turned to see him leaning against the edge of the doorway just a few feet away.

She pushed away from the wall so she was standing in the middle of the hall, arms crossed. "I don't know, Lord Roth. Speaking involves my lips moving in answer to yours."

"Which is why I've come to collect my earnings right away."

Heat traveled through her, and stupid thoughts about pride and losing at chess fled.

"Oh?"

He uncurled from the doorway and sauntered toward her. "You don't object, do you? A kiss, I believe that was my term for winning."

She couldn't say anything. The connection between her brain and mouth decided it was suddenly time for a break.

He stepped in front of her and took her hand in his, softly stroking her fingers through her gloves.

She leaned forward automatically and his fingers moved up her glove, up her forearm, blazing a continual trail upward.

He stroked the soft bare underside of her arm near her elbow. The small hairs stood on end and she shivered, pressing closer to his chest. He repeated the motion and her breasts brushed against his jacket. She could feel the heat burning from him. She could almost imagine the hot skin beneath her fingertips, restrained under those clothes.

His long fingers caressed her upper arms, the tips of his fingers grazing the sides of her breasts.

The fire spread to her cheeks and her breathing grew ragged.

And still he hadn't kissed her. Her body was running way ahead toward the end of the race. And still his lips had not touched hers.

He seemed to catch the drift of her thoughts as his hands moved over her shoulders and into the hair at the back of her neck. He tipped her head back and lowered his.

His lips hovered above hers. Just a fraction of an inch. Cinnamon and spice, heat and promise. The air between their lips swirled, drawing them closer.

"You didn't answer my question, Bella." The tips of his lips brushed against hers on each word. It took everything she had not to close the gap.

"Question, Marcus?" She looked up through her lashes and brushed her chest to his.

"You don't object to a victory kiss, do you?"

His hands reached down and curled around her waist, the tips of his fingers brushing the top of her rear. He pulled her against him another inch so they were clasped together everywhere but at the lips.

"No, no, we must keep to the terms," she said breathily, barely even remembering what they had been playing.

"Very wise of you."

He kissed her. Deliberately. Forcefully. In a way that made her dizzy and giddy. That caused her hands to reach up and curl into the soft hair at the back of *his* neck. That had her arching up into him to be just an inch closer.

She kissed him with all she had and all she was. All the love and unsated passion she had been storing since she'd first fallen for him. This kiss was like eating the finest dessert or sipping the most expensive wine. A delicious heady experience that just made her want more, more, more. Nothing could compare with kissing Marcus.

He pushed her against a wall; which wall, she had no idea. She couldn't even remember what day it was. But the wall gave her excellent leverage to push back into him. To connect them in a manner that made him groan heavily against her mouth.

The heady feeling gave way to an exhilaration unlike any she had known.

He devoured her in a way that made her feel that maybe he felt that *she* was the finest dessert or most expensive wine.

His fingers skimmed over her breast. She gasped and arched, the sensations spiking through her, adding to the fire that lit her cheeks and spread downward—tentacles of heat lacing throughout her body.

If she died at this very moment, in this very hallway, she would die a happy, happy woman.

And people would wonder what had happened to Lady Willoughby to put such a smile on her face in death. The people in the room not twenty feet away most especially.

Hold a moment.

She was in a hallway. One of Marcus's hands was wrapped around her breast, the other cupping her rear. Wantonly pressed up against a wall with no less than a dozen people a room away.

She pulled her head back, knocking it against the wall. She panted, echoing his ragged breathing.

His eyes captured hers, dark caramel and glossy. *Heated*. If she didn't move she was going to let him have his way with her right here, enjoying every minute and probably ruining her for life.

"Thing! I need to get the thing from the what's-it."

She slipped from between Marcus and the wall and turned to back away from him, his eyes still hot as he rested one hand against the abandoned paneling. His molten gaze locked with hers.

A throat cleared. "Lady Willoughby, may I send a footman to retrieve your item?"

Isabella jumped and whirled expecting to see

the Roth butler standing at attention, face perfectly blank. Perfectly blank in the way good servants observed their masters before heading down to the kitchens to gossip about them. To gossip about things like seeing their master conquer a wanton woman against a wall. But the starchy man stood discreetly around the corner, only one shiny boot in view.

"Oh, no. It's breast—I mean best—that I retrieve it."

Dear. God.

"Wait, Lady Willoughby—"

Isabella stumbled out of the house. If Marcus kissed her senseless every time she lost a game, she'd never have to worry about being disgruntled again, for she wouldn't be able to string two sentences together anyway.

She hurried down the front steps and stopped abruptly. The carriage wasn't there.

"Lady Willoughby!" the butler called.

She spun around.

"The carriages were taken to the back. Come use the back door."

"I'll just go around the house. Thank you!"

She needed the fresh air. Needed to cool her red face and heated skin. Needed to collect herself before venturing back inside where Marcus and his voyeuristic butler stood.

Her slippered feet were nearly silent as she padded down the drive. It was a pleasant night. With just a hint of a chill, the early summer weather simmering beneath. The moon was high and full, casting silvery shadows on the foliage.

She spotted her carriage parked just beyond the back. Henry, her driver, was most likely down in the servants' quarters, probably having a tipple or playing cards.

She opened the door and climbed in. She should have taken her bag inside with her earlier, but when they'd pulled into the drive she'd seen Marcus through the open door of the house and rational thought had fled.

Rummaging through her bag, she found the small wooden statue of a castle turret. She stroked it, trying to regain her balance. It was well made, but not terribly expensive, nor eye-catchingly beautiful. It was of obvious quality, though.

She had purchased it in a little shop near the Strand. Marcus had taken to it right away, and over one of their games the large rook had become their winner's trophy. She had won their last "official" match last month. They had been playing a series of unofficial ballroom matches, one move at a time, in the period since.

Sitting in the silence of the carriage, she inhaled a few deep breaths. What a night—and it wasn't yet over. She closed her eyes and relaxed. She needed to regain a modicum of her equilibrium and return to the house before they sent someone after her. With her luck, it would be the butler. She stepped out of the carriage, righted her dress, and shut the door.

Something rustled to her right. She peered into the tall bushes surrounding the tiny garden in the back. Shadows shifted and settled. A shiver of unease skimmed over her like hands too light on a piano's keys.

But no one came forth. No animal made its presence known. She brushed the feeling aside and looked through the corner window. The window provided a full view of the hallway where they had kissed. If anyone had stood out here, they would have gotten as clear a view of her wanton behavior as the butler had.

The darkness contained her mortification.

She stepped forward, and tripped, the rook clattering to the ground. She expelled a surprised breath as she landed squarely on her hands and knees atop a large canvas bag. A lumpy, shifting bag that hadn't been there previously. The thought unnerved her.

Had a servant come out while she'd been sitting in the carriage and dropped a bag of refuse?

She pushed herself up, one gloved hand fingering the bag. A bag of refuse loosely tied—tied like a burial bag.

She hastily sprung back and grabbed for

the rook, which skittered away. She felt for the wooden turret while keeping her eyes on the bag. Her fingers closed around it and she shakily stood. Her eyes stayed on the bag. They had put George in one of those when he was taken away. She swallowed and took a step backward. Perhaps she had been gone longer than five minutes. Perhaps someone would be coming out the back door right now.

The bushes rustled.

She jumped and whirled, trophy held out in front of her, eyes scanning the gardens, the dark entrance to the stables, the shadowed areas between the carriages parked in the drive. Her breathing picked back up to the erratic pace it held before she entered the carriage, but this time from terror instead of passion or mortification.

Her feet slowly moved backward, her slippers quiet, but every sound magnified tenfold as she skirted the bag. It wasn't far to the house and she was being silly. Just a flight of terrified fancy from too much spent emotion.

She didn't stop moving. One step, then another, the rook held before her, eyes scanning the bushes and carriages. She had just been in her carriage, but no one could give her enough crowns to go near the dark shadows now.

A clinking footstep. Then another. Sounds that were not hers.

Her feet kept moving backward, picking up speed. Then a large figure moved out of the shadows.

A figure with darkened features and a low-slung cap.

Chapter 13

Isabella whirled and ran as fast as she could for the main door. Inside her head the figure nipped at her heels, intent on grabbing her. Her heart clutched as if fingers had pierced her flesh and squeezed.

The door opened just as she bolted up the stairs. She threw herself up the last few and into Marcus's arms.

He let out a grunt as he caught her. "What on earth?"

"Man . . . bag . . . after me . . ."

Marcus thrust her behind him, stepped out of the doorway and peered around the edge.

"Stay here," he ordered as he grabbed his cane from the hall stand and motioned to his butler.

She mimicked the stance he had previously taken, back to the wall, peering around the edge of the door. Marcus stepped off the porch, and before she could call him back, merged into the dark shadows.

Isabella panicked.

"Come, Lady Willoughby, to the game room with the other guests."

"What? But Lord Roth just went," she pointed out the door, "out there!"

Should she follow him? No, that wouldn't make sense. She had no idea what was going on. She didn't want to be clubbed by Marcus thinking she was a stranger, or even worse, to club him with the trophy. She was liable to club anyone who startled her at this point.

"Please, Lady Willoughby, follow me. I need to inform—"

He hadn't gotten the last syllable out before she was running to the game room. James and Stephen, thick as thieves—they would know what was happening.

She saw Stephen first. "Help, Stephen, Marcus—"

"The back door, my lords," the butler wheezed behind her.

The two men and St. John took off, leaving the rest of the guests in various states of tension and bewilderment.

Calliope approached her, reaching out to soothingly remove the wooden rook from her tight grasp and place it on a side table. "Isabella?"

A bizarre sense of having been in this situation before washed over her. She and Marcus had discovered a dead body at the Pettigrews' house party the weekend she'd met Calliope.

Perhaps she was doomed to finding a body whenever she made an inroad with Marcus.

Calliope had asked her an implicit question, but something prevented her from saying anything in front of the rest of the guests. Audrey and her sister Faye seemed to understand and started talking loudly.

"I think there's a dead body in the backyard," Isabella whispered to Calliope while pulling agitatedly at her dress. How long would it take for them to return? Perhaps she should check . . .

"Oh, dear." Calliope clasped her hands together tightly.

Isabella froze. Calliope looked distressed but not surprised. "Do you know something about this?"

"One of their . . . associates . . . has gone missing."

"What?" she hissed, shock overtaking her. "You mean there is a *murdered* dead body in the backyard?"

"Shh! I don't know."

The men returned a minute later, much to everyone's relief. Isabella couldn't stop the slight shaking aftereffects, though. Marcus and Stephen concocted a tale about drunken youths in the streets and put on a convincing show, recreating the scene they had witnessed. Isabella smiled weakly when some of the guests turned to her.

"I suppose that explains it. I thought I heard someone breaking into a carriage."

One of the guests whom she didn't know well made a noise like a trampled cat and immediately left to make sure his carriage was intact.

The incident put a damper on the night's events, and Marcus managed to usher the guests out without making it appear that he was kicking them out. Isabella was about to shakily make her way through the door when his hand shot out to prevent her departure.

"Not you. Stubbins will be back in a minute."

She shook off his hand, unaccountably irritated with the explanation of drunken youths. She supposed it could be true, but they had said nothing about a body or a large bag. "What does Stubbins have to do with me leaving?"

"Stubbins is getting the carriage ready, so he can follow us. I'm accompanying you home."

Vying emotions coursed through her. "But Henry is here to drive me home."

"Would you rather I say I'm accompanying Henry?"

A servant signaled to Marcus, and he led her outside. His eyes moved constantly, his hand steady against her back. The last carriages rolled down the drive.

"What happened, Marcus? Was someone really murdered?"

His mouth tightened as he handed her up into the carriage. "Where did you hear such a thing?" He stepped inside and pulled the door closed. "No, no need to ask. Calliope had no right to worry you."

"So it's true." She gripped her hands together.

"No. It's nothing you need worry about."

"I tripped over someone's body! Someone left a body in your backyard while I was in my carriage! What do you mean it's nothing I need worry about?"

His eyes narrowed. "Did you see anyone?"

"Yes. No. I don't know." She wiped a hand across her face. "There was a man, but it could have been one of your servants."

"Probably was." His voice was clipped.

She suddenly wasn't sure she believed him. "How can you be sure?"

"I'm sure. And there's no need to worry about anything. I'm sorry you were alarmed by this. The body was being delivered to a surgeon who has been experimenting illegally on dead bodies. We know the man responsible. It was a drunken night's work. We didn't want to panic any of the guests, though, thus the tale of drunken youths.

Some don't take well to any mention of surgical practices."

She shivered and the vehicle started moving. Her rented carriage was small and Marcus's knees brushed against hers. Her house was not far, and the streets were nearly empty. They would be there in no time.

"I saw the rook in the game room," he said, changing the morbid topic.

"You earned it," she grimaced, reminded of her earlier spectacular defeat.

He smiled faintly. "I will keep it safe."

"See that you do, my lord. I plan to win it back soon."

"Still sore with me, Bella?" He leaned forward and trailed a finger along her knee, the material bunching beneath.

His eyes were warm. Friendly, mischievous, passionate. The first two emotions weren't unusual in his lighter moods. The third . . . the third made her head feel light and her breath harder to control.

He wanted her.

He *wanted* her.

She swallowed, trying to tamp down the desire. "Of course, I'm still sore. I expect you to make it up to me."

He leaned farther toward her, his lips near to hers, the soft hint of cinnamon swirling between.

"I'll do what I can."

The carriage slowed, then pulled to a stop.

Their lips were a hairbreadth apart. He brushed a hand along her cheek. "Good night, Bella."

Marcus watched her enter her house. Her housekeeper greeted her at the door, and muscles that he hadn't known were tensed relaxed.

Isabella would kill him if she discovered he had lied through his teeth. But she was the one pure thing in his life. Untainted by politics, or greed, or the seedier side of life. She was a slice of sunshine in the midst of darkness.

When he could no longer enjoy the sunrise, no longer savor the sunset, he would still have her to remember. She would be a beacon when everything eventually went dark.

What if she discovered all his terrible secrets—and that all of her obviously warm delusions of him were wrong?

He wondered for the hundredth time what he was thinking to continue with this mad venture. But what voice was he supposed to listen to? The one urging him forward? Or the one telling him to run as far and fast as he could?

He walked roughly to his carriage. Stubbins's expression was grim. "To the docks," Marcus said as he climbed inside.

Fletcher's body was being seen to. Fletcher's family had already been cared for. Now they needed to find the person responsible. The threads of the noose tightened. One more body in the ground. One more failure. One more death that he had failed to prevent.

The list of financiers was short. He had actively argued with five of them in as many months. Yet the type of man who was writing the pithy "catch me if you dare" notes was not one who had been planning long-term. That fact narrowed the list down by one. Four men. Three he had encountered the previous day.

He narrowed the list down to two very likely possibilities. They both fit the profile. It was time to increase the noise and flush out the game.

Chapter 14

"**W**hat does Roth think he's doing?" Isabella overheard Lord Ainsworth say to
Lord Blakely as she emerged from the back room
of the small antiques shop she visited each week.
She couldn't even get away from thoughts of the
man while shopping.

"He's obviously devising a plan to ruin you,"
Blakely said while handling an ancient dagger.

"Well, he will regret it soon, mark my words."
Ainsworth hissed. "Yes, you mark my words."

Ainsworth looked up and his eyes narrowed
as he recognized Isabella. "Good day, Lady Willoughby."

She nodded. "Lord Ainsworth. Lord Blakely."

Obviously Ainsworth wasn't happy with Marcus at the moment and was probably annoyed
that she had overheard their exchange. She wondered if Marcus would explain the man's ire.

Sometimes he discussed House politics, and

sometimes his lips were tighter than a clam's. Curious, though, that the two men would openly discuss Marcus in a public place, although to be fair, the shop had appeared unattended.

And people thought women gossiped.

Isabella squinted as she left the shop. The day was unaccountably bright and warm. She had one more stop to make. Ringing bells drew her to the present. She banished thoughts of Marcus wreaking vengeance and looked across the street hoping to see Bertie, who had bypassed the antiques shop and gone onward to the next stop.

She spotted her maid a block ahead peering at the milliner's window. Isabella needed to catch up to her before Bertie became too firmly attached to some dreadful bonnet sporting an overabundance of fruits and nuts.

She was about to step into the street when the bells jingled louder and raised voices shouted out a warning.

She turned toward the noise, horrified to see a carriage weaving wildly down the street, barreling toward her. Her heart jumped into her throat and she jerked back, the vehicle passing within mere inches of her—the whoosh of the reins and the heaving breaths of the horses close enough to feel. Shock held her immobile as she tried to restart her stilled heart.

"Are you well, Lady Willoughby?" Blakely

asked breathlessly as he put a hand on her arm, concern showing in his eyes. She looked at Ainsworth, who was staring after the vehicle, his lips tight. People in the street were shouting after the mad carriage, which had been traveling much faster than allowed. It had clipped two men farther down the street, and people were rushing to help.

"Yes. Yes, I'm fine. Thank you."

Blakely patted her arm and looked down the street, anger blazing in his eyes. "I heard the hooves and shouts. What the devil was that driver thinking? Pardon my language, Lady Willoughby."

"No, no, you are quite right." She was relieved to see the two injured men down the street stand with the aid of bystanders. "I was thinking something along similar lines."

Ainsworth humphed and leaned grouchily on his walking stick.

"Would you like one of us to see you home? You've had a dreadful fright," Blakely said.

She smiled weakly, still a little shaken. "No, but thank you. My maid will see me home after we finish."

"Do you shop here often?" He pointed back to the antiques shop.

She gave a wry smile. "Trying to figure out if André will give you a good deal?"

Blakely looked chagrined for a moment. "I wish to buy my betrothed a gift. I was hoping there would be something of interest you might recommend."

"You are betrothed to Lady Margaret Banner, yes?"

He smiled and it lit his blue eyes. "I am indeed." A mischievous look entered. "You wouldn't happen to know anything that would suit her, would you?"

Isabella had rarely spoken to Blakely. She knew very little about the man. Marcus disliked him intensely and there had never been much reason for their paths to cross at parties. She'd heard whispers the betrothal was on shaky grounds. It was rumored that secrets had been exposed that had Lady Margaret's father questioning the future marriage.

Yet, Blakely's eyes glowed warmly when speaking of her. It would be a shame if ugly rumors, provided they were unfounded, got in the way.

"Actually," she tapped her lower lip, "there is an exquisite peacock brooch that I think she would love. She looks so wonderful in blue. André has it in the back room. Mention that we spoke of it."

Blakely bowed low and smiled. "A thousand thanks, my lady."

"My pleasure."

"Stay away from rogue carriages," he said, and

grinned wryly. "Perhaps we will see you at the Donningtons'?"

She nodded. "Have a good day, Lord Blakely. Lord Ainsworth."

Ainsworth bowed, but he was obviously pre-occupied.

The men reentered the shop, and Isabella tried to shake off the lingering effects of the scare. She could see Bertie hurrying toward her through a break in traffic, which had backed up after the chaos had occurred. She smiled crookedly at her maid, relieved that she was near a friendly face.

"My lady, are you well?" Bertie fussed over her as they crossed the street, Isabella looking both ways continuously.

"I'm well, Bertie. Just another mad driver racing through the city streets. Did you notice if the men farther down were harmed?"

"They looked well. But when I saw you, my heart nearly stopped. That carriage almost hit you!" Bertie's face darkened. Isabella had seen that look before and prepared herself for a tirade. "They need to start locking up the drivers who imbibe too much! Can't hold their drink!"

Isabella let Bertie's rage at the miscreants of the world wash over her and felt much better as her shaking slowed and her heart fell back into a regular beat. She needed to continue her weekly browsing. The shopkeepers on her Wednesday route always had items waiting for her perusal, and she needed to find something for her mother's upcoming birthday.

The Donningtons' party was a reserved affair, since many society matrons were in attendance. Marcus was relieved to see Isabella wearing a lovely, understated gown. Yet, despite the fact that the gown was not daring or flashy, all he could concentrate on were the flashes of skin his view afforded as she moved.

He recognized the gown as one she had previously worn, but his attention had never before been captured by the graceful lines of her neck, or the way the material brushed a hidden curve when she turned. She greeted someone and he was rewarded with a beautiful view of the long column of her neck. Smooth and milky.

He planned to kiss every inch.

Their affair would be much easier if they were away from London. Perhaps a trip to Bristol? He would like to take her to his seaside estate, but Deal was a full day's ride, even with the team changes he had in place.

His eyes moved from Isabella to her companions. He stiffened. Perhaps he should ask her right now whether her plans for the evening included him. He rather thought that would gain her attention.

As he neared, he overheard their conversation.

"What a lovely brooch, Lady Margaret."

Lady Margaret Banner blushed and glanced shyly at Blakely, who was by her side. "Thank you, Lady Willoughby. It was a gift from Lord Blakely. Isn't it lovely?"

As soon as Lady Margaret's beaming eyes returned to Isabella, Blakely winked. At Isabella. Who smiled back.

Marcus didn't like that. He didn't like that one bit.

"The blue matches your eyes. What good taste Lord Blakely has," Isabella said.

Lady Margaret smiled. "Yes, doesn't he?"

"Oh, Lord Roth," Isabella said as he drew level with them, "We were just admiring Lady Margaret's new brooch."

He looked at the intricate peacock design crafted in blues. It was definitely something Isabella would like, though it wasn't something she'd wear.

"Lovely."

"Lord Blakely gifted her with it just this evening. Isn't his taste exquisite?"

Blakely smiled. Marcus didn't.

"Exquisite. I believe this is the dance you promised me."

Isabella looked confused for a second, as she ought—they had talked about no such thing, but as he expected, she held out her hand and excused herself from the other couple.

As soon as they were moving on the floor, she said, "I didn't promise you a dance."

"Didn't you?" He lowered his mouth to her ear. "I thought you promised me many, many dances. Of all varieties."

He felt her shiver and contained his look of satisfaction.

She raised a brow. "Interesting that you say that. You haven't felt the urge to dance previously this evening."

"Why, Isabella. If I'd known you were quite so eager to *dance*, I would have accommodated you sooner."

"Would you have?" She suddenly looked serious.

"Do you doubt your own charms?"

She looked away for a brief moment.

He tipped up her chin. "You do, don't you?"

"What would you have me say?"

"Something a young blade or flirtatious debutante might. That you know your own appeal. That you know the way it affects me."

She tilted her head, her long expanse of neck exposed. "But I know nothing of the kind."

"Would I be in this position, saying these things?" His thumb moved along her palm, stroking the silk glove.

She drew in a shaky breath. "Perhaps. Perhaps if you thought it a game, a way to sate the adventures of poor, lonely Lady Willoughby. A way to string her along, but never quite follow through with it."

Her eyes were serious, but he caught a fleeting glimpse of wistfulness in their depths. It was provoking.

"Why would I do that?"

"Because you want to protect me, but you don't actually desire me."

She believed what she was saying. He nearly stopped dancing.

"I don't?"

"No. I've seen you, you know. You are arrogant, selective, and fickle. You don't smile genuinely at women you are interested in . . . in *mating* with."

"I see." Women really were bemusing creatures at the best of times. "And according to your logic, since I've given you a genuine smile, I therefore cannot be interested in *mating* with you?"

Spots of rose bloomed in her cheeks, but she boldly pressed forth. "Would you have let me go into my house alone last night if you desired me?"

Last night he had gone from the ecstasy of having her wild and willing in the hallway, to being shaken to the core when she had thrust herself into his arms, stuttering about men chasing her.

Last night, after he had deposited her safely at home, he had taken care of Fletcher's body, visited the docks, and arranged a few less than desirable things. He pushed the thoughts away.

He stroked her silken palm again and pulled her into a turn. "I seem to recall a rather heated moment in my hallway last night that lays waste to your claim that I don't desire you."

Her blush deepened and her lower lip slipped between her teeth.

"And the last I checked, your neighbors took stock of the comings and goings in all the houses around," he said, deliberately pulling her against him as they moved.

"If you desired me so, would you have let me leave your house, then?" He was pleased to note that her voice had gone a little breathy, in the way he was discovering he craved. Dangerous thoughts.

"And had you shamefully enter your house the next morning?"

"Would you have made me leave in the morning? Why not keep me till noon or beyond?" Her eyes searched his.

"And return in the same dress?"

"Surely you have a wardrobe of dresses stashed for your other women," she said matter-of-factly.

He raised a brow. "Who said anything about other women staying in my home? Have you ever heard such a thing?"

She said nothing. She couldn't, because he never had. It was rumored fact that he never invited a woman home. He always took them elsewhere.

She picked up the previous threads of the conversation. "Would you have made this the fourth time in a week, the third night running, that you tempted me and then backed away? Promises, but no delights."

"No delights? I truly have been neglectful."

He slipped a finger beneath her glove and stroked the smooth skin there. Her eyes grew wide.

On the next turn he pulled her closer, her breasts brushing against his jacket, their lower bodies pressed together for half a second—just enough to stroke across.

Her sudden intake of air pleased him. On the next turn he repeated the motion.

Her hand gripped his shoulder tightly. Rose bloomed in her cheeks once more.

It wasn't just that he wanted her. He wanted to be the only thing she thought of for hours afterward. The only thought as he moved inside her. The only word on her lips as her head thrust back against her pillow and *Marcus, Marcus, Marcus* issued from her lips in a strangled, passion-filled litany.

"The neighbors aren't moving. And the dresses won't appear." She bit her lip. He wanted to reach

down and replace her teeth with his own. "How
do normal patrons conduct affairs?"

If he weren't staring at her lips, his body already responding, he might have raised a brow
and faked a haughty stare. But all he could think
of was Isabella lying on her back, legs wrapped
around him, head thrown back, and . . .

"Would you care to visit the seaside?"

She blinked, but didn't miss a step in the dance.
"The seaside?"

"Yes."

"What part of the seaside?"

"Anywhere that does not include your neighbors."

Really, he was being rather stupid about this
whole thing. Why was he continuing with this
game? For as much as he suddenly couldn't contain his desire for her, and as much as she was
baiting him, this was a game. A dangerous game
when it involved him. Better to let her play it with
someone else.

*Her legs wrapped around someone else, her head
thrown back on someone else's pillow.*

His hand tightened fractionally around her
waist and he pulled her close again.

No, this would be best for both of them. She
would have her adventure. He would get her out
of his system.

Their friendship would probably be ruined.

But it would save her from mourning him later.

"Marcus?"

He smiled. A fake smile, but the dance ended and he managed to conceal it as they walked off the floor.

"What were you talking to Blakely about?" he asked, trying to change the direction of his thoughts.

"I helped him choose the peacock brooch for Lady Margaret this afternoon. I had heard their betrothal was on shaky ground. Not that anyone has come right out and said so. I do hope things work out for them."

He stopped. "You saw Blakely this afternoon?"

"I was out browsing. I always shop on Wednesdays, you know that."

"Do you always stop to talk to Blakely?" he asked sardonically.

She raised a brow. "No. 'Tis the first I've seen him. He was most pleasant, though. I don't know why my seeing him has you in a twist."

"Blakely is not pleasant. He cares only about himself."

"He seems most infatuated with Lady Margaret."

"Seems. Believe me, Blakely cares not a whit for her."

"That is horrible of you to say."

"It's the truth."

"What about his brother? It was obvious Blakely cared for him."

Marcus paused. "He cared more about his brother after his death than he did before."

"How do you know?"

"I watch people."

"And people watch you." She pointed to Charles Ellerby and Ainsworth, who as soon as he met their eyes, averted them. They were talking in hushed tones. "What have you done this time?"

"Me? Nothing."

"I see. I have no idea what you do in the House sometimes—with your club and secret talks—but I know how you treat people. And sometimes it is very poorly."

He stepped close to her and lowered his voice. "After that dance, it sounds like I have been treating you poorly, Bella. I think I need to make it up to you."

Her breath hitched and he smiled. He backed away slowly, still conscious of where they were.

"Lord Roth, Lady Willoughby, pleasure to see you both."

Marcus wondered if he shouldn't just take Isabella's arm and steer her to the other side of the room, but before he had the opportunity, she was already looking over his shoulder.

"Lord Ainsworth, Mr. Ellerby. Are you enjoying the party?"

"Quite a crush," Charles Ellerby said. "I've heard that you've been enjoying many parties this week. My brother Fenton was telling us how fetching you looked at the Grenstridge affair."

Fenton Ellerby moved up a notch on Marcus's list of people to destroy. It wasn't a particularly hard move. He already disliked the man. Charles Ellerby earned himself a respectable first showing on the list. Traits ran in families—he knew that better than most.

Isabella's lips tightened but she gamely held her ground. "That was very kind of your brother, Mr. Ellerby. Remind me to thank him, Lord Roth." She cast a glance in his direction. "Mr. Ellerby, your brother wasn't looking especially himself at the last party. I'm afraid he looked rather ill. But that he overcame that illness to admire my form is an honor."

Point to Isabella. And he was pleased to note no affectionate attachment to Fenton Ellerby in her voice.

"The Grenstridge affair was a little out of your norm, wasn't it?"

Charles really was too new at this. He didn't have the polish or the tact for a truly threatening attack.

Isabella raised both brows. "Out of my norm? I

am on a social committee with Lady Grenstridge and involved in many children's groups with Ladies Giles, Norman, Filstitch, and Mrs. Creel, all of whom were in attendance. We held a serious discussion of prison conditions for children. Are you interested in our work? A contribution perhaps?"

Charles reeled back. Ainsworth huffed, "My wife is on that committee, Ellerby."

And checkmate. Not even support from his partner in this crime.

"I—I'll think about it. Pardon me, I see Wellington, and we have matters to discuss."

Wellington held some of the same views as Charles Ellerby, ones that differed from Marcus's, but if there was one thing Wellington despised, it was a toady.

Ainsworth looked sour and disappeared behind him.

Isabella watched after them. "Well, that was an interesting exchange."

But Marcus saw the unease in her face. The way her teeth were catching her bottom lip.

"Why are you doing this?"

She met his eyes. "Doing what?"

"Attending risqué routs. Risking the reputation you've taken such pains to build."

She shrugged, but the gesture was stilted and she glanced down. "Everyone needs a change."

He wanted to take her chin in his hand, raise her warm blue eyes to his and discover the real answer, but he settled for a flippant response in the middle of the swelling crowd. "Adventure?"

"Yes." Her relief was palpable, and it produced a sliver of unease in him. Could she want more than a quick affair? Everything about her said yes, even as her words said no.

Isabella wasn't the torrid affair type.

"You don't have to do this."

Her eyes met his again and hardened. It wasn't a look he was accustomed to seeing on her face. "Would you rather I go to Fenton Ellerby and see what adventures lie there? Marcus, if you don't want to do this, just . . . just tell me. I was serious on the dance floor. No more of this to and fro."

"I want to." His mouth responded without his permission.

Her eyes settled into their more usual expression of friendliness with a hint of underlying insecurity.

He liked Isabella. More than any other woman of his acquaintance, past or present. Probably future too.

What the devil had he gotten himself into?

A few hours later, with Isabella on his arm, he followed the stream of people leaving the house.

The Donningtons lived just outside of London proper and had a drive where the carriages couldn't be brought forth to the front. Guests made a promenade down the drive instead. More than one couple used the walk as an excuse to hang onto the arm of their chosen escort or to clutch their lady closer.

Marcus was trying to figure out how to proceed. He felt like a boy just out of school. Worried about his lady and what he could do to mess it all up.

He hadn't felt this way since before his father died. Being detached was so much easier.

It wasn't until they were halfway to the carriage that he noticed multiple pairs of eyes staring at them. Not from the other patrons; no, from the men stationed between the carriages.

He let his eyes scan the other directions. Men were circling there as well. Not apparent to anyone but a close observer.

"Marcus, are you going on to the Plessandes'?"

He calculated five to six men.

"Perhaps."

In and of itself a high number.

"Perhaps? Didn't you respond?"

He wondered where they had found so many men willing to take down a peer.

"Yes."

It was a crime punishable by death.

"Well, you should at least put in an appearance."

The person who hired them must be more bold and desperate than he'd thought.

"You know how these things work."

He had to get Isabella safely away from him before the men made their move.

"Yes, I do. And good manners dictate you should at least put in an appearance."

They would wait for the crowd to thin, or simply follow him.

"Wouldn't you rather we go somewhere else? I promised you those *dances*."

He would get her to go back to her house . . .

She paused. "When you put it that way, I doubt the Plessandes would notice our absence."

. . . while he led the beady-eyed men in footmen's garb away.

"Oh, they'll notice. Everyone will notice."

She would be safe at home while he was leading everyone else astray.

She sighed. "You are about to put forth some shockingly appalling plan where you show up at the Plessandes' and then disappear, only to reappear at my window."

He stopped surveying the scene for a moment and looked at her in consternation. "What makes you say that?"

"It's what you do. Don't tell me that you think I haven't noticed the number of times you've come to a rout only to disappear. James and Stephen always say something to the others about you being in the card room, or out getting some air, but you never are where they say until later in the evening when you suddenly reappear—cravat somewhat more starchly tied than before, tugging at your cuffs to arrange them in place."

He noticed one of the men moving forward, and he increased their pace to catch up with the foursome of guests ahead.

"I beg your pardon, I don't tug on my cuffs."

However, he was shocked that she had been so observant.

"You don't usually. Generally you are unnaturally *still*. But when you reenter a room, occasionally you make last minute adjustments. What I've just never reasoned out is whether you are meeting women or men."

He stopped dead, forward motion forgotten. "Pardon me?"

She waved and tugged him back into motion. "Not like that. Meeting men about secret diplomatic affairs. Which emperor takes after Caligula—likes horses—that type of thing."

He raised a brow. "Caligula?"

One man signaled to another.

"I had a rather eccentric history master."

Another man signaled. Something was going to happen soon.

"Mmmm. Listen, Bella, I just remembered something I forgot to share with Donnington. I'll join you in an hour or so after putting in an appearance at the Plessandes'. I promise to leave their party and come to your window posthaste."

Dusty rose grazed her cheeks. It was an excellent color on her. One he hoped to witness spread farther south.

She stopped and tapped him in the chest. "You'd better. I'll be quite sore with you if you leave me again, Roth."

He smiled at her. "Duly noted. Be careful in the crowd."

She gave him an exasperated look and headed off toward the carriage.

Satisfied that Isabella would be safe, Marcus turned to draw the men back toward the Donningtons.

Something in the air changed. An excitement laced it that had been absent previously. The men surrounded him on either side, just as he wanted them to. He walked upstream of the guests, exchanging an occasional pleasantry or barb.

The men continued to follow, but something caused him to stop, the guests fanning out around him and continuing downstream.

A tingle of alarm made the hairs on his arms stand on end.

While he still had the attention of three of the

men in his sights, the eyes of one of the men were not focused on him at all, but on something behind him.

Marcus abruptly turned, pushing through the couples he had just passed, causing a few squabbles in his wake.

His eyes swept the line of carriages, trying to locate a pile of dark hair.

There. He could see Isabella.

Two men circled her, one catching her attention and opening the door of a carriage.

A carriage that belonged to neither Isabella nor Marcus.

What a fool he had been not to have anticipated this move. He would never make it in time to keep her from getting in, but the crush of carriages would slow them down. It always took a long time to depart. He just hoped they didn't have anything planned for the time it did take.

Like leaving her dead body to be found.

He was now running, dodging and pushing people out of the way.

Her hands were on her hips and she was arguing as one man motioned her inside. He finally gave up and grabbed her arm.

The man's eyes met Marcus's as he bore down upon them.

A screeching whistle sounded, and, as at a signal, the man melted behind the lines of carriages.

At the moment, Marcus didn't care if they all went home for an ale and hot bowl of stew.

"Isabella."

His call caught her attention, and the attention of those around him. Well, the gossips would be talking about them now anyway.

"Marcus. Why are you running? I wasn't upset with you. Go talk to Donnington."

He let out a strangled laugh, slightly hysterical in nature and foreign in his mouth.

"I don't need to talk to Donnington. Let's get you home. Your carriage is ten down."

He had to work to keep his hand from shaking.

"Yes, it was very strange. A coachman I've never seen before was trying to put me into the wrong carriage. Insisted on it actually. That happened to the Pinchings two weeks past, you know. Some tipsy driver hastened them inside and they ended up riding clear to Windsor. Driver just kept on going, ignoring the trap taps."

They wove through the crowd, Marcus keeping a firm grip on Isabella while she kept talking.

"Well, you can imagine his surprise after the alcohol wore off a bit and he opened the door to two incredibly irritated passengers. Not the first or last time it will happen either, what with the way some of them drink. Lady Marvo had much the same happen to her. Luckily, the driver was one of her neighbors' grooms and so she ended up pretty much home. I can't imagine it being a very pleasing experience, all the same."

His fists clenched. It wouldn't have been a pleasing experience at all, of that he was sure. "Let's get you into the correct carriage, then."

He surveyed the scene. No use pretending he wasn't looking for the men who had been there. He'd already tipped his hat in that direction. The whistle had done its trick. Not only had the man with Isabella disappeared, but none of the other men were present either. The eyes of the ton, however, were glued on them.

Not a single excuse for his running back to her crossed his mind, so he assumed his frosty facade, and the eyes of the less bold immediately averted.

"By the by, why were you running?"

"I just realized that where I really needed to be was right here."

Her eyes softened. "Oh, that's sweet of you."

Something like guilt squirmed uncomfortably in his gut. "Yes, well, let's get you to your carriage."

The groom opened the door as they approached. Isabella entered and Marcus got in after her.

She stared at him.

He stared back.

"What are you doing?" she whispered urgently.

"I'm riding with you."

She looked sharply outside, where people were milling, trying to peer inside.

"Why?" she hissed.

He couldn't very well tell her that her life could be in danger. He wasn't sure he was quite ready to contemplate that himself.

"Your carriage is farther down the drive than mine," he said.

"Marcus . . . " She shot another furtive glance out the carriage door. The groom's eyes were wide as he shifted from foot to foot trying to decide whether to shut the door. "This isn't exactly subtle. We are at a proper party."

"No one much cared that Nelson lived with Lady Hamilton and Sir William. And Mrs. Flitchley is accepted in polite society, and everyone knows she is Lord Tinken's mistress."

Isabella looked gobsmacked. "First of all, yes they did, yes they do. Secondly, are you saying you want me to be your mistress and let everyone know it?" She was as ruffled as any cat he'd seen.

Her words caught up to his brain.

His best choice of action was to exit the carriage. Swiftly. But then he'd be leaving her in here, alone, ripe for the pickings by men who wanted to use her to no doubt get back at him somehow.

He had always known he would lose her. Would lose all of his friends. But he didn't want to *lose* her, lose her. He wanted her to be happy and go on with life, with some nice man who valued her. Well, maybe he could live without picturing another man. But he didn't want her to be a corpse on the side of the road because of him. He didn't think he could bear it.

"Well?" she asked, brows knit together and a brook-no-arguments look in her eye.

And then all of a sudden, the prayers he hadn't made were answered. He caught a glimpse of St. John and Faye Kendrick, Audrey's sister, bickering as they walked down the drive.

"We'll discuss it in a few hours, I promise. Stay here."

He jumped from the carriage and told the groom, somewhat tersely, to keep the door open.

Faye smiled when she saw him. St. John nodded, while still glaring at Faye.

"Faye, I need you to accompany Isabella home. Invite yourself in for tea and check inside. I'll send my carriage to pick you up in an hour."

He kept an eye on Isabella's carriage to make sure she remained inside, the groom stayed frozen in place, and no one else entered.

Faye shrugged. "Shall do. Just send the Marston carriage after me. It's down by yours."

The thing he liked best about Faye was her willingness to go along with any scheme and wait until later to ask questions. That and her coolness under pressure. He had brought her into their covert group after Audrey and Stephen had married. Having been raised on the streets since she was eight, Faye more than pulled her weight, and had connections to the underground that the rest of them never would.

St. John had not been pleased at having a female member join the group. Marcus thought it probably had more to do with the fact that Faye was the only beautiful woman St. John couldn't get in bed.

Faye walked away without a by-your-leave, and St. John's eyes narrowed as he watched her wave to Isabella and enter the carriage.

Marcus nodded at the nervous looking groom, who then closed the door and vaulted onto his seat.

"What was that about?" St. John asked irritably. Things were never dull around Faye and St. John. They loathed each other with equal intensity.

"There were men here who went after Isabella instead of me."

St. John's eyes turned sharply to the carriage as it rolled down the drive. "And you just let her drive off? And with Kendrick?"

Marcus was arrogant. His arrogance defined him in some ways. But he prided himself on never being arrogant enough not to trust the people he had chosen.

"Faye can handle anything that comes their way. Besides, Isabella is no dull blade."

"Does she know she's in danger?"

Marcus ignored the steady stream of guilt pouring down his spine. "No. I'm sure it hasn't crossed her mind. Why would it? You know we keep that part of life separated and secret. She thinks we deal with dignitaries."

"Still—"

"Still, that is why I'm going to follow them," he said, walking to his carriage. St. John followed.

Marcus noticed his driver looking around oddly.

"What is it Stubbins?"

He handed him a note. "This was given to me by a carriage hand a minute ago. He said another driver gave it to him. Said it was important. I haven't had a chance to talk to the other man, though."

Marcus opened the note and felt the blood drain from his face.

Chapter 15

I have to admit that your recent choice of bed partner has me bewildered. Lady Willoughby? But it is of interest to me that you already held her in regard—as opposed to your previous women. I wonder if you will weep for her loss?

Two carriage mishaps in one day? One for show, one for play?

She won't be so lucky again.

Cold rage settled over him. His heart beat a wild rhythm, as if playing the allegro con brio of Beethoven's Symphony Five.

"Sinjun, round up the others. Have them meet at Isabella's house. I will go after Isabella and Faye."

"Are they in danger?"

"Perhaps. Just get the others, I'll explain there. Stubbins, I'll need you to talk to the other driver later. You know who it is?"

Stubbins gave a nod; Marcus nodded back and hopped inside.

He was trying to decide how to explain to Isabella that she had become a target. And what did the message mean about a second carriage incident?

How was he going to protect her?

It was too late to push her away. He couldn't pretend not to care. The ploy would be completely transparent. They would go after her anyway.

They would go after her anyway.

He tapped the note, thinking hard.

He'd take her to one of his estates. He had already mentioned the seaside to her. He knew every inch of his lands. If they came after her, they would be the foxes in the hunt. If they gave up on doing her harm, even better.

And in that case, did he need to tell Isabella anything? It would be awkward, no doubt, and would ruin the few remaining illusions she had of him. If they could just catch the villains without her being any the wiser . . .

But then, what if she was unprepared? What if he missed something?

No. He would tell her in a few days. There would be no way for the note writer to rally before then. By that time Isabella would be safely ensconced in the country with security measures in place. Otherwise, she might accidentally give something away.

A crack of distant thunder echoed through the night. The plan sounded bad even to his desperate ears.

He watched through the window as the houses passed, the clippity-clop of the horse hooves on the street drawing them closer.

When they were a block away, he could see the lights in the front window of Isabella's house. Shadows shifted as figures moved through the room. He kept from panicking. It was just Faye, Isabella, and her staff. Nothing more than that.

He saw a man across the street, an illuminated tip lifted to his mouth. Smoking and watching.

Marcus rapped the trap and Stubbins's head appeared. "Turn left here and stop a few houses in."

Stubbins did as directed and Marcus exited.

"There's a man watching Lady Willoughby's house. We need to capture him."

Stubbins nodded and pulled out a club.

"I'll give you five minutes to get around the block and into a good position before I flush him toward you."

Stubbins nodded again, familiar with the drill, and disappeared down the back street.

A man of few words, Stubbins, but priceless.

Marcus gripped his walking stick and tapped his pocket watch. He stood behind the fragrant bushes of the corner house and watched through the branches as the man continued his vigil.

The street was very open, and there wasn't much cover for covert spying, but even so, the man was obviously a beginner. Faye had assuredly noticed him. The nosier neighbors probably had too.

Unluckily for the man, the watch hadn't been called yet. The members of the watch were much nicer fellows than Marcus.

He glanced at his pocket watch before tucking it away and rounding the corner. He stepped along the walk toward the man. Step, stick, step. Step, stick, step.

The man noticed him at once, but hesitated before moving in the opposite direction, shuffling away.

Marcus kept his pace, nice and even, and the man didn't panic—not even when Stubbins clubbed him on the head.

When Marcus reached them, Stubbins was dragging the man into the low bushes. Since there wasn't much in the way of hiding places, Stubbins would have to hurry back to get the carriage.

"Can't be helped," Marcus said, shaking his head at Stubbins's nonverbal inquiry. "Get the carriage, grab him and go. We can worry about the neighbors seeing us later. Come back here after you drop him—if he awakens, see what you can learn. On your return, park wherever Angelford and Marston do."

Stubbins nodded and left to get the carriage.

Marcus bent down and rifled through the man's pockets. Two pounds. A hefty sum for a run of the mill man on the grayer side of the law.

Assured that the man wouldn't be going anywhere until Stubbins could take care of him, Marcus crossed the street and walked to Isabella's. Sure enough, he caught a glimpse of Faye peering from a side window. She had most likely observed the entire incident.

Isabella's housekeeper opened the door before he reached the steps and he ducked inside.

"Marcus! What are you doing here?" Isabella peered outside before shooing him into the small room in the back.

"I decided to drop by for a game and tea."

"A game and tea?" She shot a furtive glance in Faye's direction. "I don't understand."

"How would you like to travel to Deal tomorrow?"

"Deal? Tomorrow? But that's Thursday."

She looked adorably clueless.

"Is Thursday not good?"

"There's afternoon tea with Mrs. Creel. A planning session with Ladies Norman and Filstitch. A rout, which I know you are invited to, at Lady Giles's—"

He leaned down and brushed two fingers along her cheek. "Do you really want to attend those instead of coming to the seaside with me?"

Her eyes met his. "Well, it isn't that I wouldn't love to go with you, Marcus." She glanced again at Faye, who had busied herself in the corner looking at fashion plates. "But—"

"But you'd rather keep your social engagements?"

She nibbled her delectable lower lip. "I've accepted dozens of invitations."

"Cancel them."

She looked aghast. "Marcus, you know I cannot. Nothing short of death would be accepted without comment."

"Then let them comment."

She nibbled her lip some more.

"It's nothing that can't be solved later."

She looked up at him. Did he mean marriage? Or just a good hard rumor cleansing?

She could hear the rolling wheels and clopping hooves of a carriage stopping out front. She had thirteen to a dozen that it was either the Angelfords or the Marstons. She cast a look at Faye again, who was pretending interest elsewhere. Something was happening.

A minute later her suspicions were confirmed as James and Calliope walked through the door.

"The twins are asleep, so we thought we'd drop in for a visit." Calliope smiled. She looked impeccable as usual, but for her hair loosely knotted at her neck. Not a style that would have taken more than five minutes to create.

It was well after midnight and they had obviously been roused from home. This was no casual visit.

Stephen popped into the house a second later, golden hair mussed, followed by Viscount St. John, who was still attired in his evening clothes. By rights, St. John's and Faye's presence could be explained—though she knew the two of them less well than the others. At least they had been out tonight. The other three had the look of being roused from their beds.

"What did we miss?" Stephen said cheerfully.

Isabella surveyed the room. Everyone met her gaze, but their expressions were widely varied. Marcus's face gave away nothing. Stephen had his normal friendly face on—the one meant to disarm even the harshest hag. Angelford was expressionless, but his eyes were a degree warmer than usual. St. John looked two steps away from a severe case of ennui, though his eyes flicked between the window and the occupants with regular frequency. Faye was smiling mysteriously. Nothing too unusual there. The girl was always two steps ahead when it came to some things, and one step behind when it came to others. Since Faye had been helping to hold her captive for the past half hour, this was definitely one of the times she was two steps ahead.

Her gaze finally came to rest on Calliope, usually her ally. Calliope looked confused but hopeful.

Hopeful?

"What is this about? Not to be too rude, but what are all of you doing in my house at this hour?"

Calliope gave her a look that suggested she hadn't a clue. Isabella was about to ask another question, followed by maybe two to two dozen others, when Marcus took her arm and gently pulled her into the corner.

She could hear the others forcing conversation in the background. It just made it all the worse.

"What are they doing here?" she hissed, waving a hand at her "guests." "For that matter, what are *you* doing here? What happened to the sneak through the window plan? That was a horrible plan, but it's a good sight better than this one!"

"I thought it would be nice to visit the seaside, to visit my estate, as I said before. Get away from curious eyes and probing questions." His eyes were penetrating and there was a look in them—a look he often got in the midst of a particularly cutthroat game.

"What does that have to do with these five?" She pointed sharply to the others.

"They are here to help you pack and take care of rearranging schedules and alibis."

"Pack? Schedules and alibis? Are we off to rob stagecoaches?"

"I promised delights, did I not? You made your case, and I accepted. We both agree that getting away from London would be the easiest thing to do."

She had a feeling he had just moved a piece on an imaginary chessboard.

"While I agree that it would be marvelous to go to the seaside with you, we can't just—*I* can't just—drop everything and leave without so much as a warning! In the middle of the night, if your packing and alibi nonsense is to be believed!"

"No one will remember a thing about your departure in a few weeks."

"No one will remember—" She broke off, speechless. "Better just to announce myself your mistress and be done with it. It would make for less talk!"

"I thought you wanted to do this?"

"What game do you play? You know I do. But why not wait for two weeks? Most everyone will be gone. All parties scattered to the corners of Britain. No notes of regret or other talk necessary. You can have the entire summer to have me do your bidding."

His eyes examined her face, searching for something. She tried to hide her hope and desire. There was a flare of something in his gaze—something like triumph. "Unforeseen events have taken place. I'm leaving London tonight. I want you to come with me. It is your decision. After this I may get called away for months."

And just like that he called checkmate. She knew it. He knew it. If she wanted to have this affair, he was explicitly stating that this was the only way. The chance wouldn't come again.

"I'll send the notes," she whispered, trying to keep her voice from breaking.

He brushed her cheek. "It will be right, Isabella. Go upstairs. Calliope and Faye will help you pack."

Isabella went almost unwillingly upstairs, and Marcus felt more than a twinge of conscience. Were he to explain what was happening, he would have to explain everything. And what if . . . what if she thought he deserved the consequences?

No, better to follow through on his current path and worry later about her reaction.

"Lady Willoughby doesn't look too pleased. Courting gone afoul, Roth?"

. Marcus just shoved the note Stubbins had given him to Stephen, who read it, whistled, and passed it on.

"Reminds me of that business a couple years back," Stephen said.

"Just another madman seeking revenge."

"That's what happens when you play power games," Stephen quipped.

James elbowed him.

Stephen sighed and his face took on a serious expression. "Have you thought this through?" He held up a hand to stave off comments as Marcus's eyes narrowed. "Have you thought this through in regards to Isabella?" he clarified.

"Of course."

"Are you going to tell her why you are leaving so precipitously?"

"No."

"And if they don't take the bait and follow you?"

"Then I trust you will catch them here. Leaving is as much for her safety as for setting the bait. There's a good chance they won't take the bait, after all. It all depends on the level of desperation behind the revenge. There seems to be quite a good bit of it."

"But in the meantime, are you going to play with her, string her along?"

His eyes narrowed at Stephen. "I won't be stringing her along."

"We don't want to see her hurt."

"And you think I do?" he said sharply.

James gave a dissecting glance. "I don't think you know what you want."

Marcus's teeth ground against each other. "I don't want to see her hurt."

"So you will marry her, then?"

Ice gripped his heart.

"Marcus?"

"One has nothing to do with the other," he said coldly.

"Have you asked her that?"

"She's the one who initiated this."

James raised his brows.

"Ask her. I'm not going to discuss it."

The room was silent for a tense moment.

Marcus raked a hand through his hair. "I need to go over plans for the next few days. Are you with me in this?"

They all nodded, Stephen more slowly than James and St. John.

"Stephen, I need you to take your seat and mine."

While Stephen gaped, Marcus plotted. This was actually going to be a good plan on several fronts. He needed Stephen to become more involved in the House so that when he was unable to serve, Stephen could at least grudgingly do so.

"James, Sinjun, you'll need to help him."

"I don't need help." Stephen sounded outraged for once.

James gave him a sardonic look. "You don't even like being a duke. If you didn't care about people so much, I'd be concerned about your dependents. As it is, your estates are quite healthy, everyone on them is happy, but the political prestige of your title rests solely in Roth's hands."

Stephen wielded power, they all did, but Stephen's power was of a different kind. He could fleece a miser out of all his money yet leave him smiling at having lost every penny. His power was in dealing with people, not paper, and Marcus knew he would be a force in Parliament if they could persuade him to sit in the sessions.

"Roth enjoys that type of intrigue," Stephen said to James. "He doesn't want me stepping in and thinking for myself on the House floor. And neither do I. We share the same views, he's just willing to play. I'm quite happy having him as my proxy."

"Well, I'm not going to be able to serve as your proxy for much longer," Marcus snapped. "You'll have to be mine."

They all looked at him.

Damn.

Stephen's gaze was most piercing. "Why is that?"

Marcus made sure his face was set in careless lines. "Payback. If I'm off playing with Isabella's heart and keeping her out of reach of the villains who want everyone near me dead . . . you get to do this in my stead."

He reviewed his words and frowned. "I don't think any of you will be targeted. Injuring peers is too risky. But watch your backs."

St. John tossed his head arrogantly, the distinctive white streak settling back across his eyes. "As if we'd do otherwise."

Stephen stuck his thumb out toward St. John. "Give Sinjun the House tasks."

"No, he and James already play. And I already speak partially in your name. I need you to take my part. I have everything you'll need at my house. These two will help with the rest."

Stephen sighed. "Very well. But I'm registering my vote against all of this."

Isabella penned the notes of regret with the help of Bertie and her housekeeper, who held all the correspondence. "She regretted to inform them she was retiring from town earlier than first thought. Something unexpected had come up. She would see them upon her return." And so forth.

She penned an additional note to her mother, telling her she'd been invited on a trip and would write again soon. She knew her mother would worry otherwise. She felt a pang of guilt. Her mother would worry anyway. There weren't enough details in her note to satisfy—and her mother wasn't stupid.

She'd probably get an earful when next she saw her.

She had achieved in one week what she thought it would take months to do—retire from London with Marcus. She wasn't so sure of her own charms or naive enough not to question the haste—or the reason why there were currently five other people in her house who clearly had some other purpose for being here than to see Marcus and her off on some spontaneous trip.

Hopefully, during their trip he would confide in her. She was in the middle of the game, and he was clearly holding the most material on the board while her queen scurried about.

She would have to move her pieces cautiously until she could get a firm handle on his new strategy.

She intended to win.

Chapter 16

Isabella dragged herself into the carriage, her baggage already safely stowed. Dawn crept over the houses and the barest amount of activity began in the streets. The dawn of a new beginning or the calm before the glare of the midday sun?

She unfolded the coach blanket on her seat and shook out the tidy creases before draping it around her shoulders.

The door opened and Marcus stepped inside. The tails of his coat brushed her knees, and she pulled the edges of the furry blanket more tightly around her.

He ran his fingers through his dark hair as he sat down, but the haphazard locks refused to look anything other than skillfully arranged. There were darker smudges under his eyes, but they just added to the overall dangerous gleam within. Did the man never look bad?

He leaned back and closed his eyes briefly, then

trained them on her. Golden predatory eyes surveying their prey.

"You look tired."

"Tired? I look wretched. Being told to pack after midnight, then bustled into a carriage before the sun is up, tends to promote a less than desirable mien. The waning hours are rarely kind to us mere mortals—our eyes grow pinched like dried fruit, our skin turns gray as if drained by leeches, our disposition is less than sunny."

The demon across from her smiled.

As the coach began to move, she positioned herself in place from long practice.

"I didn't say you didn't look desirable. Merely tired."

"It was implied."

He reached over and tucked a loose edge of the blanket under her thigh. The skin burned beneath. "Sleepy eyes, rumpled clothing, and tousled hair can be both desirable and a sign of tiredness."

She put a hand to her hair to smooth it. "What did you do with Bertie?"

"She's in the other carriage, have no fear."

Isabella had relinquished her fears along with her baggage an hour ago when she'd finally become too tired to care.

She wondered if she could just nod off sitting upright, the way the elderly ladies occasionally did at balls. She envied the way Marcus lounged on the seat across from her. Her stays would in no way permit such an action. And there was no Bertie to lean against.

But there was Marcus.

"Since we are now on our way, will you tell me why you so suddenly decided to visit your seaside estate?"

"Will it not be easier to conduct an affair there?" His voice held a teasing note, but his eyes were serious.

Ire bit into her. She was in over her head—floundering while he made jokes and controlled the reins. Spiriting her off to the country was all well and good—definitely good for conducting an affair—but did it have to be at dawn? An ache from the lack of sleep settled behind her eyes. And where in Mary's name was her pillow? Bertie couldn't have forgotten her pillow, could she? She needed her pillow.

She looked around the coach, her eyes coming back to rest on Marcus. He looked as if he expected a response. Oh, right. "Yes, I suppose it might," she said grudgingly.

He raised a brow. "You don't seem so keen all of a sudden, Bella."

She waved a hand. It was well-known in her household that no one interfered with her sleeping hours if they didn't want a cranky mistress. Her thoughts began to slip into the haze. She'd find out answers to whatever it was she wanted to know later. "Budge over."

His brows lifted, but he slid left. She pushed off her seat and settled next to him. His shoulder was soft, the feel of the cloth comfortable against her cheek.

He chuckled, the low vibrations strumming through her as she drifted off to sleep.

She didn't feel the long fingers brushing the hair from her face, the lips that grazed the top of her head, or the blanket securely tucked around her.

Isabella woke to gentle rocking, her cheek pressed against something warm and firm. She tried stretching her legs, but pain radiated near her hip and her left leg felt tingly, as if it had long since fallen asleep.

Her right hand pressed into her pillow. It was round and long. What had gotten the goose down feathers into such a state? It was as if she were sleeping on a leg. A hard leg.

She opened her eyes and lurched upward. Papers fluttered to the floor.

She tried to sit upright, but her stays thought otherwise, and her pained hip and deadened leg remained firmly in place. Unable to maintain the precarious position, she slipped and fell right back into his leg.

A muffled chuckle met her reddened ears. Mortified, she put her hands on his leg to prop herself up, one hand higher than proper, if putting a hand on any part of a man's leg could be deemed proper. His laughter ended abruptly.

She pushed upward. Just before she was fully upright, his hands scooped under her arms and lifted her, much like a cat about to be chastened. Or cuddled.

"You looked so uncomfortable after an hour or two that I thought this would be better."

He settled her onto the seat. She had been quite capable of settling herself, she thought grumpily.

"My dignity begs to differ."

"You fall so gracefully, though." He leaned forward and pushed the ruffled curls back from her face. "And if I'm to have lips so near my . . . leg . . . would that they were yours."

She was horrified to feel the heat rise, red hot and licking, to her skin.

She was saved from answering by a rap on the door. "My lord, my lady. We have arrived at The Green Man."

Isabella hastily tried to tidy herself. Marcus smiled. He gave her a few moments before opening the door.

Bertie was anxiously peering around the groom. Marcus helped Isabella down, then her maid took charge, directing her to a room where she could freshen up.

Her legs were so stiff that she tried her best not to hobble inside.

As soon as they were shown to the room, Bertie began fussing.

"Oh, my lady. What have you done?"

Isabella looked in the tall mirror. Her hair was mussed on one side from sleeping, her clothing in disarray, and there was a rose print on her left cheek from pressing against Marcus's shoulder and leg.

She looked as if she had experienced half an orgasm. One only on her left side.

She giggled, then hobbled over to the table mirror and chair so Bertie could put her to rights.

"You can't even walk! What did that man do to you?"

Bertie had never sounded so scandalized.

"Oh, Bertie, settle down. I think it's quite obvious what happened."

Her maid looked even more horrified. "Are you hurt badly? Is there any bleeding?"

"Bertie! I slept the entire way." She pointed to her hair, cheek, and clothing. "On my left side. Honestly, woman. What are you thinking?"

"That you were alone in a carriage with Lord Roth, whom you've fancied forever, and came out rumpled like a demirep the morning after," she said baldly.

"Yes, well . . . " She busied herself fiddling with

a comb on the table. "I can assure you that I am rumpled from sleep, and that is all."

"If you say so, my lady."

"Bertie, in all the many years you've known me, have I ever been less grumpy than when I haven't slept?"

"No." Bertie set to removing the pins from her hair.

"And this morning when I entered that carriage?"

"Grumpy."

"And when I exited the carriage?"

"Well-sexed."

"Bertie!"

"Fine," she said grudgingly. "Less grumpy."

"There you have it."

"As if the attentions of the gentleman in question wouldn't rouse you to wakefulness and settle your grumpiness."

"I thought you said just the other day that I was the grumpiest sleeper you knew?"

Her maid mumbled as she repositioned the pins and patted her hair into place.

Her cheek returned to her normal shade, and her traveling dress was shaken out and straightened.

Marcus was determined to travel to his estate in Deal in one day, and seemed to have a network of fresh teams in place to do just that.

After a light meal they were off again, silent

companions in small quarters. In addition to the lingering discomfort from the previous ride, her nerves were on edge. There was nothing for it. They were alone—and awake—no family, friends, or acquaintances to interrupt, push, or cast a shadow. Bertie was in the other carriage, probably chewing her nails and wailing silently about the state of her baby.

"Would you like to play?"

She looked up sharply to see him pulling a portable chessboard from his valise.

"Yes."

They set up the board, Marcus giving her his beloved black pieces and claiming white.

"Do you have a sudden fascination for the valiant side?" she asked.

He shrugged, a smile hovering on his lips. "Heaven forbid that I do something nice."

He moved his pawn forward for the king's gambit.

She raised a brow and accepted the move. "Do play the same way you did in our last game. I know exactly how to beat you this time."

"I wouldn't dream of giving you a boring game, Bella. Never you."

"I know you wouldn't. 'Tis why I choose to play with you. You are why I keep coming back to the board." She gave him a playful smile, but his eyes regarded her seriously.

She waited for him to say something, but he moved his pawn to take one of hers.

Her fingers brushed against his as she moved her pawn in a mirror move. The top of her fingers brushed beneath his pads, leaving shimmers in the wake.

"Will you play for me when we reach Grand Manor? I remember you saying you had purchased one of the new Broadwoods."

He toyed with his bishop. "It's an exceptional instrument. Seven octaves. There is nothing better on which to play Beethoven. The Viennese Stein in the town house is excellent, of course—the best for playing Mozart."

"So you plan to brood in Deal?"

"Beethoven doesn't brood. He struggles. He triumphs."

She moved her knight. "Do you struggle, Marcus? It seems to me you more often triumph."

He noticeably paused over his own knight, to her surprise. "Some struggles don't end in triumph."

"Of course they don't. But you are not one for whom struggle is a daily word."

"Am I not?"

His eyes grew darker and more brooding. The carriage wheels hit a rut and the board jostled precariously.

"Do you have a cursed illness? Are you poor in

friends? Can you not afford a crumb of bread?"
she asked lightly.

"I have not forgotten your husband. He was
very sickly, was he not?"

She jerked, and the piece she had been about to
move clattered to the floor. She bent to retrieve it,
but he deftly picked it up and handed it to her, his
fingers letting it go after a minute tug.

"George was ill toward the end, yes," she said,
moving her piece and only glancing up at him
after.

He looked as if he were debating something.

"I heard from Stephen that you were donating
a large sum to the Botanical Society in your husband's name," he finally said.

That hadn't been what he was going to say, she
was sure of it.

"Yes. We both loved to garden. His love of it
carried him through to the end."

"That, and his love of you."

She remained silent and made another move.

"You should have told me you were donating
so much. I will donate as well."

She looked up sharply. "You hate gardening. You are the only person I know that dislikes
flowers—every single variety of them."

"But you like them."

Her heart beat faster. "You know I do."

He said nothing. She wished he would.

Another bump jarred the carriage, and he moved the board more securely onto his lap.

His silence unnerved her.

"Are you finally going to share why we are in such haste?"

"No."

"No?"

Heavy lids concealed his eyes as he studied the board. "There were a few problems in Parliament. Too many new hotheads in both Houses. It was a good time to leave."

"When have problems and hotheads ever rattled you? And why would either necessitate leaving London as we did—stealing away in the early morning?"

He didn't answer for a minute. His hand caressed his queen.

"I could have stayed in the city. But I wanted to ply my fingers over that beautiful . . . Broadwood."

His fingers flexed and his eyes studied her. She wanted the real answer, but was willing to wait him out. Especially when he looked at her like that.

"I'm sure the Broadwood can't wait for you to play her," she said, heat traveling down her limbs.

He shifted the board again to compensate for the rocking.

She moved four pieces closer to his territory in the next turns.

The board was nestled in his lap. So close as to almost be touching his stomach. Yet there were several good uncovered inches between.

Looking at the uncovered space and then up at his pensive expression, her hand strayed nearer. His expression changed. Tightened. Grew fierce. He was moving his pieces around the board in a strange fashion, giving her access to his king, but allowing his king to shift. Just a square one way or the other, always staying near the center back. Always giving her reason to move her pieces closer, circling, in order to capture him.

She estimated ten moves until she would have him in checkmate. She was leaning so far forward that when his hand darted out to move a piece at her end, it brushed her breast.

Her eyes locked with his, and when the carriage hit another bump, the chessboard slid to the floor, the pieces scattering, and he was reaching for her instead of his chess queen.

He pulled her onto his lap so she was straddling him, her dress tucked between their legs and flowing to the floor behind.

He kissed her, all that latent passion hidden in his eyes pulling apart and encompassing her.

His arms pulled her tighter against him, her breasts forcibly brushing her chemise as they shifted together.

He tugged her dress up. She could feel his

arousal. His hardness seeking her softness, the answering call to her passion.

She pulled back from the kiss, her lips full and parted, her hair flowing from its pins where his hands had loosened them.

His trousers pressed against her, rubbing. Producing an aching need to be filled. His eyes locked with hers, the motion of the carriage rocking them against each other over and over.

His eyes were dark gold and possessive.

She reached for the top of his trousers, wanting nothing more than to be locked together with him, complete, but he bucked up, causing her to gasp and grip his shoulders. His fingers slipped under the silk of her dress. She arched into him, and his free hand pulled her mouth to his.

The kiss was hot, his tongue hot upon hers, stroking and claiming.

His hand moved against her, one finger buried within her. Her body throbbed, the sensations so intense that she moaned against his mouth. It was not the completion she wanted, but a slight appeasement to the mounting ache. Yet when he pushed up against her again, the friction and feelings were too much, and she came apart in his arms, shivering and shaking and crying his name.

Her head dropped to his chest and she could feel his heart thudding against her cheek. The most glorious feeling. In the arms of the man she loved.

He stroked her hair, his breathing harsh, but not the harshness of postcoital bliss. Rather the harshness of a man right before the throes. Like a man punishing himself.

She stilled.

She reached for him, between them, but he stopped her hand. His arms encircled her and his forehead rested against hers.

"Why don't you let—"

"We are almost there. Your skirts can hide things that my clothes never will."

She accepted his words, but it muted her pleasure a bit. She had just come apart in his arms, and they were almost to his estate—somewhere they could indulge freely. She knew she should be pleased, not unsettled with actions that could be explained away.

It was dusk by the time they arrived. Near the longest day of the year, the hour was late.

The servants were lined up to welcome their master home. Isabella recognized a few who served at Marcus's other estates and those who traveled with him. She had never been to Grand Manor, however. Marcus rarely brought anyone here.

The manor lived up to its name from the outside, but she expected no less. In the waning light she could see the gently curving gardens and the ivy covered walls.

Two footmen held huge lanterns near the large doors. Although the servants eagerly welcomed Marcus, there was a somber undertone, a hidden sadness.

It was said that his parents were buried on this estate and had lived their last years cloistered within its walls.

She wondered what secrets lay inside.

"My lady." Bertie touched her arm. "We can be shown to our rooms while Lord Roth speaks with his staff."

Isabella nodded. An older maid led them forward. Marcus nodded to them. She would see him later.

The foyer was exquisite yet understated. Gentle yellows, golds, and taupes, with darker accent colors. Hints to something deeper.

They climbed the grand staircase to rooms on the first floor. Her suite was done in blues—cornflower, sky, and navy—with gold leaf. Very much suited to her.

"Supper will commence in an hour," the maid said. "Is there anything I can have sent up in the interim? Cheese, bread, and tea, perhaps?"

"That would be lovely."

Bertie and another maid began removing items

from the cases, and a maid returned forthwith with the food. Isabella ate a few bites, then set off to explore until dinner.

She poked through the open rooms on the first floor, but stayed away from the east wing, where the family rooms were located. No need to invade his territory yet. She had been wandering for a while when she entered the portrait gallery.

The gallery was long and reasonably wide. She loved browsing through family galleries. They told one so much about the history and attitudes of a line. August Stewart. George Stewart, Charles Stewart, Benjamin Stewart. Two more Charleses, two more Augusts, another George and Benjamin.

Marcus's ancestors had commissioned family portraits whenever the heir was around eight. The two parents were seated, and a frilly or severely dressed boy, depending on the time period, stood behind them in all the pictures.

Judging from the portraits, a single boy child was the family trait and the immediate line had gone unbroken for three hundred years—quite a feat. A male child surviving from one generation to the next, and producing the next male heir. She noted that the last three men—Marcus's father, grandfather, and great-grandfather—had died at a rather young age, in contrast to the earlier forebears, who, judging from their portraits, looked robust and considerably older.

She tried to recall from her social history lessons what she knew of Marcus's father and grandfather, but her recollections were hazy. If she remembered correctly, they had both retreated from society, dying in seclusion a few years later. If that was true in the case of the great-grandfather, she wondered why there wasn't gossip about a family curse. There was nothing the ton liked quite so well as a family curse.

That society hadn't discerned one was probably a good indication that there either wasn't anything worth talking about or that it had been hushed up incredibly well.

"I see I've found you in the midst of the moldering family portraits," Marcus drawled, lounging against the door.

"How did your great-grandfather August die?"

Marcus froze for a split second before walking toward her.

"He was ill."

"Lung fever?"

"No. A wasting sickness."

He gazed at the portrait in front of her, and she looked again. A vibrant man entering his prime. It was hard to believe he could have wasted away.

"That's terribly sad. He looks as if he has his whole life ahead of him."

Marcus's eyes narrowed. "He doesn't."

"Well, no, he's been dead for—" She checked the date. "—seventy years."

He turned so he was standing in front of her, his back to the portrait wall. "Bertie was going to fetch you, but I decided to come instead. Are you hungry?"

She was, and propriety demanded she accede forthwith, but she longingly looked to the end of the gallery where the portraits of Marcus and his parents hung.

"Yes, but do you mind if I take a peep at the rest of the gallery?"

"If you wish." His voice was stiff.

She stepped past his ancestors' portraits and stopped before the most recent one. Her memory of his parents was vague. Though they had cut ties with her parents—and everyone else—when she was still young, she could remember a charming woman devoted to her husband and a stern man who would occasionally pass her treats when no one was looking.

"Your mother was quite lovely."

"Yes."

She admired the fierce lines. "It's a strong painting."

"Painters sometimes take liberties."

She looked sharply at him. "I remember she was particularly devoted to your father."

"Yes. Particularly."

She bit her lip, but curiosity got the better of her. "How did she die?" She had always wondered.

"Wasting sickness."

"She caught it from your father?"

He smiled mirthlessly. "In a way, I suppose. She was a delicate woman. Upstanding and kind. But not strong. My father's death took its toll on her. She passed soon after."

"Do you blame her for leaving you?"

"I was eighteen. Plenty old enough not to be 'left.' I missed them both, of course. We were quite close before my father took ill."

Isabella didn't think any age was old enough to lose a loved one, but she knew better than to say so to Marcus. He wouldn't appreciate the sentiment.

She looked to the right, to his portrait. He appeared very dashing with a sword in his hand, hair slightly mussed and a serious look on his face.

Next to it was a setter at point.

"Lovely child," she said lightly. The painting of the dog was in the spot where his own family portrait would hang someday.

"I thought him quite quiet as a newborn."

He took her hand in his arm as they walked back down the portrait hall.

"In that case, you will most likely be sorely disappointed in your next."

"We are allowed only one." His smile was forced.

"It is better than being allowed none," she quipped.

He turned and touched her cheek, his thumb rubbing across her chin. "You will marry again and have many beautiful children."

Her lips parted but she didn't know how to reply. She wanted to marry *him*. Have children, or a child, with him. It didn't take a lot of thinking to realize that perhaps she shouldn't broach that topic yet.

They descended the stairs to the dining room, and Isabella clasped her hopes and dreams tightly to her chest.

Chapter 17

Dinner progressed without further comment. They made small talk about the day's trip and discussed some of the more interesting things that happened in Parliament that week. Unlike many men, Marcus never treated her as anything less than an equal.

That didn't mean he told her everything. She had a feeling that even James ground his teeth when Marcus became mysterious or less than forthcoming in his answers.

They retired to the music room after dinner. It was a lovely room, with windows on three sides and enormous burgundy drapes edged with gold. Candle sconces created deep golden light and gave the room a heavy, intimate feeling.

She stretched her fingers along the piano top. It was one of the largest pianos she had seen. His Viennese in London was much smaller, as were the Broadwoods he had at the other houses she'd visited.

"It's beautiful."

His fingers drifted over the keys as he watched her.

"Play me something," she said teasingly.

Graceful, flowing fingers pressed into the keys, pulling the notes from the board and pushing them into the room. The notes connected with the air, bounced off the ceiling and walls and pierced her.

She sank down beside him. She loved Beethoven's Piano Sonata 32, still new enough to intrigue but performed enough to be familiar. Marcus played Beethoven like no other she knew—both the darker, stormier pieces, and the lighter, more optimistic ones. It was fascinating to watch such a dark and virile man play light but emotionally complex pieces. Amusing, but poignant at the same time. As with the darker music, something channeled within him and through the piano. Emotions that he rarely expressed flowed through his fingers.

As he pulled the opening threads, delicate and gossamer, and pushed into a crescendo, she closed her eyes and recalled the first moment she had spied him in a practice room at his parents' Devon estate. She had wandered off and had seen the dark-haired boy furiously playing, the top of his head moving back and forth, up and down the keyboard, until he held the last note. She had been mesmerized, then he had looked up and pierced her with that unforgettable gaze.

She opened her eyes to see him regarding her. The playful middle section of the piece playing beneath his fingers, the hints of darkness covered, uncovered, and overlaid by more optimistic chords and runs. It was technically demanding, but there was also something so ambivalent, so tearing, about the piece. Was the darkness encroaching? Or was it being overcome?

The sweet, tapered coda sounded as the final notes played on her heartbeats. Three . . . two . . . one.

The last note echoed in the stillness of the air.

Even when he rose and took her hand, the spell wasn't broken. It increased in strength, and then she felt herself escorted up the stairs, standing in front of her door, Marcus before her, the door at her back. She smiled, opened the door, and walked inside.

Knowing he would follow.

Chapter 18

Bertie was waiting up for her, but after a long look, she retreated through the side door, closing it behind her.

Marcus's strong, capable hands pulled her from her dress, slowly unwrapping her stays. One artistic finger and thumb pulled the lacings through one hole and then another. Unthreading, unhurried.

Just like the last notes of the sonata.

It had been so long since she had felt the touch of a man's fingers on her clothes. And Marcus's . . .

His hands moved from her half undone stays to her hair and worked at the pins within. One pin, then another, joined each other on the tabletop. He was methodical. And the heat in her belly extended outward as he liberated one more lock, one more stay from its bindings.

Her hair tumbled down in waves as it was freed,

and she closed her eyes and sighed. It always felt so good to have her hair free. The released pressure from her scalp felt wonderful.

His fingers combed through and lightly pushed her head forward so her hair curtained her face and his hands pressed against the back of her neck, massaging upward and into the locks.

She grew unsteady on her feet and rocked into him. He stilled, then his hands trailed down her back, across her soft, thin chemise and back to her stays, attending to them again, the thread getting longer and longer as he progressed, the tingles spreading from her stomach downward, pooling below.

The heat pounded in that pool, as if it had a drumming heartbeat of its own.

She needed something to soothe the heat.

He unthreaded the final lace and the ribbon fluttered to the ground, coiling there. Her shift slid down and followed it to the floor.

He pulled her back against him. The hard planes of his body pressed to the soft curves of hers.

His arms reached around and traveled up the front of her thin chemise, the silk bunching beneath his fingertips. They moved from her hips, past her navel, around the peaks of her breasts and down her arms.

His head bent down to hers, his lips next to her ear. "This is your last chance, Bella."

"I know," she whispered, arching back into him.

It didn't matter that she was interpreting his statement differently than he had intended. It wasn't her last chance to get away, it was her last chance to get him.

"And what is your answer?"

"Yes. Of course, yes."

She turned in his arms and pulled his head down, bringing his lips to hers. It was a sweet feeling. The taste, the passion, the knowledge that she was finally going to have the man she'd loved for so long.

The kiss was gentle. His mouth moved softly across hers, with little coaxing needed to open and explore. She deepened the kiss, swiping her tongue across his, and he leisurely followed. The urgency of the carriage, or of the hallway in his London house, was gone. They had all night. But there was urgency of a different kind. Urgency to get closer, to complete a bond.

The shoulder muscles beneath her hands worked as he pulled back the coverlet and sheets on her bed.

He broke the kiss and moved down her body, gripping the edge of her chemise, his smile devilish. He spun her around so she faced the four poster. He lifted the silk slowly, pulling the hem from her ankles up her calves. She could just see the tips of his fingers and the bunching material of the silk as it rose.

She could feel every movement on her skin. Every touch sent spikes of pleasure through her body.

He placed a kiss behind her right knee, then her left, causing her knees to buckle. She eeped.

He chuckled, the warm tones sending just as many pleasant shivers through her as his roaming hands.

She placed both hands on the bedpost to remain upright, gripping the smooth, faceted wood, while his hands reached ever higher.

The silk pulled over her thighs, under and against her curls, as his hand slipped around. She gripped the wood harder. The silk flowed over her hips, freeing her, a cool breeze wrapping between her legs. She felt him rise behind her, one hand reaching up to move her hair to the side, his lips pressing against her nape, dropping her head forward so she was fully splayed out—arms in front, head down.

His hands continued their ascent, pulling the silk over her breasts, pausing for a moment to circle them gently before pulling the chemise up past her neck and along her arms, so conveniently straightened in front of her.

She breathed heavily as he draped himself over her back, pushing the garment forward. She felt him, firm against her bare rear, pushing lightly against her, and heat flared everywhere.

She let go of the post, and the garment dripped to the floor in a haze of silk. He ran his hands down her sides, her back clasped against his front.

"If you could see yourself like this, Bella." She arched back into him as his hand caressed her breast.

He straightened, turned her around and laid her on the bed; a buffet, naked and ripe for devouring. She had never felt more beautiful then she did at that moment as his darkening eyes caressed her. His hands moved roughly at his shirt and she couldn't contain a satisfied smile. She traced the brocade of the partially turned down coverlet while he disrobed, her eyes feasting on every new bit of skin uncovered.

When his fingers hooked into his trousers, she held her breath. And then those too were gone.

The bed depressed as he straddled her torso, kneeling above her. His fingers traced a path up her leg.

"What is it you want, Bella?"

His fingers curled into her, playing with the curls between her legs.

She arched into his fingers and they slipped between the curls, rubbing in gentle strokes. She gripped the edge of the counterpane and the sheets bunched in her hands.

"You. I want you," she groaned, arching back as one finger, then two, slipped inside.

He crawled forward, like a large cat, his chest brushing against hers, his fingers playing a magical tune. "Do you want me to make love to you, Bella?"

She panted as one finger crooked upward and rubbed a spot deep within her.

"Yes." She couldn't catch her breath.

He skimmed downward, his chest brushing across hers again, his breath caressing the tip of her right breast. "To sink deep within you?"

He took the tip of her breast in his warm mouth.

"Yessss." The sound was dragged from her.

"To claim you?"

His finger crooked again and his thumb rubbed a spot outside and she saw stars for a moment.

"Oh, God, yes," she moaned. She felt as if she had imbibed too much wine. The canopy of the four poster wobbled in her vision, golden lights dancing behind her eyes.

"Please." She was on fire. She would beg until he relented, would promise him anything.

His fingers withdrew and he scooted her up so her head lay against a pillow and his hands buried into her hair, tilting her head back for a kiss, hot and heavy, but still with that underlying care, that tenderness he had shown throughout.

He moved between her legs and she parted them, letting them fall to the side before wrapping around him. Bringing him closer, nudging him forward.

He brushed against her and she felt the tip of him nudge and then slide along her, wet and slick.

She kissed him more fiercely, so high on the edge that she wanted him inside her now. The edge of completion beating at her for release.

She pulled back and looked in his eyes. "Make love to me, Marcus. Now."

With a deep thrust he slid smoothly inside her, and the bed knocked against the wall behind. Her heart shifted up into her throat and her eyes rolled back.

It felt so wonderful. Nothing else could feel this good. He was stretching her, the length of him moving inside her. And she had never felt the like. Never been privy to the heavy sensual experience of lovemaking, only that of care and friendship.

He shuddered as he moved deeper, more firmly within her, so far up that tingles seemed to radiate from the center out.

He stopped and they lay there for a moment, breathing heavily and looking into each other's eyes. He pulled back, and when he pushed forward once more, she took back everything she had said about the first stroke, because the second was even better.

He pushed in fully again and the bed ricocheted against the wall, her body writhing beneath his.

A fine mist gathered across her skin and she forgot how to breathe properly. But breathing properly was the least of her concerns as the heat spread, to her toes, to her ears. He withdrew and thrust again and she felt a tightness begging for release.

She slipped her hands up to his shoulders and into the hair at his nape, the thick edges curling around her fingers.

He kissed her, his tongue hot against hers, his lips devouring hers. Then he leaned back to watch her as he thrust again. In and out, in and out. She threw her head back and clutched onto him.

The sensations spread everywhere, and then all of a sudden coalesced where they were joined together.

She arched wantonly against him, calling his name over and over as the sensations tightened, peaked, and a thousand lights exploded in the back of her eyes.

He moved faster and faster within her, jaggedly; as if he were a dying man seeking his last breath of air. As if he could do nothing else except finish what they had started. And then he said something she couldn't hear, pulled out of her abruptly, shuddered violently, and emptied himself into the bedding beneath.

She froze, her panting cut abruptly. The exquisite sensations overlaid with confusion.

Instead of the completion, the ultimate joining, he was next to her, apart, shuddering alone, not locked together with her in a supremely satisfied embrace.

A hollowness crept upon her.

She wiped a hand across the hair plastered to her forehead and tried to get her breathing back under control. "Marcus?"

He turned to her and smiled. A smile that lit parts of his eyes usually shadowed.

"Yes, Bella?"

She tentatively smiled back and swallowed her question, unwilling to dim that light for even a second. "Nothing."

He kissed her, softly and tenderly.

She loved him. They had just shared an earth shattering experience.

And she could have cried.

Chapter 19

He watched her sleep. Watched the morning light pierce through a crack in the draperies and gently caress her cheekbones. A fairy princess, a changeling in disguise.

She twitched and stretched, her eyes blinking sleepily, a crooked smile curling her lips. "Good morning," she whispered.

He leaned down and kissed her on her sun-drenched cheek. She was still sleepy and warm. Comforting.

"I need to visit some of the tenants. Would you care to join me this morning?"

She cast a rueful glance at her well-indented pillow, then looked back to him. "I'd love to join you."

Marcus was confident they had not been followed to Deal yet. There hadn't been time enough for the Crosby gang, or anyone else, to have discovered their whereabouts and orga-

nized a strike. But he fully expected someone in-
tending harm to show up tomorrow or the next
day.

He and his men would be ready.

He signaled to a few of them as he and Isabella
made their way to the stables after breakfast. Better to be safe, especially with Isabella venturing
beyond the confines of the estate.

He assisted her into the saddle, letting his hands
linger on her waist and enjoying the faint blush
that spread across her cheeks. That she could still
blush amused him.

"Feeling feisty today, are we, Lord Roth?"

His mouth curved and he felt some of the
weight he had been carrying for so long—too
long—lighten. Mounting his own horse and
keeping the reins firm, he leaned in close, his
lips brushing her ear. "I can't seem to control my
hands around you, Bella."

She returned the gesture, though her mare
snorted in protest as the reins sagged. Her lips
touched the skin behind his ear, causing all of the
hairs in the vicinity to stand at attention. "Whoever said I wanted you in control of yourself,
Marcus? Not I, I assure you," she whispered.

She pulled back, her skin a beautiful rose, her
eyes sparkling in challenge. She nudged her horse
and trotted toward the wooded path, a princess
entering her fairy kingdom.

Yes, Isabella Willoughby was a changeling, no doubt about it. And he could pretend for now that he was charging forth to make her his.

They rode along the seafront. The waves beckoned, whipped from breakers to froth along the sand. Hints of a distant storm played on the breeze. He could see his men amongst the trees. Watching, waiting. The shadows grew shorter as the sun rose to its zenith. He looked to Isabella, but she seemed to be only interested in the ride, the wind whipping her clothes and pulling strands of hair from her coiffure.

They reentered the woods and stopped at a stream that wound through the property. Now that Isabella wasn't giving her horse its head, she was having more difficulty.

"Shhh, just over here."

"Bella, you are being too gentle. Make her go where you want her to go."

She shot him a disgruntled glance. He listened in amusement as she tried to reason with the horse. Isabella was an adequate rider, but she was too gentle.

When her horse turned to head back to the stables, Marcus whistled sharply and the horse's ears went back.

"Isabella, just make her go where you want her to go. Be firm. Even aggressive."

She gave him a pointed stare. "Good advice for dealing with domineering men, as well."

His lips curved involuntarily. "I can't say I disagree."

Her cheeks turned rosy and she switched her gaze back to her horse's mane. "I don't want to hurt her. This is why I don't ride."

"You aren't going to hurt her. Be firm."

She tugged on the reins. Marcus could have sworn the horse gave a resigned snort before tromping over to join her mate.

Marcus hid a smile at Isabella's glare and led her to a medium-sized cottage in the south glen. Constance and Timothy Slattery were his favorite tenants.

The door to the little house opened as he lifted Isabella down.

"My lord!" A stout woman tumbled out of the house.

"Mrs. Slattery." He accepted her squeeze. "Good to see you."

"It's good to be seen, your lordship!"

Timothy strode out, as tall and thin as his wife was short and round.

"Isabella, this is Mr. and Mrs. Slattery. Meet Lady Willoughby."

"Ah, call us Constance and Timothy, milady. Come inside, come inside. The wind has picked up something fierce." Constance shuffled Isabella into the cottage. Timothy watched the two women disappear and turned to look at Marcus.

"Good to see company, your lordship."

Marcus raised a brow, feigning ignorance. "Have you missed my company so much?"

Timothy shook his head. "Not yer company I was referencing."

Marcus hadn't brought anyone to the estate in years. And he had never brought a woman. The servants at the manor could barely keep quiet about it, even within his hearing.

"I'll have to send the steward over more often."

"Fine, keep yer lips buttoned." Timothy cast a shrewd glance his way. "Connie has sweet buns."

"I know. I've been telling you that for years."

Timothy muttered about the notions of youth, but Marcus could see the smile lurking around the corners of his mouth. He released a little more of the stiffness that had settled almost permanently on his shoulders.

The inside of the cottage was unchanged from the last time he had visited. A cheery fire flared, a pot simmered above it. Large rugs and colorful, homemade tapestries covered the floors and walls. Marcus was directed into a chair at the head of the deeply gouged, but highly polished, oak table and watched avidly as Constance plunked a pile of sweet, sticky buns on the tabletop.

He reached for one and felt the slap of a wooden spoon against his knuckles.

"Yer lordship or not, the lady be getting one first."

Isabella's face switched from shock at seeing the sharp rap of wood to noble knuckles, into amusement. "Thank you, Constance."

She separated a bun, holding it delicately between her fingers before taking a small bite. Marcus forgot about the buns the moment Isabella took her first bite; her expression changing from amusement to bliss. He wanted to taste something indeed. Every last bite.

She gave a low moan. "Oh, these are wonderful, Constance. How do you make them?"

"'Tis a family secret. But I'll tell you this bit." Constance launched into the merits of baking ingredients, and Marcus plucked a bun and watched the different expressions flutter across Isabella's face as she conversed with his tenant.

"Yes, good to have company," Timothy murmured, as he relaxed into his chair, a secret smile on his face.

Marcus took a bite and nearly moaned himself as the honey dripped down his throat. "How has everything been? I've received positive reports, but you know I'd rather hear the news from you."

"The couple on the border has been having some trouble. Wife had triplets in March. 'Twas a miracle all survived. Three babes." He shook his head. "We've all been pitching in. Might want to take a look. They inherited from Bill Hanney who passed last year. 'Tis his nephew."

Marcus nodded. "I spoke with him briefly after Bill Hanney passed and approved the turnover. I'll make sure to visit and send Sarah with some extra baskets."

Timothy nodded. "Bit of a trouble spot with poachers, but think we've taken care of them. I've noticed there's been an increase of men patrolling the grounds since you've been here."

"Yes. There will be for the next week or so. Be cautious," he said softly, not wanting Isabella to hear. Timothy seemed to understand as he just nodded.

"Rents are acceptable. Everyone is managing well. Even saving a bit."

"Good," Marcus said.

Timothy looked up as Constance and Isabella finished their conversation.

"Connie's still after me something fierce," Timothy said, raising his voice. "Anything you can do about that, your lordship?"

"And brave her wrath? I think not."

"I always said ye was a smart man, your lordship," Constance said.

A mischievous light entered Isabella's eyes, but

a knock at the door saved him from her rebuttal.

"Enter," Constance called.

A woman poked her head in the door, her eyes going wide as she saw Marcus. "Your lordship!"

"Good afternoon, Mrs. Derning."

"Good afternoon, my lord! It's wonderful to see you. Will you be coming round today?"

"If it is a good time for you."

"Of course, of course. Always a good time for you to visit. I'll let Nathaniel know." She glanced down at her sack. He could see her mentally tallying her supplies. She'd probably hustle home to make one of her famous stews. One thing he loved about visiting his tenants was enjoying the regional delicacies with which he was stuffed. Even his French chef in London, renowned and always in danger of being whisked away from him, couldn't compete with the salt-of-the-earth English fare, the generations' old family recipes, and the care with which every dish was made.

Good will and delicious food. That the other landowners didn't take advantage of building lasting relationships with their tenants was to their own stupidity.

Marcus introduced Lizzie Derning to Isabella.

"What can I do for you, Lizzie dear?" Constance asked.

"Pamela's out of the tisane, and so is Sally.

Mistress Mally won't be back through until next week. She went up north to help the Busby's. Do you have any more?"

"Of the Handler herbs? No dear, I'm afraid the fennel is all gone."

Isabella perked up. "Are you trying to make The Helping Handler?"

Lizzie Derning gave her a surprised glance. "Yes, my lady."

"Do you have nasturtium?"

Constance looked mystified. "Yes."

"You can substitute the nasturtium for the fennel."

Lizzie's mouth dropped. "Are you sure?"

Isabella smiled. "Yes. As long as the person you are brewing it for has suffered no previous malefic effects from nasturtium."

Lizzie shook her head as Constance left to fetch the herb. "Mr. Derning will be too pleased to be rid of his pain. A husband is no delight when ill, I'll tell you!"

Isabella laughed, but Marcus could feel the discomfort beneath the timbre. A whisper of cool air slid down his spine.

The women chattered about cures and brewed the tisane, while Marcus devoured the sweet buns and Timothy whittled. It was a pleasant, homey scene. It reminded him of when he used to escape from the estate—from his father's sick-bed, from his mother's permanently engraved face, from the impenetrable air of despair. He would run here and be fed sticky buns until he was overflowing. Isabella fit right in—but then, she always fit in.

Isabella wasn't the problem.

"Just like the old days, eh?"

Marcus turned to Timothy and saw Isabella's smile as she stirred a pot. Saw in his mind's eye that smile turning to worry and despair.

"No, hopefully never like the old days," he said softly.

They spent another half hour with the Slatterys before continuing their rounds of the estate. Cheerful faces greeted them everywhere. And if they were a bit too watchful, too evaluative, too hopeful, Isabella made no mention.

Every time the topic of his parents was broached, he deftly steered the conversation away.

Their final stop was the Hanneys. Marcus had never met Mrs. Hanney, but found her to be pleasant. Mr. Hanney had made a good impression when Marcus had met him the previous year. Isabella immediately fussed over the three babies and helped Mrs. Hanney calm them down. He wasn't sure if the look of complete adoration on the part of Mrs. Hanney was as a result of Isabella's help or the way that Isabella made people comfortable.

If only he—

No.

He looked at Isabella, sitting in a sturdy, utilitarian chair with a babe on her lap and one in a basket at her side. The third child was in Mrs. Hanney's arms, but Marcus barely spared them a glance. No, Isabella was the only person his eyes would focus upon. He could see the wistful look on her face as she brushed the fine strands of hair on the baby's head. As she stroked the cheek of the tiny body in the basket. As she tucked the blankets more securely around both.

His normal, rational, cold thinking was under siege. Battered by emotions he didn't want. Crushed by the blossoming of things he wanted so badly he could taste. Emotions that would never leave, but relationships that could only slip from his grasp.

No, not slip. He would fling them from his grasp. He couldn't afford not to.

Marcus tried to focus on what Mr. Hanney was saying, but the words blended together into a cacophonic dissonance. As if someone had brutalized a piece of his beloved Mozart.

He pushed away the impending headache. He wouldn't ruin this now. There was still time. There had to be.

Chapter 20

Isabella planted a tenth set of sainfoin conicals. The deep pink, red-veined flowers stood proudly in the small plot she had been given by the head gardener. Shoots of lucerne, yellow pimpernel, and chicory were interspersed throughout the plot, giving a colorful and wild look to the space.

The gardener at Grand Manor had been averse at first—suggesting that she would do better to make suggestions and have his workers do the manual labor. He didn't want some outsider mucking about in his gardens. It had taken a considerable amount of flattery and a lengthy discussion regarding the virtues of one plant and flower species versus another to convince him of her passion and knowledge of horticulture.

In the end she had triumphed completely, and he had given her the freedom to take what she wanted from the greenhouse.

He'd seemed entirely pleased with the results the last time he had walked past. Everyone was happy.

Actually, it wasn't just the head gardener who ventured by. She frequently saw two of his assistants, several brawny servants she had seen around Marcus in London, and even Stubbins on occasion. If she didn't know better, she'd think they were concerned about her stealing some hidden treasure in the flower beds.

She hadn't been alone in the gardens for more than a minute or two all afternoon.

One of the brawnier men walked by, looking around in all directions.

"Good afternoon . . . Mr. Freem, was it?"

He stopped, focused on her and gave a bow.

"You seem to enjoy the gardens so well, I was wondering where you thought I should put this last sainfoin?"

The man's eyes widened. "I wouldn't know, my lady."

"But you have been out here so often."

"I often take walks in the gardens." He shrugged helplessly. It was an amusing gesture on so large a man.

"Are you just taking the air, then?"

She watched as he rubbed the back of his head and a bead of sweat trickled down his brow. "Yes, I needed some air."

Sure he did.

"But surely you have an opinion. Where should I place this one? Over here?" She pointed. "Or there?"

"Er, over there looks right."

She pretended to think a moment before nodding. "Very good. Good afternoon to you, Mr. Freem."

The man took off without a second spared.

She shook her head and continued digging the spot "over there" that she had already started.

"Frightening the help, Bella?"

She froze, a pleasant feeling overtaking her. The slight pains from bending and crouching forgotten.

"You mean the men sent to watch me?"

"Men sent to watch you?"

She turned to see him drop gracefully onto a garden bench, his long legs spread in front.

"I'm not stupid, Marcus. I haven't questioned you about what happened the other night, because I *wanted* to come with you. Because I trust you and was willing to remain ignorant and silent until you were ready to trust me."

He raised a brow. "It is no wonder you won that trophy back. That last sentence was beautifully framed to play on my guilt."

"Thank you." She put her trowel down and waited.

He didn't fidget. Sometimes she wished he would. It just wasn't normal that he held himself in so controlled a manner all the time—allowing only a limited range of facial expressions and ten different meanings behind the height of his raised brow.

"I like watching you garden," he said.

"I like watching you shift the conversation."

"You have a lovely assortment there."

"You have a lovely mouth."

His eyes sparked and there was a subtle shift in his body position.

She wondered if her boldness was the result of the new confidence blooming within her. She had never consciously thought herself unworthy, but perhaps it had been simmering below the surface. A consequence of an unrequited love.

Not that Marcus had declared his love. Or even completed the act she found holy. But his actions had declared her desirable. And she found the feeling irresistible.

"I like the pink ones best," he said. "The dusky pink tips, the swollen red lips. They remind me of something."

She wet her lips and clasped her work gloves. "They remind *me* that you are too good at getting what you want. In this case, a topic change."

He leaned back, again a subtle shift, and perused the edges of the garden before focusing back on her.

"What do you want to know, Bella?"

"Why do your men keep walking by? Why are you studying everything in the vicinity the same way they do?"

"You don't believe we are all interested in taking a pleasant walk through the fragrant gardens? Near a beautiful woman?"

She was under no illusions as to her own looks, but that did not diminish the pleasure at being called beautiful.

"No. I don't believe it."

He leaned forward. "And what do I need to do to convince you of your beauty?"

"Marcus, that is not what I meant." She picked up the trowel and shook it at him. "Why is everyone so alert and anxious?"

He watched her. She imagined him tracing the iron scrolls beneath his hand, but as usual he didn't move, just watched.

"There have been threats made against me."

Her mouth dropped open.

"And against you."

Her jaw snapped shut. "Me? Threats? What type of threats?"

"Unpleasant ones."

"Why?"

"You have often been seen in my company. I've

been paying you too much attention. We were probably seen kissing at my house that night."

That jolted her for a second. Having looked through the window before falling on the body bag, she'd thought about how visible they had been. But she'd been concerned about tittering gossip, not about—

"So you have some jealous woman clamoring after you? Marcus, how many affairs have you been having?"

His eyes sparked. "I haven't been having any 'affairs.' You are my first."

Oh. "Then all those other women . . . "

One brow raised.

" . . . you weren't carrying on relationships with them?"

She had hoped not. Had vainly thought no women had held his attention.

"No."

Her relieved mind circled back. "Then who is threatening you?"

"Someone politically."

"Threatening with what? Political suicide?"

"Something a bit more dire than that."

Her mind stopped working. "Someone is threatening to kill you?"

"Yes."

She blinked. He was dead calm. The first part of the conversation came back to her.

"And me?"

"Yes."

One part of her mind couldn't quite grasp what he was saying. She stood up. "And you knew about this before and are just now telling me?"

"You are perfectly safe here. I would never allow you to be harmed."

She sputtered. She didn't know what to say even as warmth flooded her at his last words. "Why—Why would you say nothing to me about this in London? At my house?" She thought of her five unexpected guests. "Obviously I'm the last to know."

She gripped the trowel more tightly. "Did you bring me here out of pity for involving me?"

His eyes narrowed. "No."

"But you were never going to tell me, if you could help it. Isn't that true?"

He said nothing for a few seconds. "Yes."

She angrily stepped back and her foot landed on one of her plants. She looked down at the mangled stalk and knelt to straighten it and pat it back into place as best she could.

Fuming, she stabbed a stick into the soil, ripped a swatch of cloth and tied it around the plant and stake to keep it upright. The actions gave her a few extra moments of needed perspective.

"I want to know why this person is after you, and now me. And don't banter with 'it's political.'

I could do with the tiniest morsel of information if you don't want me hopping into the first carriage to Deal."

His body went rigid. "You can't go into Deal."

"Well, obviously, as there are people out there that you say want to kill me. Kill me!" She repeated a bit hysterically. "But so help me, I will take half your servants and rent out an entire inn in Deal on *your* credit until I can get back to London if you don't give me something more to go on."

He was breathing hard. She could see his chest lifting.

"I've made enemies over the years."

"Yes, well, you aren't the nicest person at times and you champion unpopular causes. I'm sure there are all types of people who don't like you and vice versa. That doesn't mean they want to kill you," she said pointedly.

"I've made some bitter enemies. Men I've ruined."

Her eyes scrunched. "Ruined in what way? Cutting them? Saying rude things?"

"Making sure they can never reenter society again."

Isabella felt the breath leave her, a cold feeling in its place. "Lord Yarnley didn't just 'move' to the Continent then. The rumors were true?"

"Yes."

"And Blakely? He is hanging onto the very fringe. Your doing as well?"

His mouth tightened. "Yes."

"How many more?"

He swallowed. That he was nervous calmed her somewhat. "A few."

"Why?" she whispered.

"Different reasons. Yarnley was up to his neck in illegal trafficking. Blakely has ruined three estates, two peers, and he can't stop gambling, though he has kept that under wraps. He is after the Banners for their money. Not unusual, but it sickens my stomach to see the Banner chit look at him as if he created the stars."

"He loves her. I can see it."

"He doesn't love her. He is using her."

She swallowed. She wondered if he was the only one. "And the others? What about Ainsworth?"

"Ainsworth is an idiot. I've done little to him above pointing out what everyone else knows. The others . . . " He moved his hand over the iron. "Some were engaged in illegal activities—much easier to run them off than to have them arrested and the Houses defaced. Not all of them have been political. We deal with an . . . interesting element from the underbelly of society."

"So you are saying that instead of having a crazy person from society after us, we may have a crazy person from the underworld after us?"

"More than possible. Though there is likely a connection to the ton."

"I see," she whispered, looking at the spade in her hand. She couldn't believe this. It all seemed so unreal. Someone wanted to kill him. Someone wanted to kill *her*. "Who was the body in the bag the other night, Roth? Not some poor soul that had been left for a nameless surgeon, I'll bet."

He flinched a bit at her use of his title.

"No."

"You lied to me." She felt strangely calm about it.

"Yes."

"Why?"

"I didn't want you to worry. It was none of your concern."

She nodded. "None of my concern. I see. Perhaps not, but I do trust you not to lie to me. You could have told me it was none of my concern at the time."

"You would have been hurt."

"And you think I'm not hurt now?" she said viciously.

He started to say something, but she held up her hand.

"Perhaps at supper—I'm feeling distinctly ungenerous at the moment. I'm going inside. You need not worry about me venturing out again. I'll stay inside as long as you do. As much as I'm displeased with you at the moment, I don't want to see anyone hurt."

She turned and walked inside without waiting for an answer.

Supper was a taut affair. Isabella had determined in the intervening hours between their confrontation and the meal that she wasn't ready to cede complete control to Marcus just because she loved him. She wasn't going to let him lead her around blindly, as he had in order to get her away from London in the first place, by dangling her affection and desperation in front of her.

She picked at her fish. *Desperation.* Just thinking the word made her lose her appetite.

Looking up to see Marcus watching her, she had a feeling her desperation wasn't completely conquered.

"What should we talk about, my lord?"

His fork clinked against the dish. "How about you stop calling me my lord?"

"Lord Roth?"

"Isabella . . ."

"Roth?"

"You are being petty."

She bristled, upset at herself as well as at him for having the nerve to point it out. "Pardon my descent into the infantine."

He said nothing.

"I take umbrage to being the only petty one in this conversation," she ground out.

"Do you want me to apologize?"

She pointedly poked at her asparagus.

"I apologize for not telling you about this in London."

She sighed. He sounded contrite, or as contrite as Marcus could sound. She didn't know what she wanted. His undying declaration?

"I know."

"But it's not enough," he said resignedly.

She shifted in her seat. "I just wish you trusted me. I suppose that is what hurts most."

He put his fork down carefully on his plate. "I trust you, Bella."

"Not really, you don't."

"Why do you say that?"

"There are other things you are keeping secret."

"I can't tell you my every secret. Especially not those that are not my secrets to tell."

"I don't want you to share someone else's secrets. I just want . . . "

"Yes?"

. . . *yours*.

". . . I just want you to trust me," she finished somewhat lamely.

"I do."

And somehow that made things worse than before. Because as much as he said he trusted her, he didn't trust her completely. Probably didn't trust anyone completely. Did she even know what she was asking for?

Could he love her if he didn't trust her completely?

Maybe. She didn't know. And that was the problem. She wanted so badly for him to return her love that she was scrambling to decipher the clues as to whether he did or did not.

A servant walked in. "My lord, there is an urgent messenger to see you." The servant looked uncomfortably in her direction.

She pushed her chair back, and Marcus rose with her.

"Please do not feel the need to stay on my account," she said. "I believe I will retire early. Good evening to you."

The words came out more tersely than she'd intended, but she needed to think things over. She didn't want the looming sense of desperation that clung to her to taint her thoughts before she had a chance to reason them through.

She walked from the room, leaving a pair of narrowed eyes following her wake.

Marcus dismissed the messenger and mounted his horse alongside his men.

"Your lordship?" one of the men queried.

Marcus caught a glimpse of a rose-gowned figure in the ivy-crowned first floor window. Long, dark hair flowed loosely around her shoulders, one gloved hand rested on the pane. Caught like a fairy princess in a gilded cage.

His mouth tightened. He whirled his horse toward the woods. "Let's head out."

It was time to remove the threat.

They rode hard and fast into the dark forest. Hooves pounded along the path, kicking up clods of dirt. Marcus ducked to avoid a low lying branch and leaned forward as his mount soared over a fallen log.

With each stride his pent up anger, his guilt, his frustration increased. The responsibility for the deaths of his men and the threat directed toward Isabella was so near, so tangible.

They slowed the horses some fifteen minutes later near the stream that divided the forest. He took two deep breaths, trying to center himself amidst the overwhelming need for revenge.

"They are just to the west, my lord, using the abandoned cabin in the glen. Our men are already stationed near their camp."

Marcus nodded. "Good. You two." He pointed at two of the men. "Go around north and circle in. Wait for the signal."

The two riders took off north. He motioned to the other two men. "Same orders, but south."

He waited with Stubbins at the edge of the river as the riders receded from view.

"It's time, Stubbins. Past time."

"Yes, my lord."

They headed straight west, straight into the heart of the enemy's camp, straight to where vengeance beckoned.

Marcus broke through the trees. A startled shout echoed in the clearing as two men stumbled from the cottage and ran in different directions. Marcus watched through narrowed eyes and rode around the side of the cabin in time to see a third man falling from the back window. The man, upon seeing him, fled toward the edge of camp, toward a horse tethered to a great oak.

Marcus could see his men emerging from their spots, hemming in the campsite and roughly capturing the other two. He rode forward and swung his horse to a stop, blocking the fleeing man from reaching his mount.

"Going somewhere?" He asked, his tone mild.

"J-just to my horse, sir. We haven't done nothing wrong. Swears it on my honor, I do." The man sported an ingratiating smile.

"And pray tell, what are you doing in this clearing, on private land, at this hour?"

"Just resting our heads. We didn't mean any harm." The man's smile turned crooked and disarming.

"The rifles are just for show then? For any large, wild animals that might come round?"

Marcus watched the man's smile dip as he saw the cache of weapons resting on a crate, clearly visible through the open front door. The man cast nervous glances as each route of escape was closed off by more men surrounding the site.

He regained his smile quickly. "Ye've caught us out, sir. We were poaching. A sad business. Take me to the local constable. I'll pay me fine." He smiled ingratiatingly again.

"Tie them up," Marcus said, speaking to the men behind him, but keeping his eyes on the reedy fellow in front. "We'll make use of the cabin these three so precipitously vacated."

The man's eyes went wide. "Now, now, don't be hasty, your lordship. My family, we're just so hungry. One or two little rabbits, who'd notice?"

Whereas in a normal case Marcus might have been darkly amused by the man's ploys, nothing about the current situation was amusing. "When one of those rabbits answers to the title of lady, I'd say a great many would notice."

The ingratiating look vanished from the man's face. "I don't know what ye speak of."

Ah, there was that street accent coming through. Marcus smiled. "That's not a problem. We'll help jog your memory."

He motioned to Stubbins, who hauled the man

up the steps and thrust him into the cabin.

There was very little inside except for a few blankets, two chairs, and the weapons. These men were better at their jobs than some he'd seen. They hadn't lit a fire outside. They hadn't called attention to themselves with candles or cooking. If his men hadn't been canvassing the grounds on an hourly basis, they may have escaped detection. With the door closed, the cabin looked abandoned.

Marcus signaled and the two hulking men who had run out the front door were carted off to the back. He trusted his men to keep them far enough away so that one man could not overhear another's confession.

Stubbins bound the lanky talker to one of the room's old wooden chairs.

"Now see here, I haven't done nothing wrong yet. I admitted to wanting to poach. I'll pay for my transgressions. But I don't even have a shot rabbit or deer on me." He exhaled sharply. "What are you doing to my legs?"

Stubbins secured each of his ankles to a leg with thin, but strong, ropes.

"Just making things comfortable."

"Comfortable would be in me bed wrapped up with a woman. You gonna make that happen?"

"Perhaps if you answer my questions honestly and quickly you might live long enough to find some pox ridden bird in London," Marcus said while circling his prey.

The man's eyes narrowed as he tried to follow Marcus's movements. "I told ye all ye needed to know. Now send me to the constable."

"Do you know who I am?"

There was a brief hesitation. "Yes."

"Good. Do you know what I do?"

"Attack poor men who are trying to feed their families?"

"Mmmm. If that is what you believe, and if you are who you claim, you must feel yourself in dire straits."

The man's lips compressed. One layer peeled away. No more talk about poachers.

Marcus continued circling the man bound to the chair and his voice regained a mild timbre. "What is your name?"

The man snorted. Marcus smiled. The criminal had deluded himself into thinking he still had options.

He pulled a chair over. "Such an easy question. Perhaps if you indulge us, you can prevent any . . . unpleasantness . . . before it begins."

"Ye don't scare me. I don't believe what they say. Think yer so high and mighty. Ye wouldn't dare get your hands dirty."

Marcus lifted a brow. "No? Even if that were true, you obviously haven't thought things through. I have five men here, friends of three murdered men, who would be more than happy to get their hands dirty."

He could hear one of his men crack his knuckles behind him.

A trickle of sweat forged a path down a thin grit-laden cheek. "Ye don't scare me."

"I see. Does that mean you won't tell me your name?"

The man's lips tightened.

"Very well. I think I'll call you Judas."

Judas's lips tightened further.

"Or I can call you something else? But Judas will be so fitting after tonight." Marcus leaned forward and was pleased when Judas's head moved back. "You can begin your redemption upon the morrow."

"I'm not telling ye nothing."

Marcus lazily rose and snapped his fingers. A long thin box was placed in his hand. He walked around Judas and stroked the box. "Is that so?"

He sat down in the chair again and idly opened the box, taking his time to undo the cloth wrapping inside.

He pulled out a metal rod, dull and heavy, and placed it on Judas's knees. The man flinched and tried to pull his knees in, but they were bound to the chair legs so he couldn't move far.

"Did you know Dudley Jones, by any chance?"

Everyone on the streets knew about Dudley Jones. Judas's eyes went wide before he tried to school his expression back into a cool mask. "No."

"Ah. Shame. Good boy, Dudley, before he fell in with the wrong types. He became a very, very naughty boy, which got him chased by—well—a different sort of wrong type."

"Don't care none."

"Shame what happened to his face. They say his mother can't even recognize him now." Marcus smiled, but he knew it was no smile at all. Stephen called it the devil's grin.

Marcus removed a hammer from the box and Judas's eyes bugged. He stroked the head of the hammer, and placed that on Judas's knees, too. Judas tried to shake the tool off, but both the hammer and rod stayed in place, shifting with the roll of his knees.

"But you assuredly aren't vain, not with that face." Marcus smiled again. He was pleased to note that his smile triggered a response on its own, as two more beads of sweat pearled on Judas's chin.

He pulled out a long knife. Sharp and wicked looking. "Your tongue, however . . . now that would be a shame to lose." He pretended an avid interest in the sharpness of the blade. "Tommy the Tongue. Isn't that what they call you, Judas?"

Judas/Tommy was panicked now—red faced, short rapid breaths, pooling sweat.

"They call you that for your ability to talk your way out of anything, I hear tell. That's quite a reputation to bear in this situation, Judas. How will I ever believe what you say?"

His head was as far back as it could go. "Now then, yer lordship, don't be hasty." Marcus could see that Tommy was starting to believe. The knowledge that Marcus knew his true identity was an unexpected blow—exactly as it had been meant to be.

"I'm never hasty, Judas." He stroked the flat edge of the knife. "Precise to a fault, maybe. But never hasty. I'm surprised my reputation hasn't preceded me. Perhaps I need to rectify that. Shall I leave your fingers so that you can still write and tell the story? Like Charles Anthony? Do you know how to write?"

"N-yes!"

"Mmmm, see there. I don't believe you do. What if we put it to the test? You write a sentence of my choosing, and if you succeed, I'll let you keep your fingers?"

"No," he whispered. "I don't write."

Marcus gave him another cold smile. "That wasn't so hard now, was it? I knew Tommy the Tongue would know when to quit." Marcus looked over his shoulder calmly. "I win that bet,

Stubbins. That's another pound you owe me."

Tommy was fully panicked now. The wonders of a nasty reputation and a solid dose of fear. It didn't even matter if Marcus had done any of the things he threatened. The key was that Tommy believed he had. The streets whispered it in hushed tones.

Tommy's cohorts looked dim at best. They would roll over easily, but their information would not be complete. It would be enough to verify Tommy's, but it wouldn't be complete. No, Tommy was the nut to crack. The one who would have the real information.

"And Brian Brisby? Have you heard of him?"

Tommy started to shake his head, then nodded. "Disappeared," he muttered.

"Yes, Brian was once in your position. He was a good man, though, and gave up his information. Reformed. Perhaps he has been set up with a new identity, a new life. Wouldn't that be nice, Judas?"

He nodded shakily, his eyes trailing the knife that Marcus continued to lazily wave.

"So let's begin with your name again. What is it?"

"Tommy Anderson."

Marcus nodded. "And why are you here?"

"To watch you."

Marcus shook his head. "No, no. That won't

do." He slid the tip of the knife down Tommy's knee.

"To-to grab the lady."

Marcus threw his white hot rage beneath a cold smile. "And what were you going to do with the lady once you had her?"

"Return to London."

Marcus split the seam next to Tommy's knee with the knife's edge.

Tommy squealed. "As long as she didn't give us any trouble," he hastily amended.

"You were told you could dispose of her otherwise, I'm sure."

Tommy looked like he was about to cry. "We wouldn't have. No good killing womenfolk. We just needed to hold her. To use her to get to you."

"If only your statement were true, Judas. I would really like to let you go." Marcus feigned a sigh. "But I know that it's not true. Someone already tried to kill her."

He moved suddenly, the sharp edge of the knife pressed against Tommy's throat. "And I will kill anyone who tries again, do you understand that?"

The rank smell of urine permeated the air, giving Marcus Tommy's answer.

Even if he hadn't been a believer before, Tommy believed him now. Which was good, because this wasn't a bluff. Marcus wasn't going to let anyone harm Isabella. He would hunt down and destroy the perpetrators. And nobody was going to stand in his way.

"Now, let's try again."

Isabella played with the lace stitches on her nightgown. She had promised herself that she wouldn't seek him out. That she would stay in bed and wake tomorrow and see how things progressed. But the nagging feeling that she was needed somewhere, somewhere downstairs, was becoming increasingly clear.

She would just take a quick peek downstairs. If he wasn't there, she could return to bed, with only her earlier thoughts plaguing her. If he was there, well, she would see.

She pushed back the covers and slid from the bed.

Her door opened soundlessly and she padded across the soft runner, down the hall. She slipped down the stairs, following the sound of her heart. Sound echoed from the music room as she neared. The stormy and brooding notes of Beethoven's Piano Sonata 14 pounded from within, not played with any underlying tenderness or uncertainty, but as if to purge demons from his very soul.

Her hand rested against the frame of the door as she watched him hunched over the instrument, fingers skittering down the keys and thumping the bass rhythm.

The piano really was magnificent.

The player even more so.

Dark locks obscured portions of his face, but his eyes were still visible. Locked onto the board, the keys below, the hammers underneath, the strings twanging and producing the melancholic, angst-ridden sounds that he wanted. Needed.

Her heart beat in her chest. She was at a loss. She didn't know what it was he so desperately needed. Something she was obviously unable to give.

His eyes shifted to her, through the hanging locks, and then back to the keys below, hammering just a little bit harder on the board, playing a little bit faster from the already too frenzied pace.

Her hand slipped from the frame and her feet carried her across the separating space. Her fingers played across the piano lid, feeling the vibrations from within as he continued the driving pace.

Seeking something at the end of a journey. Comfort? Redemption?

Her other hand found its way into his hair, pulling it back from his face. Her fingers touched the side of his face, offering solace.

He shuddered and missed a note. Then he was

reaching for her, hands on her waist, pulling her between his parted thighs, backside to the piano keys as the movements banged off key.

He kissed her, devouring her like the notes of the music in the night. Dark and deep and overwhelming.

She returned the kiss with all the emotion she had. She didn't like fighting with him. Didn't like the fact that he had used her and lied to her. Didn't like the haunted look in his eyes. Eyes that usually only showed what he wanted them to. Never fear.

Fear of what?

She looked at him and fell into his golden eyes.

He couldn't stop looking at her, absorbing every detail in the shifting light. She was beautiful, her features dark and mysterious in the shadows, splayed as she was over the piano. His hand started just under her throat and stroked down the length of her, thumb curling into the heat between her legs, hot through the thin gown. She arched upon the keys and lid, her head thrown back.

This woman was different from the very proper lady of the ballrooms, from the slightly daring Isabella of the recent weeks, or even the warmly passionate Bella of last night.

She was hot and wild and worried. Worried

about him. No one had worried about his state of being in a very long time. Not as a primary concern.

It was intoxicating. And terrifying.

He inched up her gown and trailed his fingers along the smooth skin beneath, from her thighs to the crowning curls. He replaced his fingers with his mouth. She squeaked and bucked. He anchored her in place and thrust his tongue within.

She moaned, grabbed his hair and pulled; her head dropping back as he greedily watched. He held her in place, circling her sensitive spots and mercilessly playing inside.

She edged up the piano backward, arching, moaning, and moving her way up one inch at a time, allowing him to do anything he desired. Her bare feet dangled, hitting the keys and plunking a discordant tune that echoed her jagged breathing.

Lifting her hips, he slid her farther up the lid, her gown still bunched beneath, letting him move her around without harm.

He reached for the top of her gown, the two peaks there seeking attention as she squirmed beneath him.

His hands brushed lightly over the top, making her wiggle and arch. He took one more taste of her in order to hear those delicious sounds. He was the composer and she his most beautiful creation. He pulled her back down toward him and slid her off the piano.

She grabbed his head and forcefully kissed him, melding her body to his. She was wild and free, and he had the dangerous thought that he could get used to this side of her *very* easily. As long as she stayed his good friend he could keep her at arm's length. But as his good friend by day and this passionate creature at night? No, he wasn't so sure that arm's length was quite far enough.

He pulled her closer.

Sweet Isabella. His sweet Isabella.

He stripped her gown and chemise and tossed them onto the keys and edge of the piano lid. She stood naked before him in the flickering light, a small bit of sanity returning to her open face as self-consciousness flickered across.

That wouldn't do at all.

He pushed back, just an inch, and performed an exaggerated perusal of her body. She automatically pulled her arms in front of her, which he batted away. "You are beautiful. And you are mine. And I don't like my artwork hidden."

He pulled her to him and somehow managed to get his trousers undone and her settled on his lap in one motion. He gently pushed her torso back so she relaxed against the edge of the keyboard, cushioned by her dress.

He could see her entirely. The glazed look in her eyes, her heavy hair gone awry, the way her heaving breaths lifted her breasts. Up, down, up, down. A fine sheen of perspiration pearling her skin. The way the shadows played against her stomach, her hips, her thighs.

The gorgeous, glistening area in between.

He leaned forward, shifting her on his lap as he moved, and pulled her right nipple between his lips. Her hands found his hair again, tugging at the back, urging him closer.

"Marcus," she whispered, her voice breathy and erotic.

He looked up at her though his lashes, his tongue lazily tracing her breast, sucking at her nipple. Her eyes were heavy and pleading, her panting seductive and entreating. Her bottom was inching up his legs, trying to get closer.

She was miles past ready.

He thrust two fingers into her.

The keys violently depressed beneath her as she threw her head back once more and wailed to their tune. He scooted the bench forward with his other hand. Her beautiful legs dropped over the back edges of the bench and brought her into perfect alignment.

They brushed together.

Her head lifted and she met his eyes. There was so much emotion there he didn't want to define, didn't dare, but it poured through him.

He reached up with both hands and framed her cheeks. He bent forward for a soft kiss before pulling back.

"Bella."

He buried his fingers all the way to the top knuckles in her glorious hair, at the same time he buried himself within her.

She let out a silent scream and arched her back, pushing down on him further.

And then she was riding him, and he was pushing her against the cushion, against the keys, the length of him spearing her and filling her.

Love swirled around her. Their actions swirled within.

The pace was fast and deep. He pushed against the top walls inside of her, sliding against her most sensitive areas without.

And she fell apart, coming violently among the cresting waves and opened stars.

He felt her breaking and wished with all he had that he might join her there. But he closed his eyes to her, sense prevailing, and lifted her up and away from him the very second before he too found violent release.

He shuddered and pressed his forehead to hers, too broken to risk seeing the confusion in her eyes, the unhidden pain. The same look she'd worn last night, but most likely magnified tenfold.

He could never explain. He was Lord Roth. Arrogant, a pacesetter, beyond capable in anything he tried; loved, respected, and hated alike.

Never would he admit, least of all to Isabella, that something was very much wrong with him.

Chapter 21

Isabella planted a sprig of thyme and watched Marcus shuffle papers from the corner of her eye.

He had overridden all of her hesitations for coming out to garden today. Now that she knew more about the activities that surrounded his darker side, she supposed that he was more used to living on the edge of danger than she.

Not that it was too difficult. She had little experience with danger. She had even written off the carriage incident—both carriage incidents—as accidents. Why would she presume her life to be in danger? She had had no prior reason to think in those terms.

There were no guards actively patrolling today, though she knew they hovered on the edges of the grounds and property. Marcus had accompanied her from the outset.

She had heard a version of what had taken place

the previous night after dinner. She was under no illusions that the account had been abridged.

The garden they had chosen was close to the manor. Small dog-rose hedgerows surrounded the garden, and pale pink flowers and thorns dotted the low bushes, bestowing a colorful yet prickly atmosphere. It was the cook's garden, with multiple herbs and spices planted throughout.

The walls were low enough so they could see out and others, namely brawny servants, could see in.

From the side of her gaze she saw Marcus put his ledger aside to watch her.

They had declared a tentative truce. Neither had spoken directly about their argument the day before or what had occurred in the music room; instead, they silently agreed to go forward.

She hoped their relationship would progress naturally. She didn't know what Marcus was thinking. She rarely did, and the thought rankled.

Where not knowing had once been a mysterious and seductive thing, now it was frustrating and nail-biting.

"What are you planting?"

She patted the soil into place. "Feverfew. Especially good for headaches."

He leaned forward. "Really? What types of headaches?"

She shrugged. "All types. Though some healers swear by lavender or betony. Ladies mantle or chamomile. If you had an especially severe headache, willow bark is what I would recommend."

"And you think the herbs work? They are different from what the quack doctors conceive?"

She shot him a smile. "Not all doctors are half trained. Besides, there is a time-tested tradition with some of these remedies. They've been used for years."

Marcus's face took on a brooding expression. "I see. So they would have been tried years ago?"

Isabella shrugged. "Perhaps. It all depends on whose advice was sought. Why do you ask?" Curiosity pricked a memory. "Did your father have head pains? I seem to remember your mother asking after remedies."

His face shut down. He touched a plant near him. "And this?"

She reached over and batted his hand away. "'Tis foxglove. It's been mistaken for comfrey more than once, to a deadly result. I should ask the gardener about moving it. Even if it is not in the herb plot, still, it does no good in the vicinity if a hapless servant were to pick it for tea."

He examined the stalks. "Looks as if someone picked some already."

She absently looked. "Probably for a basket. If

you need me to brew you something for a headache, I can make you a tisane."

"I don't need anything for a headache."

She patted some parsley into place, ignoring
him. "This is parsley."

"I at least know that much."

"Well, I know you said something about not
liking to get your hands dirty. Thinking with your
mind, not with your hands."

His eyes sparked. "Did I? I don't mind dirty-
ing my hands at all where certain things are concerned."

"Did you know parsley wine is known for its
. . . more *uplifting* qualities?"

He leaned forward and pulled an escaped lock
of her hair around his finger. "Is it? What other
fascinating things do your herbs do?"

"Promote healing. Increase vigor. Stop death.
Increase urges."

"What types of urges do you have, my lady?"

"Ones that need no increase from parsley wine."

His lips brushed across hers. Anyone could see
them, but suddenly she didn't care. She parted
her lips for a soft, promising open-mouthed kiss.

A throat cleared.

Isabella pulled back, face flaming as a liveried
servant stood uncomfortably between two hedgerows.

She tugged her overly large bonnet and grabbed

another plant, her spade spiking into the soil at random.

Marcus leaned back on the bench. "Yes?"

"News from London, my lord."

The steady stream of messengers was starting to irritate her.

Isabella picked up the basket she had brought with her and stood. The gardeners would clean up the tools and extra plants. She wasn't fool enough to stay outside while Marcus went in. Not that he would allow it anyway.

She trooped upstairs to bathe and nap. Bertie was always nagging her about staying out in the sun, but with a wide-brimmed bonnet and a parasol, she never had any worries. But the sun tended to drain her energy even fully covered, and a nap sounded divine. She wanted to be alert for anything Marcus had planned later.

"You are sure?"

The messenger nodded. "Yes. The Crosby gang has all been rounded up. The information you sent led straight to them. The head of the gang admitted to writing the notes. One of the boys is a printer's devil. We got him through the ink. He led us to the stragglers."

Marcus reread the paper in his hand. It was from James and essentially said the same thing, but was signed by his friend's hand.

"Something still seems off."

He had sent the information with his fastest rider as soon as he had finished questioning the man they'd captured. He knew James and the others would take care of the roundup. But he didn't like being so far away from London. The ploy had served its purpose. It had more than served its purpose. If the note was to be believed, they had captured the lot.

Still . . . it felt like something was missing, but he couldn't be sure if it was a genuine feeling or one promoted by missing out on the London capture and the closure of it.

"Could be we don't have every last one," the messenger said, "but the majority are in our control, as well as the leader, of that we are sure."

"And their plans?"

"To capture Lady Willoughby and use her against you. It was revenge."

"All of their plans are dead or have been revoked?"

"Yes."

He tapped the note. He knew no one else had ventured near the estate. His men were the best, and they knew every inch of the property, as had been shown the day before.

"My lord?"

Isabella would be free to return to town. She could leave him whenever she chose.

"Yes?"

When would she do it?

"Would you like me to relay anything?"

Usually he had plenty of correspondence. Today he had none. He had not been able to write a line. Too many thoughts. Too many fears.

And the scariest thing was . . .

"No. Thank you."

. . . what if she *didn't* leave him?

They had been playing picquet for half an hour. She had beaten him at chess, though it had been close. His mind had been elsewhere all day and through supper.

"What is on your mind, Marcus?"

He swirled the wine in his glass, the dark burgundy catching the light on the crystal. "The villains have been rousted."

A weight lifted from her shoulders. She was beyond relieved. He looked anything but.

"This is a good thing, no? Why do you act as if someone has died?"

"Not died, Bella. I just feel something is off, is all. But we can leave for town at any time."

Some of the weight settled back on, but with it was its own brand of relief. "Well, then we should stay."

He hummed a noncommittal noise.

"If you feel that everything has not been

cleared up satisfactorily, I would rather we stay here."

That, and she wanted to keep him for herself as long as possible.

"You do not find it a bore so far from the city?"

He knew she didn't, so she sent him a disparaging glance. "You know I don't. Besides, I like being with you. Having you all to myself."

He smiled. "Such a greedy creature you've become. Count me impressed."

"I'm sure."

They played a few more tricks. A flickering light from the hall caught her attention, and her eyes grazed a family portrait of Marcus and his parents. He looked to be about twelve, just growing into the man he would become.

"Why do those of your family have only one child? It is a legend of your line."

He stiffened, but played his card. "Instead of the heir and the spare, a good English tradition?"

She bit her lip. "Even beyond those reasons, many people desire a larger family."

"Why did your family stop with one?"

"Mother said they just weren't blessed with more. I don't believe it was a case of not wanting more, just that it didn't happen."

"Perhaps thus it was so in my line."

His tone suggested that he did not care for the line of questioning.

"Would you prefer more than one child if given the choice?"

"I would prefer none at all."

She swallowed and looked away, her eyes catching on the portrait again. His parents were seated closely together, their hands interlaced. "Your parents were happily married."

"Yes."

"A terrible hit for your mother when your father died."

"She died broken."

"A broken heart?"

"A broken spirit."

"What do you mean?"

He said nothing, playing another card.

"Were you there, with her?"

"I was there through it all."

His choice of words was odd, but before she had a chance to question him, he changed the subject.

"Who heads the donation committee for the Botanical Society?"

She let him change it.

"Mrs. Creel."

"Ah. Perhaps I will give the money to you instead. Mrs. Creel holds little liking for me."

"It's because you turned up your nose at her cousin." She gave him a disapproving glance.

"Ah yes, Yarnley. Got himself into a fine mess.

Deserved every upturned nose he received."

"For some bad credit?"

"For his illegal activities and indiscretions."

"Surely you are not saying that he was turned out for an affair? There is more than one well-born child who looks like a peer who is not his father. A woman may face such disgrace, but not a man."

"Not for an affair. For many, many affairs, some of which were with girls not old enough to decide otherwise."

Her eyes widened. "You jest."

"No."

"I've never understood what other women saw in Yarnley. He was unctuous, and always reminded me of a circling raptor."

"Like a man hunting prey."

"Oh, and I thought you were the one who hunted prey, Marcus."

He cocked a brow. "Do you see yourself as a dove, Bella?"

"Perhaps a sparrow."

"Is it your wish that I hunt you? I can't think of a more delicious meal."

Heat rose in her cheeks. "I would never deny you a good meal, Marcus."

He put down his cards and touched her cheeks, bringing her across the table for a rather ravaging kiss. Her cards slipped from her fingers to clatter softly on the table.

She was leaning over the table trying to get closer to him. Her breasts grazed the top, brushing cards from the surface.

He drew back. "While last night was quite lovely, I think I'd prefer the softness of a real bed."

She ached at the look in his eyes.

He took her hand and led her upstairs. The artwork on the walls and the bolted rugs passed by in a haze as he turned toward the family wing. His fingers caressed hers as he opened his door, and she caught the back of a valet leaving through a side door.

It was the first time she had seen his bedroom, his domain. The colors were gloriously dark and thick, permeating the room with a warm cocoon effect. The furnishings were sparse, the middle of the room completely bare, everything pushed to the edges. No rugs in sight

The entire scene was neat. A gloriously appointed spartan atmosphere. Not quite a dark cave, for the fabrics were rich and luxurious, from the drapes to the turned-down bedding. But cluttered it was not.

She started to say something, but his mouth claimed hers, and when she could speak, she found something infinitely better to say.

"About that bed?" she whispered.

He smiled against her mouth and backed her

toward the bed. He started to remove her dress, and when his hand dipped down the back, he smiled again.

"I'm shocked, Bella. No stays?"

She'd felt naked without them, and her dress had looked a bit odd, but the feeling of being naked, bare to him beneath, had kept her on the edge since she had changed for dinner. Bertie had just shaken her head and muttered.

She had loved having him unwrap her the first time they'd made love, but it took a long time, and she didn't want to wait tonight.

While they were here in the house, and it didn't matter if her clothes fit properly, she could get away with it.

"I'm surprised you didn't notice, Marcus. I've been a bit lumpy all night."

His hands moved to cup her breasts. "You are always *beautifully* lumpy."

She smiled. "Just what a lady wants to hear."

He leaned forward to kiss her again. She was both pliant and demanding. Dominant and submissive. A give and take that enflamed him.

Someone who could challenge and support.

She wrapped her arms around his neck and he aligned their bodies. Her dress was nearly un-latched. One more and it would fall away, leaving only her chemise beneath. No stays. He chuckled against her mouth and then relieved her of the rest of her clothing.

As far as he was concerned, she could stay naked. She didn't need to wear anything to give her the perfect female dress form. She was perfect to him just as she was.

He whispered that against her lips and fiercely sucked in her beautiful little gasp.

He worked his fingers into her hair and released the pins. Her favorite golden comb clattered to the floor. He wondered if he could kick it under the bed, to keep it for later.

Her beautiful thick hair wrapped around him as it fell to brush her breasts, to caress the middle of her back. It encased him, luring him closer, capturing him within.

Her small fingers brushed the top of his trousers, tugged and pushed down. They dropped to the floor.

He ran his hands up her arms and heard her breath hitch. He deepened the kiss. Her fingers danced along his shirt, unbuttoning and pulling until it fell from his shoulders and bunched at his elbows, hanging loosely behind. Her fingers ran over his chest, and he felt obliged to return the favor.

Soft, smooth skin. Cool and heated, the heat beating further down, but clamoring to rise.

He bent down and took the tip of her breast into his mouth. She clutched him, her bottom half arching into him and giving him better access to the feast.

Bed . . . yes.

He nudged her forward, laying her down on top, licking and sucking, embracing all of the sounds she made. Her hands threaded through his hair.

He pulled a finger down her stomach and farther down to where the heat had risen. She was already wet, and he groaned against her breast, causing her to moan in response.

"Bella . . ."

He kissed her, and she hungrily wrapped her legs around him. He shifted and nudged against her, his mouth on hers, his fingers caressing her neglected breast. He could feel her coating his tip. The softest, warm, wet velvet on the most sensitive part of his body. He hovered there while he kissed her thoroughly. For the next few hours he wanted her lips to be bright red, her eyes to be unfocused, and his name to be the only sound she could produce.

She wiggled against him, and he slipped in half an inch more. He shuddered and kept her in place, their heartbeats and ragged breathing allowing just the smallest back and forth, in and out, as he hovered. She wiggled again and panted against his lips.

He looked into her glossy eyes. Passion over-rode nearly everything else, but he could read the trust, the . . .

He kissed her again, more fiercely, and she bucked. He slid another half inch inside. She squeezed him, closing around him to hold him there, to urge him further inside. He fought from thrusting deeply, spearing her so that he touched her soul.

"Marcus . . . "

The sound was from heaven. His name on her lips, forming the syllables as a plea.

He buried himself completely inside her and shuddered. She arched and whimpered his name. He set about making sure she made more of those sounds. It could have been thirty seconds, it could have been two hours. He was aware of nothing but being inside her, kissing her, looking deep into her eyes and seeing all manner of things re-flected there.

A mixture of feelings, some soft, some scream-ing, echoing through him.

He was aware of nothing but the complete and utter desire to make her his forever.

He dove deeply into her, lifting back out and diving in again. He held her eyes on a particularly long thrust, and when he pulled back, she began to pulse around him. He thrust in and out to keep her on the wave, to keep her pleasure as high as possible, his own feelings and sensations building around and through hers.

She arched back. "I love you, Marcus."

He peaked abruptly, violently, and spilled himself inside her. He held her fiercely, riding out the last of the overpowering waves with her, trying to get as close as he could to being one with her.

It was glorious and terrifying.

She gasped and bucked, making the most delicious sounds as she repeated her love over and over.

He held her tight.

Sated and crazed.

She loved him.

He closed his eyes. He knew she loved him. Knew deep within that she wouldn't have made love to him otherwise, no matter what he had tried to convince himself of. And he had taken advantage of that love. That trust. Willfully disregarded the future and selfishly taken the present.

He had completed the most intimate of acts with her. The evidence was between them, as perfect and horrifying as it could be. He had never found his release in anyone else. No one but Isabella. Perfect Isabella.

Panic rushed through him. The old fears and the new choking him. What had he *done*?

He disentangled himself and let his feet slip off

the bed and onto the floor, his head in his hands, his breathing haggard.

He could still hear her deep breaths, could feel her light shudders. He should have been holding her. Should have been assuring her that everything was fine. That he loved her too.

But he couldn't do that. Everything was not fine. Not even close to fine.

A small hand curled over his shoulder. "Marcus?"

"Yes, Isabella?"

Her hand stopped momentarily, before continuing its path down and around his chest, hugging him back to her as she rose to sit behind him.

He closed his eyes.

So right. So wrong. Contingency plans had to be enforced. He had to do this. Selfishness, pure selfishness, had created this, and selfishness would finish it. It was in the best interests of everyone. Isabella, for obvious reasons; him, for not seeing that shattered, irrevocable expression on her face; and the best interests of any children who would have to suffer the same as he had.

"What are you doing?" Her voice was hesitant, still laced with the confidence she had gained a few days ago, but with the old insecurities seeping back through.

He laughed humorlessly. "I'm brooding."

Her hand stilled. "Brooding? Why?"

He didn't answer.

"Did I do something wrong?" He could hear the thread of panic lacing her voice.

No. She did everything right. That was the problem.

"No, you did nothing wrong." He couldn't bring himself to crush her completely. He reached up and touched her hand.

A throbbing pain in his head pulled his attention. He smiled mirthlessly. Excellent. Right on time.

She wrapped her fingers around his. "Then what is making you brood?"

"Life's little ironies."

Her hand dropped from his shoulder, her fingers from his, and he turned to see her move self-consciously, covering herself with the coverlet.

He could have cursed everything from England to China in that moment. He reached up to touch her cheek, but dropped his hand at the last second. Her blue eyes grew glassy.

The glorious blue of her eyes, one more color he might never see again.

He forced a smooth face and even a small smile. "Bella, we need to leave for London in the morning."

Her knuckles were white around the coverlet. "Why now? Why suddenly now and not before we came up here? Before we . . . "

The headache beat more insistently against his skull. Lights danced at the edges of his eyes. He didn't know what he was going to do if he blacked out or lost his eyesight while talking to her.

"Is it—Is it because the villain has been caught and now you have no further need of me?"

"No."

Yes. But not for the reasons she thought. He had a terrible feeling he would always need her.

"Is it—Is it because I said I loved you?"

He froze. The pounding of his headache, the heavy beat of his heart, a clock somewhere in the distance, all pressed together around him.

"No."

Yes. She *couldn't* love him.

"Is it because of the way we made love? The— The ending?" Again he could hear the insecurities.

"No."

Yes. It had been an irreparable mistake.

"I don't believe you. One of those has to be the reason. Tell me which." Her voice was pleading.

"No." The pain spiked.

"Damn it, don't just keep saying no!"

Her breathing was harsh. She could barely formulate thoughts. She'd even taken to swearing.

Something passed through his eyes, but as usual, the emotion was too quick to decipher.

He winced suddenly, as though in physical pain. "We could have made a child," he said harshly.

Her arms immediately wrapped around her middle. "I know you said you don't want a—"

"I don't, dammit. I *can't*."

"I wouldn't blame you if it happened," she whispered.

"It doesn't matter."

She hugged her middle more tightly. "I would cherish such a thing."

"No," he gritted out, his face more expressive than she had ever seen it, though not set in the expressions she would have hoped. Determination and pain, not love and tenderness.

Pain beat inside her. "I most definitely would!"

"I won't have a child."

"You wouldn't have to marry me," she whispered, looking him in the eye. Golden eyes on a child's face. "I'd go away. I'd still cherish him or her."

"That would solve nothing. This was all madness. What was I thinking? What brand of selfishness have I wrought?" he said, more to himself than her.

She felt the tears. They choked at her throat and moved upward to her eyes.

She wouldn't let them spill. "I never knew you for a coward, Marcus."

He gave a short unpleasant laugh. "Welcome to the most unpleasant reality, Isabella. I'm not your hero, I'm not the rakish, all powerful protector that you want so badly. I'm a man with many, many flaws. Most of them decidedly unpleasant."

She swallowed heavily. "I know."

"Do you? No, I don't think you do."

"You do me little credit."

His eyes narrowed on hers. "I give you much credit. More so than I give anyone else. But in this, I know I'm right."

How could he say things like that one moment and then crush her the next? "Marcus—"

He made a slicing motion with his hand. "No. You are going to London tomorrow. You will find someone more suited to you. Someone who wants marriage and children and gardens filled with ever blooming flowers."

She gripped the counterpane so tightly her knuckles hurt. "This is all because you spilled yourself within me? That there's a higher possibility of a child? But there's always been the remote possibility of a child."

His eyes were piercing. "That was merely my reminder of how very idiotic this whole plan was."

She saw blurred red. "Idiotic? You seemed just fine with this idiotic plan two hours ago!"

"I let myself forget. It was time I remembered."

"Remembered what?" she cried. "Why couldn't you just stay in your *forgetful* state?"

"It's not in your best interest."

"My best interest?" She was nearly hysterical. "Does this look like my best interest?"

"No." He looked away. "But you will thank me. One day."

Her eyes focused for a second. "Thank you?"

"Yes."

She looked to the side. "I'd thank you to be honest with me."

His head turned back to hers. "I am being honest with you. There will be nothing more between us other than friendship."

Somehow that seemed unlikely. This would be the end of their friendship too.

But the way he had kissed her, the way he had held her, the way he had looked at her as they . . . The way his eyes had flashed and his body had responded when she said she loved him.

"I love you, Marcus," she whispered. "If only—"

She swallowed.

"—if only you could love me."

He said nothing.

The moments stretched and her hands shook as she waited for him to say something, anything. *Anything*.

He turned away. "I'm sorry Isabella." His voice

was dull and dead. His eyes unfocused as if he didn't even see her.

She closed her eyes, the pain too great, the soft light in the room too bright and garish and mocking. She had taken the risks and she had lost. Badly.

She could stay and plead, cajole and beg, and it wouldn't make one whit of difference. She knew Marcus, no matter what he said; she knew the core of him. And once he made his mind up like this, he was implacable.

Totally implacable.

And she didn't know what to say when he had shut her out so completely. There was no rational argument, because whatever was behind this was driven by emotion. Something wholly uncharacteristic for Marcus, who tended toward strategic, rational thinking.

And when he made up his mind . . . implacable.

She opened her eyes and lifted her chin, wobbling though it was.

She gathered her clothing, slipping on her chemise and messily layering her dress over top—laces, buttons, and connectors askew. Just enough to clothe her, so she could walk from his room to hers without going naked. It was not as if the servants were stupid. They knew exactly what was going on between the two of them. Or what had been going on between the two of them.

Tucking the rest of her garments under her arm, she looked at him. Her voice was no more than a whisper, as if saying the words softly would make them less real.

"Good-bye, Marcus."

He continued his silent vigil staring at the wall away from her. She didn't merit a response. Wasn't even worth a look.

A wave of sadness and despair crashed through her, and for a moment she found it difficult to breathe.

The silence grew so painful that she could stand it no longer. She turned on her heel and focused on the door. Her steps echoed through the room and the door seemed farther with every empty step.

She touched the handle and waited.

Nothing. Emptiness.

She walked out the door and listened as it clicked behind her.

Chapter 22

One week and many wet handkerchiefs later, Isabella was still having trouble dragging herself out of bed and to town functions. She had left Grand Manor as early as Bertie had been able to bully the grooms into readying a coach. Not that it had been too hard. Marcus had apparently given instructions sometime between her leaving his room and Bertie's bullying that she was to leave whenever she wanted.

She wondered what he would have done had she just stayed at the manor.

Probably left her there. Well-protected, well-cared for, and utterly forgotten.

Bertie popped her head in the door. "My lady, Lady Angelford and her children are in the drawing room."

"Thank you, Bertie. I'll be right down."

She listlessly patted her hair into place, then trudged down the stairs.

"Good afternoon, Calliope." She forced a smile. "Good afternoon, Lord William, Lady Mary."

The two babies beamed and returned to playing with a string and two blocks. Their nanny hovered behind.

Calliope smiled, though it didn't quite reach her eyes, worried as she looked. "Good afternoon, Isabella. How are you today?"

"As well as the day is sunny."

The weather had been miserable for the past week.

Her friend gamely continued. "Are you ready to go to the Marstons?"

No.

"Yes, let's be on our way."

The fivesome entered the carriage and Isabella found herself with a small body pressed next to her, an adorable little face and two huge blue eyes peering up.

Her throat tightened. Mary reached up to play with a long feather in her bonnet, and Isabella bent to let her feel it, her arm going round the little body and hugging her close.

Calliope chattered about a rout that evening and other plans for the next few days. Ever since Isabella had arrived back in London last week, Calliope had been stuck to her side. It would be just like Marcus to have said something to Calliope. Nothing specific, just a veiled hint, as he had at the masquerade. There were other times that he'd probably done the same thing, now that she thought about it. She smiled bitterly. Always keeping track of and protecting her.

But she appreciated Calliope's concern. Calliope tried to cheer her up by bringing the children around and asking after home remedies, or tried to keep her busy by bringing sick plants in need of care. Bertie, on the other hand, was causing her to go spare with her wailing diatribes of "his wretched lordship" or "her poor lamb."

And her mother . . . well, her mother had threatened to return to London unless she confessed everything. Not satisfied with the vague misdirection sent her way, doubtless her mother would be on her doorstep within a week if she didn't discover a way to placate her.

The problem was, for the first time she had taken a risk and ended up with consequences she didn't know how to fix. She had *known* the risks, but her rosy optimism had colored the risks as less harsh than she now knew them to be. She'd thought that Marcus not returning her affection *before* had hurt . . . she hadn't known the meaning of pain.

The Marston town house loomed ahead, with its double front draped with hanging plants and creeping ferns. Stephen loved his plants as much as Isabella loved her gardens. She usually enjoyed visiting, to see his newest creations and what he was experimenting on. Today she couldn't be less interested.

Sterns, their butler, greeted them all at the door.

He bowed. "Good afternoon, Lady Angelford, Lord William, Lady Mary, Lady Willoughby, Miss Johnson."

Calliope twinkled at him, hoisting Mary higher in her arms. "Afternoon, Sterns. How have you been? How's your knee?"

He drew himself up and looked down his nose imperiously. "I know not of what you speak."

Calliope ignored him and peered down at his left leg.

The butler drew back, offended. Or at least, mock offended. He had been Calliope's butler for a few months while Stephen and she had been plotting, before she was married to James. So the two of them were good friends.

"I could make you a tisane, Sterns," Isabella offered.

He sniffed. "I do not need a tisane."

Calliope nodded vigorously behind him in the fashion of saying, *"Yes, he does."*

"Of course you don't. But you could share it with the others in the household, could you not? I would like to see if it is effective."

"For the good of the others I might be able to

do that, Lady Willoughby. The weather has been quite poor this week."

Calliope smirked, but wiped it off when Sterns turned back to her. She set Mary down.

"This way," the butler said.

Though Sterns was leading them, there was little need, as they very well knew the way. But he was a stickler for propriety. Or, at least the aspects of propriety that he felt necessary.

Audrey started to rise to greet them, but they shooed her back down in her chair—her pregnant belly extended far forward. William opened his mouth and a large belch echoed forth. Mary gummed the arm of a chair and grinned—around the wood—at Isabella.

Calliope sank into the seat across from Audrey and smiled wryly, peeling her wood-chewing child away and onto her lap. "And just think, soon you'll be stuck with one too."

Isabella busied herself with helping serve tea, eyes on the teapot and making sure to pour correctly. She hadn't spilled a drop in years, but with a heavy film clouding her eyes, pouring became more difficult.

"Isabella, what is this I hear about you and Roth being estranged after your trip seaside?"

The teapot jerked in her hand and a small drop hit the table with a splat. Isabella had less in common with Audrey than with either Stephen or

Calliope, but Audrey was immensely loyal and someone she was glad to have in her corner. She always cut to the heart of things. But sometimes it was hard being on the receiving end of her frankness.

Calliope studied her teacup, as if she could see something fascinating in its depths.

Isabella cleared her throat. "It was a lovely trip."

It *had* been a lovely trip, all the way up until the end.

"And?"

"And it was time to return to town."

"But you were barely there a week. And after all the struggle with leaving . . . "

She took a fortifying sip of her tea. "Luckily my absence has hardly been remarked upon due to the duration."

Actually there had been one or two comments, but it was as if people didn't know what to make of things.

"That doesn't explain why you returned so quickly."

She put her cup down. "The villains were caught, were they not?"

Audrey was watching her closely. "How much do you know of that business?"

"Only what Marcus would tell me."

"Do you want to know more?"

She did. And yet, she didn't. What was the point now?

She was getting maudlin again.

"Yes, I'd like to know more."

"You know Roth looks into matters for the Foreign Office, correct?"

"Yes. I understood them to be diplomatic matters, but have started reforming my opinion."

Audrey smiled. "That is what they want everyone to believe."

"Telling our secrets, dear wife?"

Stephen strolled in, and Audrey visibly brightened. Isabella watched him place a kiss on top of her head. Watched her lean into his body. Watched William and Mary playing next to Calliope, their heads bowed together as they held some secret conversation without words. Isabella felt more in common with Miss Johnson, the nanny, at the moment. Though the nanny had a smile on her face, an easy air of belonging to the Angelford family. Isabella thought a smile might crack right off her face if she attempted one in this idyllic scene.

Maudlin? She was going to become downright weepy in a second. And for what? This was a familiar scene. She had been in this tableau before with these exact same people. But she had never felt the longing and loss quite so keenly.

"Too many secrets from Isabella here."

He looked at the nanny. "Miss Johnson, we

have just finished the nursery. Would you care to take William and Mary up? Sterns is outside and can show you the way."

Miss Johnson nodded and disappeared with the two children on her hips.

They sat in silence for a moment. Isabella saw Audrey motion to Stephen with her hand.

He took a breath. "Isabella, the matters we take care of for the Office are complicated. Some of us started working there as a lark in our youth, some had something to prove, others just wanted to serve their country during the war in a way that was allowed—most heirs are not allowed to serve in the forces, for obvious reasons."

"Some of what we do in the office spills over into other sections of life, most noticeably government dealings. When you get used to making life or death decisions and dealing with less than stellar segments of society, you sometimes tend toward, well . . . ruthlessness."

She waited for him to say more. They all looked expectantly at her.

"Yes?" she said tentatively.

"We tend to make enemies."

She waited for him to continue. He seemed to be waiting for the same.

"The villains will never be caught. Not totally. There will always be another."

Ah.

"And even if Marcus leaves, there will always be someone who wishes him harm."

"Yes, he does tend to produce that reaction." She wouldn't mind an opportunity with a cudgel herself.

"If you are with him, you will be in danger too."

Isabella was mystified. "You think I'll change my mind. Why would you think this would make me feel any differently about Marcus?"

Stephen smiled wryly. "We didn't, but I can guarantee you that Marcus feels that way."

She put her teacup down. "But that is not the full reason. It may be part of the reason, but it is not the full reason behind his . . . rejection."

Lines appeared around Stephen's eyes. Audrey and Calliope alternated between throwing out theories and comforting her, but Stephen remained silent and watchful.

She gripped her teacup and was both relieved and disappointed when Sterns reappeared to say that William had become fussy.

A round of fussing over the babies and intermittent conversation broke the tense atmosphere, and before she knew it, the visit was over.

Stephen gripped her hand as she walked toward the door. She felt a piece of paper slide into her gloved fingers.

"It's always useful to have a sister-in-law with

continuing ties to the underworld. Though it took a great deal of convincing for Faye to hand this over, you will find what it is you seek." He paused and touched the tendril of a hanging fern. "I do hope."

She walked outside, a bit unnerved, and opened the note as the rest of the group exited behind.

The note said: *7 Hampley Lane, Wednesdays at one p.m.*

Odd. She turned to say something to Stephen, but he simply smiled mysteriously, and perhaps a bit sadly, as Sterns closed the door and his visage disappeared.

Two days later she found herself in front of a brick building located on a side street just off the busiest street in the district, Bertie at her side. She could see the carriages moving past on the thoroughfare, but few people turned to look down the small residential passage that resembled an alley more than a street.

Stephen's mysteriousness and later refusal to answer her questions made her uneasy, especially given his comment about underworld ties and her recent craziness about being a target. But she trusted him, almost as much as she trusted Marcus, and if she thought about it rationally, underworld ties could merely mean information.

A sign to the side of the door read: "MARY
CHATWOOD'S HOME."

Isabella wasn't sure she wanted to enter. Usually such a sign meant a group home—and sometimes new information was a dream destroyer.
What if this Mary Chatwood were somehow re-
lated to Marcus? What if she were his mistress, or
long hidden wife, and there were dozens of their
children inside?

Would Stephen do that to her? Make her find
out with her own eyes?

She knocked on the door. A small, elderly
woman answered—her hair in a bun, wire glasses
on the end of her nose. She propped her hand
against the door and took a moment to inspect
Isabella and her maid behind her. Her eyes grew
wide and joyful.

"Are you from the Ladies' Society? We had just
thought to contact them. We didn't expect a response so soon."

The home had to be some sort of charity if
they'd contacted the Ladies' Society. Isabella relaxed fractionally. She was in fact a member of the
Ladies' Society, so she didn't feel too much guilt
when she replied in the affirmative.

The woman's smile dimmed somewhat and she
wrung her hands. "Oh, but we never have guests
in on Wednesdays. It's the one day closed to all."

Isabella waited patiently, hoping that the

woman would keep control of the conversation and allow her to just follow along. "Simone is in charge of contacting patrons," the woman continued, "and I was sure she said she would invite you in for a Monday. What was Simone thinking?"

"Oh. I must have mistaken the date," Isabella said. "I'm sure the note must have said Monday. Right, Bertie?" She didn't want to get the faceless Simone in trouble for something she didn't do.

"Yes, my lady, it must have been the other appointment for Wednesday." Bertie floundered, poor dear.

The woman at the door peered behind Isabella and Bertie. "Oh, that happens to me too on occasion. Is it just you that has come to visit?"

Isabella smiled. "Yes. Is that a problem?"

"Not usually, no. But it's Wednesday," she said, mostly to herself.

Isabella had no idea why Wednesday was important and different from other weekdays, but she could make outside inquiries into the matter. She wasn't going to force her way in and make the woman uncomfortable just because the note had said Wednesdays at one. Perhaps she'd be able to wheedle the information out another way.

"It's not a problem," she said. "Perhaps you might schedule me in for another day? My name is Lady Willoughby."

The woman stared at her for a moment before

breaking into a relieved smile. "Oh! Well come right in then."

She motioned her inside, and Isabella bemusedly followed.

"It's so nice to meet you! I'm Mrs. Horncastle. I run the home. I've heard so many lovely things about you."

Isabella automatically nodded, baffled. She saw Bertie shrug helplessly in response. "Why thank you."

"Do you want the full tour? Or do you wish to attend the reading? No one is allowed, you know," she said conspiratorially.

She went from baffled to completely confused, but said, "Of course."

"It's so good to see Mr. Stewart having a bit more fun. Such a lonely man." Her smile dimmed a bit.

Mr. Stewart? Marcus's family name was Stewart, but no one would ever call him Mr. Stewart.

"Does Mr. Stewart come by often?"

"Only on Wednesdays. It's the reason for restricting others."

"And it's acceptable that I be here?"

Had Marcus said something? Hope beat in her chest.

"Oh, yes. The Duke of Marston made a sizable contribution last week when he stopped by. He said that Mr. Stewart had told him you were also to be allowed inside any time you pleased."

Isabella smiled weakly, the hope fading. Something—no, multiple somethings—didn't fit. If Stephen had used his title, Marcus would be using his. No, she didn't think Marcus was aware at all of what Stephen was doing.

"Mr. Stewart is here?"

"Yes, he is in the reading room. Would you like to see him?"

"No," she said, more strongly than she'd intended. Mrs. Horncastle's eyes widened. She took a deep breath. "No, please, I don't wish to disturb him. Perhaps, if we could just oversee the room?"

"Oh, yes, a tour. How neglectful of me. Please, right this way."

Isabella was led into a large room filled with neatly stacked toys, some of which she had never seen before—strange blocks and tops. The neatness of the scene made her blink. Everything was in its place, much like how Marcus always had his things. A sort of spartan feel in an otherwise obviously lived-in room. She reached down and picked up a stuffed bear from a bin. When faced with so many toys, some things required no explanation.

"How many children do you house?"

"Twenty. Poor dears. And another twenty adults. We used to have more, but Mr. Stewart has been finding them work, and while some of them return here to live when not at work, others have found homes. The hope shines from them. All of them. It's almost too much for my poor heart." She wiped at her eyes.

Isabella tried to understand what she was being told, but it wasn't making any sense. "What type of work?"

"Two women on stage—one for the opera, another for a small theater. Four men and women in factories, separating items. A dozen in the fields—they don't live here anymore, of course. One man to help with a lighthouse, of all things. Says he can hear the ships coming! Why, he even got one man into a chamber group that is playing in society! Exceptional violinist, but no one would hire him." She tsked.

"Why wouldn't anyone hire him?"

Mrs. Horncastle looked at her strangely. "Because he is blind, of course."

Isabella looked around the room and swallowed heavily. Of course. Oh, God. Oh, God, of course.

"You keep the rooms so clean, and with so many children around," she whispered.

"Yes, wouldn't want the dears to trip on anything. They are excellent at navigating and finding what they need, but if something is out of place . . . well, no one wants an accident. So they always make sure to put things back. Everything has its place," she said happily.

Everything had its place. His clothes, his furniture, the lack of rugs in his room, the way the rugs were nearly bolted in place through the rest of the house. The spartan setting, so much less to run into.

She clutched the bear to her and lowered her head.

"My lady?"

She shook her head. She wanted to curl up in the corner and sob, but she couldn't. Not here.

She took a breath and lifted her head. "Is it possible to observe them?"

"Oh, yes. There's a small window at the back. All the children will be in there. They love story time."

The woman motioned to the door, but Isabella's feet wouldn't move. She squeezed the bear, took a deep breath and placed it in the bin, then put one foot in front of the other.

The window was tiny, but she could see through it, could hear from an open door around the corner Marcus reading a story. All the children sat in rapt attention, leaning forward as he read about a monk and a parakeet.

" . . . and the parakeet flew high into the trees . . . "

His voice, deep and like caramel, melted over

her. He turned the page, continuing the tale, though she no longer heard the words.

There were adults seated in the room as well, sitting on chairs near the edges or holding children on their laps. It was such an odd scene that for a second she doubted what she was seeing. But no, it was Marcus, most definitely, and he was *reading* to a room full of children and even some adults.

Children who obviously adored him. Children that he said he never wanted.

She pulled away and pressed against the wall, shutting her eyes as she tried to make sense of it.

"My lady?" The whisper came from her right.

She opened her eyes and looked at Bertie, then at Mrs. Horncastle, who was motioning her into another room, away from the reading.

"What do you think of the house?" Mrs. Horncastle asked when they were out of earshot.

"It's wonderful. We will, of course, be supporting the Mary Chatwood Home."

"Oh, splendid." She clapped her hands together. "Would you like to wait for Mr. Stewart?"

"No, no. Let me give you my card. And please, don't tell Mr. Stewart I was here."

She looked perplexed. "Whyever not?"

"We are planning a surprise for him. I assume the Duke of Marston told you to keep his visit a secret as well."

Stephen obviously had said nothing to Marcus.

"He did. It's most vexing, though. Mr. Stewart has paid for nearly everything in the home. I don't feel right keeping anything from him. But you say there will be a surprise and you will tell him soon?"

"Yes."

"Good. He has taken care of us these past fifteen years. Since his parents passed, poor dear."

"Oh?"

She didn't want to pry, but there was little on earth that could stop her at the moment from trying to find out more.

"Yes," Mrs. Horncastle said. "But I'll be saying no more." The woman's eyes sharpened with loyalty.

"Of course. Thank you, Mrs. Horncastle." She pressed one of her cards into the woman's hand. "I will be in touch soon."

She turned from the woman and exited the room and home as fast as dignity allowed.

She had many stops to make.

Chapter 23

It had taken nearly a week to find everything she needed. She'd visited herbalists, midwives, doctors, and quacks of every variety. She had scoured apothecaries all over town, argued with gardeners, pillaged gardens, and cajoled men who were specialists in every type of medicine.

She was two steps closer. Two steps in slippered shoes. She just didn't have all the facts to make the last step, which required Wellington boots.

She'd have to confront Marcus.

She closed her eyes and breathed in the fresh, rich jasmine mixed with the last breaths from the dying lilacs. She was looking forward to the confrontation with a sort of savage intensity.

She strolled nonchalantly around the stone terrace, the uneven pavers nudging the soles of her slippers. He would be here tonight. Everyone left in town was expected to attend the Clarence rout, and Stephen had assured her that Marcus would attend. She hadn't seen him since returning to London. They had somehow managed to attend separate functions, no doubt Marcus's doing, knowing which ones she would attend based partially on Calliope and partially on past knowledge.

But he wouldn't escape tonight.

She had even considered wearing her red dress. Her battle dress. But she'd settled on the flowing navy gown designed by Madame Giselle, thinking that perhaps she should try some less obvious tactics before declaring war. It was a strategic move.

Isabella continued her stroll and admired a clematis vine that the Clarences' gardener had trained to hang *just so*. It required patience to tweak and arrange the creeping vines. She might be grumpy in the mornings and a sore loser at chess, but if there was one emotion she understood, it was patience for a worthy quest.

Mrs. Waterbee stared down her nose and crinkled it as if a foul odor passed beneath as she strolled by. She had experienced a similar reaction from a few others, but Isabella had come not to care as she might once have. There was nothing wrong with what she had done. She loved Marcus, and if she wasn't deluding herself, the sentiment was quite possibly returned.

So let them sniff. She would fight for him, beat down his barriers with all the patience she could muster, and if she won, then wild boars wouldn't drag her happiness down.

If she lost, then at least she would lose fighting to the end.

She smiled pleasantly at Mrs. Waterbee and continued her circuit.

"Lady Willoughby."

Fenton Ellerby appeared next to her, a rush of too much masculine perfume overtaking her. He took her gloved hand in his, and she held back a weary sigh while maintaining a smile.

"Good evening, Mr. Ellerby. How have you been?"

He leaned in close. "Not as well as I would have been in your company." He gripped her fingers and she had to tug them back.

She smoothed the silk of her gloves and took a discreet step backward. "How kind of you to say."

He stepped forward, his too charming smile hitching the edges of his mouth. "Not as kind as you are to grace us with your brilliant presence once more."

"Such charm, Mr. Ellerby."

She smiled and began walking again, forcing him to walk alongside her.

"I have noticed that you seem out of spirits lately, Lady Willoughby."

"I think it comes with the end of the season, does it not, Mr. Ellerby? The feeling of awaying to the countryside, while pleasant, stokes the melancholy the end of the season brings."

A few people were openly staring at them, questioning looks plastered on their faces, where just two weeks ago naught would have been thought out of place.

"I know exactly what you mean. Which is why it is always pleasant to be near others. To let the melancholy drown in the happiness between two people."

Did women really fall for this drivel?

"Mmmm . . . "

He touched her bare elbow. "Walk with me in the gardens?"

She stepped away, and his hand dropped. "I think not."

He smiled charmingly. "There are many people outside. Just a quick stroll to relieve the heat before I must go inside and claim a few dances of others."

A few of the ladies were gazing adoringly in his direction. And indeed there was a knot of people in the gardens, much of the ballroom having spilled outside during the orchestral break. While there was no way she would disappear with him into the extensive gardens, a brief stroll on the lawn between sets would be good for her feet. The grass would make a pleasant change from the uneven stones, and they would still be in total view of the guests—nothing noteworthy to report beyond Ellerby's attention to her.

She wasn't naive enough to get herself into a situation with Ellerby. And any ancillary gossip about them would die quickly with nothing to support it. Ellerby was the only one willing to speak with her outside the stuffy ballroom—the others unsure of what the relationship was with Marcus and how to react. She could use some conversation, however bad, while waiting.

"Not in the gardens, Mr. Ellerby. But here on the lawn we can continue our conversation."

His smile grew. "It will be my pleasure, Lady Willoughby."

Marcus stalked into Ainsworth's cluttered study, hand gripped tightly around his walking stick. He needed to straighten out a few things with the man before he dropped by the Clarence rout. Isabella would be there, and he needed all his defenses in play.

It would be the first time they'd see each other since she left the manor—though not the first time he had seen her. He had discreetly followed her to town, secretly staying at the same inn instead of pushing forth to London. Once in town, he had checked on her every couple of days, but never let her see him. She had been drawn and pale at the beginning, and he could have drowned in his own guilt.

But something had happened last week between his checks. Her head was once again held high, her eyes focused, and her step determined. He could practically smell her determination. He had no idea what had happened, and couldn't use his resources to find out. Calliope, Stephen, and the others had all been tight-lipped—and more than a little irritated with him, for good reason.

Still, he stood by his decision. It was the right one. Not only for her, but for him as well. At least this way he could self-destruct without witnesses, without pity. Without seeing that look in her eyes, the love turned to resentment.

"Evening, Roth," Ainsworth said grumpily.

"Ainsworth."

He dropped into the low-backed mahogany chair on the other side of the large walnut desk and watched Ainsworth nervously fiddle with his quill.

"You called this meeting, Roth. Get on with it."

He set his walking stick against the chair and folded his hands. "You sent a note to my men warning them about an attack today. An attack that we were able to foil. Why?"

Ainsworth gave a humorless chuckle. "Should've known you'd discover I sent the note."

"Why did you?"

He clutched the nib of the quill. "Because I don't hold with the way things are going."

"But you held with the way things were?"

The nib broke. "Listen, I didn't want to be involved in this mess in the first place, but I got myself into a spot of trouble. It's always finding me." He tossed the quill to the side.

Marcus thought that perhaps he had that statement in the reverse order, but said nothing.

"I was told they were going to remove you. Maybe injure you a bit, but nothing permanent. Just enough to take you out of the House proceedings."

If only they'd waited, they wouldn't have had to do a thing. Bitterness crept into his thoughts.

"I didn't want to do it, Roth, you have to believe me. And then things went bad." Ainsworth swallowed. "Out of control. I panicked and started making up information instead."

Marcus held his temper. "What type of information?"

"Things I heard, schedules of people around

town and in the Houses. I have the accounts information. I have access. I'm not as dumb as people
think I am."

Marcus withheld comment on the last point. "I
see. And why did you do it?"

Ainsworth looked pained. "He made me do
it. Has information I don't want to get out. Said
what we were doing was going to shift power
back where it was needed."

"Who?"

Ainsworth looked down at the papers littering
his desk. "Ellerby."

"Charles Ellerby doesn't have enough—"

He shook his head. "Not Charles, Fenton."

Fenton Ellerby?

Ellerby had spent two terms in the Commons before being voted out. He recalled the
man's outrage, his bitter feelings about how
the Lords was a full-term position, but the
Commons . . .

The Commons weren't restricted to birth.

Cold current ran through him. Suddenly, all
sorts of things clicked into place. Why Fenton
Ellerby always looked vaguely familiar. Why he
didn't get involved in politics anymore. Why he
worked the ladies the way he did.

And what power he might be trying to bring
back.

Marcus narrowed his eyes. "Fenton Ellerby was—*is*—blackmailing you."

Ainsworth grimaced, but nodded. "I needed that subsidy to pay off the greedy bastard."

His suspicion over Ainsworth's subsidy had been correct after all. "You could have him out of the country at the very least for such an action."

"And expose what Ellerby knows? I think not," Ainsworth said, tightly.

"I don't know what it is that Ellerby knows, but you chose your allies poorly."

"I know. I realized it when I saw that carriage nearly hit Lady Willoughby. She's friends with my wife, for God's sake. She's a member of the ton. That's when I stopped giving information. I had no idea why he wanted her schedule at first, but it was easy enough to obtain, her being friends with my wife and all."

Marcus's heart stopped. He pushed back the chair and staggered upright, gripping his walking stick for support.

"What the devil is with you, Roth?"

Marcus barely paid him attention as he quickly stepped to the door. "We'll talk later, Ainsworth. As much as I'd like to ram this stick down your gullet, you did the right thing in the end. I'll help you if I can."

Ainsworth nodded tightly, but Marcus didn't

spare him another thought as he raced out the door to his carriage.

Isabella was in grave danger.

And he was the one responsible yet again. He had told her she was safe.

Chapter 24

"**M**r. Ellerby, I'd as soon remain here on the lawn, or better yet, on the terrace."

"But there is a particularly nice rosebush just on the edge of the garden. I know you are fond of flowers. I myself have composed no less than ten sonnets about the folds of roses."

"Lovely," she said, not budging from her spot on the spongy grass.

"Just a tiny peek? I promise it will be worth it."

"No, but thank you for the invitation."

The strains of a melody drifted on the air. She watched the last few people in the gardens drift back toward the doors, the rest of the guests on the terrace also moving, and she took that as her cue to return inside.

His hand smoothly wrapped around her elbow. "But I insist."

She gave him a withering stare. "Mr. Ellerby, this grows tiresome. I acceded to your wish for a stroll. Don't you have dances to lead?"

It wasn't a particularly genteel thing to say, but she was past feeling bad for being rude. She had no idea why Ellerby was even playing at interest in her. She wasn't his style or the type of woman he usually chased, and furthermore, she had given him no returned interest. No reason to assume she would "come 'round." Perhaps it was the challenge, but even that should have become tiring for him by now.

"A dance to lead you to a flowering bush."

She moved away from him, but he pulled her back, none too gently.

"Remove your hand from me at once."

"Not until you do as I say. You are coming with me."

She twisted. "No, I most certainly am not."

"You are, or I will dispose of you right here."

She stopped and stared at him, unsure she had heard him correctly. "Dispose of me?"

He tugged her and she stumbled.

"And if I don't come with you . . . you will dispose of me 'here'? As opposed to somewhere else?"

"Stop talking."

"What are you playing at, Ellerby?"

"If there was one thing I could do differently about this whole scheme, it would be to sew your lips together. You think you are so high and mighty."

She looked around her. Everyone had gone in, but the doors were still open. She could still scream and bring them all running. That thought calmed her.

"Many people saw us out here together—some of them will remember we are missing in the next few minutes and come to investigate, if only for a piece of gossip. What are you going to say when I go missing and people question you?"

"That you wished to sit in the gardens. That you were heartbroken from Roth's callous treatment. That I acceded to your wishes," he said snidely, "to leave you alone.

"I will, of course, pretend to be crushed that I couldn't change your mind," he went on in a nasty tone. "That you were so depressed, embarrassed, and in despair you pitched yourself into the Thames."

She twisted her arm again. "Hardly likely."

His hand tightened further on her arm and his face pushed into hers. "It doesn't matter if it's likely or not. People will believe me. And you are in disgrace."

"Hardly disgrace. Society barely believes I would have the nerve to so 'disgrace' myself."

"Is that why you've been getting so many narrowed, probing stares tonight? Do you believe your own lies, Lady Willoughby?"

"I suppose I do at that, Mr. Ellerby. It seems we have something in common after all."

His face purpled.

She didn't know why she was so deadly calm. Perhaps it was the unreality of the situation. Fenton Ellerby was threatening her life. Somehow it seemed comical. Although he might have killed people—the body in Marcus's yard attested to that. Or hired people to do it. Little better than cowardice.

"You're a coward, Mr. Ellerby. A little boy experiencing a tantrum. Unable to act like a man."

If she ever spoke to Marcus again, she'd have to apologize for calling him a coward. Not that he didn't somewhat deserve it, but his actions stemmed from a fear to protect others, and not from his own selfish indulgences.

"I am not a coward! I *am* a man. I am more than you will ever know. I should be serving in the Lords. I should be the one wielding the power. Roth should never have deposed my—"

His mouth snapped shut and he gripped her arm even more tightly, pushing her backward toward the gardens, an area that opened to the rest of the estate. She would be beyond the call for help soon, and her arm *hurt*.

She lifted her foot from the grass and kneed him between the legs. He released her instantly and pitched over onto the grass, groaning and holding himself.

She leaned down. "See you inside, Mr. Ellerby, if you aren't too much of a coward to hear what I tell the rest of the assembly about what happened out here and where this bruise on my arm came from."

She turned to walk up to the house, and blinked to see Marcus and Viscount St. John pulling up short not ten feet away. St. John was breathing heavily and smirking. Dark rage painted Marcus's features.

"Good evening, gentlemen." She pushed forward to the house, rubbing her arm.

Marcus's hand shot out and his fingers curled around her other arm. Unlike Ellerby's grip, however, his was warm and comforting.

"You dropped Ellerby."

The anger and fear in his voice melted her ire for a moment. "My father taught me a few tricks to defend myself. I told you I could take care of myself weeks ago."

"So you did." His eyes dropped to her bruised arm and he ran soft fingers over the purpling patch of skin. "Sinjun, take care of Ellerby, will you? I'll *speak* with him later."

St. John followed his instruction, handling Ellerby none too carefully as he half dragged the moaning man across the grounds.

They were both silent for what felt like several minutes, just staring at each other before Isabella said, "Do you know what that was about?"

Marcus studied her for several more seconds. "Fenton Ellerby is the illegitimate son of Yarnley."

She blinked. "Come again?"

"Baron Yarnley was known for his liaisons. He carried on an affair with Ellerby's mother while she was married. Fenton was the result. It never crossed my mind, but it should have. He and his brother Charles look nothing alike."

"So he was trying to bring Yarnley back to power?"

"Yes. And if he couldn't, to take revenge. He is the heir to the Ellerby estates, but he would much rather be the heir to Yarnley's title and estates, which due to his birth he never will."

"But why the elaborate plans, the revenge?"

Marcus shook his head. "I'm sure Yarnley promised him all manner of things."

"But he could never gain his title."

"No, but we don't know what Yarnley promised. He had the king's ear before he was disgraced. Perhaps he promised Ellerby a new title to be given by the king, not that he was or is in any position to make such a promise. My men are on their way to speak to Yarnley and discover the truth."

"And he was after you because you disgraced his father?"

Marcus's lips tightened. "Yes. It was probably Yarnley's idea in the first place. Take away my men, take away my power, take away anything that meant something to me."

She wet her suddenly dry lips.

"Oh."

He pivoted and began walking. Away. Away from her.

"Wait, Marcus."

He stopped and turned back to her. It was difficult to breathe all of a sudden.

"I know. I know about the orphanage, the home. I know why you keep everything so stringently in place."

His entire body went motionless, as if he were a marble statue placed amidst the rosebushes.

"Do you?"

She took a step toward him. "I can help. I've been researching all sorts of remedies to stave off the onset."

He laughed. The sound caused her to run her hands up and down her bare arms. "Stave off the onset?"

He closed the gap between them and ran his hands down her arms and over the top of hers. His lips whispered against her ear.

"What is it that you think you know, Bella? That I am going blind? Oh, I assure you, the end result will be much worse than that."

She shivered. "What do you mean?"

"Did you know my father's organs failed?" he asked, almost conversationally. "One at a time. He would have fits. He would cough up blood. So much that we couldn't stem it. He went blind early on. Early enough that he didn't see the effects on his limbs, didn't see the marks."

His fingers moved into her hair and tilted her head back.

"He couldn't move from bed. Weak, so weak that everything had to be done for him. He was a proud man. Arrogant. Hated the fact that he had to be helped at first. But finally worn down to not even having that. Not even caring about pride. Just wanting relief."

His lips caressed hers, and she closed her eyes against the relief in having him touch her once more, against the pain of his words.

"So what is it that you think you know, Bella?"

He pulled away and she stared up at him.

"Do you think you can save me? That somehow you can circumvent what happened to my father, and his father before, though my father and mother both spent endless amounts of money to find treatment? Spent hours with doctors and men who claimed to have a secret cure?"

"I just want to be there with you. No matter what happens."

Pain flashed through his eyes and he pushed away from her.

"Is that so? Why?"

"Because I love you."

A humorless sound escaped him. "And you think that's enough?"

"Yes."

"How pleasant for you that you can think so well." His eyes narrowed. "Tell me, how did you feel when your husband, George, was ill? Did you sit at his side writing sonnets? Pretending that everything would be fine?"

"That's not fair."

"No, it most definitely is not. How did you feel, Bella?" Her name came out as a caress.

"I was scared."

"But how did you really feel? Did you begrudge him, just a little, for being ill? For the hardship it caused? For the sleepless nights and empty days?"

"The days were never empty."

"No, they were filled with taking care of a man beyond your care."

"I've learned more since then. Spent my time trying to increase my knowledge."

"And you think this will help you with the next ill man you decide to care for?"

"No!"

"Do you find it satisfying to take care of ill

men? Do you find me a challenge, or a way to atone?"

She swallowed. "I keep thinking you can't hurt me anymore than you already have. You keep proving me wrong."

She thought she saw raw pain in his eyes, but he started circling her again.

"I'm just trying to keep you from making a dreadful mistake."

"I won't. And if I do, I make it willingly."

He was silent for a second. "Did you help George?"

"Yes, as much as I could."

"Did you sit at his bedside?"

"Yes."

"Did you read stories to him?"

"Yes!"

"Did you trudge up and down those long stairs to cleanse him, strip linens, tend his wounds, feed him? Too consumed in your own feeling of guilt to send a servant?"

She pressed her lips together.

"Bella, did you feel guilt?"

"I felt guilt," she whispered.

"Because he was ill and you were not? Because for a moment, just a moment, you wished you were elsewhere?"

"Yes—" Her voice broke.

"And upon his death? You felt pain, surely, but

also a sense of relief. That finally, finally, it was over. That you weren't sure if you could have taken another day. That you didn't know why this had happened to you?"

She couldn't answer, tears distorted her vision, something blocked her throat, her head shook from side to side in denial. Denial that could not pass her lips.

A tear slipped down her cheek. Then another. And another.

He stopped in front of her and wiped the tears. Gently. Carefully.

"The pain never goes away, does it, Bella? It just sits there eating away at you. You've always thought yourself a good person, yet you think, 'How could you be good with feelings like this?'"

She brokenly nodded.

"And you keep it buried inside, not sharing it with anyone else, for what if they confirmed it—confirmed that you are all of the evil things you've been thinking?"

"Yes."

"And maybe if you shove it down as far as you can, if you ignore it for long enough, it will go away."

"Yes."

He lifted her chin. "It will never go away until you accept it. Accept that you are having thoughts that anyone would in your situation.

For doing far more than most to make your husband's life easier, to make his ending, if not happy, then peaceful. For loving him, even when you resented—not him, but the situation forced upon you both."

"If you believe this, then why—"

"Why am I pushing you away?"

"Yes."

"Because I am intimately acquainted with all of these feelings. Who do you think took care of my father? Who was at my mother's side during her waning days? Who could not do enough to make his mother want to stay here rather than to give up and join her husband?"

"But—"

"But nothing. I wouldn't wish it on my worst enemy. And you think that I would pull you into my world? Have a child knowing that in ten, fifteen years he or she might have to go through the same?"

"But it might not happen to you. You don't know that you will have the same illness, the same result."

"I've started experiencing symptoms already." He said it so nonchalantly that she wanted to scream. "That doesn't mean I might not live to be a healthy seventy-year-old with scads of children and grandchildren, all healthy. But I am not willing to take the chance, Bella. And that's the thing that separates us. Call me too prideful, too arrogant, a coward. But I will not take the chance. I will not put someone else in that position. I won't put *myself* in the position—of the victim, of the patient."

"And until that day? You will not live life? You will escape to the country and hide? Throw yourself over a cliff?"

"Nothing quite so dramatic, I'm sure."

"You didn't answer my question. Until that day?"

"Can you honestly tell me that if I invited you in, if we set up some semblance of a home, that you would leave me when I asked?"

She swallowed. "Yes, yes I would."

The right side of his mouth lifted and he wiped the last tear from her cheek. "You are a terrible liar, Bella."

"What if—What if I'm pregnant now, what then?"

His thumb paused on the edge of her cheekbone.

"You want children, Bella. I see it in your eyes every time you look at Audrey, at Calliope's two, at the children in the streets. I can see the hope in your eyes right now at the possibility of being pregnant. But any children I have would be tainted with my blood. My *pure*, rich blood," he said scathingly.

"And if I am?"

His hand dropped. "And if you are already pregnant? I don't know."

"You rejected me because of that. Because of what you deemed a grave mistake on your part."

"I don't want to be another mournful flower buried in your garden plot."

"And you think that I wouldn't mourn you anyway, relationship or not?"

He said nothing, but his eyes tightened.

"Do you love me at all? Even a little?"

Desperation. She couldn't help the desperation.

"I think I've always loved you, Bella." He said it so quietly that she had to strain to hear him.

Her mind spun, her emotions veering from irrepressible joy to confusion and terror. "What? Then why?"

"I've explained why."

He turned to go, and she had to leap forward to grab him.

"Marcus, none of this—the revelations, the pain—makes me love you any less."

"But deep down it will make you resent me more. It will keep you from some of the things that you desire so desperately. And all of that tears a hole deep within my heart."

Oh, God, he was leaving her. Leaving her when she'd never even known she had him. "I don't know what the future holds. And neither do you.

I could be hit by a carriage next week. I could fall down a flight of stairs. You don't know."

His hand knotted beneath hers. "No, but those are accidents. This is something that probably will happen, something that can be prepared for. Something known."

"I know that I don't want to be apart from you. To waste time we could have together."

"Bella—"

"*No* . . . no, don't say it."

She put her head down, leaned against his shoulder. "If—"

She cleared her suddenly hoarse throat.

"If you change your mind at all—even a little— I will be waiting."

She pressed her lips to his, memorizing the way they felt. The way he felt against her. Having him this near.

She didn't know if it would be the last time.

Chapter 25

Marcus ran a hand through his already mussed hair. He didn't know why he was here. No, he knew. But he still couldn't believe it.

He could blame it on too many long sleepless nights since he'd left Isabella at the Clarence rout. Too many nights of seeing her face and wondering about the future.

He could blame it on love and kittens and all that Byronic sap.

He could blame it on arrogance. Or justice. Or epiphanies. Or fate.

But it was all just a cover for hope. Hope. That thin thread, threatening to break completely free for years, had now started gathering bindings at an alarming rate. Bindings that he had striven to chip away at first. To cleave them. But it was a tenacious thing, hope. And somehow it had rebelled against him and taken control.

A thin butler answered the door and directed him to a small study near the back.

Blakely rested against the back of his chair insolently, but anger shone in his eyes. "Roth, to what do I owe the *pleasure*? I thought for sure my secretary must be mistaken at your summons to meet."

Marcus went for blunt force. "Why did you care for your brother Fred more in death than in life?"

"What is this?" Blakely half rose. "You dare come into my house—"

"Sit down, Blakely. I can help you out of your little predicament, but I want some answers in return."

Blakely's glare was white hot. "My little predicament? You help me? You have unbelievable nerve. Why someone hasn't taken you down before, I'll never know."

Irritation lashed against its bindings. "I cover my back. I make sure I have other options in place before my arrogance grows too large. I don't gamble away my fortunes and lands. I don't lose my betrothed out of stupidity." He narrowed his eyes. "Now answer the question."

"I lost Frederick," Blakely gritted out between clenched teeth. "I never appreciated him while he was living. He followed me around, got in my way. But after he was gone I missed that. Couldn't stand that he wasn't there annoying me at every turn. I vowed not to let it happen again—taking someone I cared about for granted."

He clasped his hands together a bit shakily. "But I was already in over my head by then. There was little I could do to salvage things. I really do love Lady Margaret." Blakely swallowed heavily—a large gulp of pride. "I don't want to lose her."

Marcus balled his fists. No, losing love was not an option. "That's why I'm going to help you."

"Because you care so much for lovers torn apart?" Blakely said scathingly.

Marcus looked back more calmly than he felt. "Because I can. And I carry some of the burden for your secrets finding their way to Banner's ears." He watched Blakely's eyes narrow. "Do you want my help?"

In another situation, Blakely's internal battle with his pride might have been amusing. Here, it was not. "Yes," he said with no little difficulty.

"I will give you the funds you need. You must show me that you will not use them foully. Not gamble them away."

"Why?"

Marcus raised a brow. "Because I ask it of you, and because I can give you back your credibility if you comply. I can give you back your betrothed with her father's blessing. But you have to make the change."

The hungry light lit Blakely's eyes on the second statement. Isabella had been right—Blakely truly did care. She had been right, and not just about this.

"What do you get in return?"

Marcus studied him, debating. "I get to sleep at night without seeing that pitiful yearning look in your eyes. But this is a onetime deal, Blakely."

Blakely took it. Marcus knew he would. He and Blakely were too alike in some respects.

They worked through the afternoon on the documents and funds Blakely would need, sarcastic and barbed comments underlying it all. Marcus left hours later thinking that someday he might even come to like the man.

He felt better. Lighter. Cleansed, if just a bit. Isabella would be pleased with him, if she knew.

And on that note, he had one more thing to do.

Marcus knocked on the door. A bright blond head appeared and looked at him in surprise. "Marcus?"

Who knew that hope could engender such fear?

"Stephen, I need to talk."

Chapter 26

Isabella took the steps one at a time, heavily. The sun was on its downward path, and she was weary. Her butler opened the door, and she smiled wearily at him as she handed him her pelisse and parasol.

She started to untie her bonnet. "Were there any callers while I was—"

A melody, high and steady, drifted from the back of the house. From the small, intimate room where she kept the upright.

Isabella passed her butler and moved cautiously down the hall, as if she would frighten away whoever was playing if she moved too fast.

She stood in the doorway and leaned a hand heavily against the frame in support. Marcus sat at the piano playing a lively piece of Mozart.

She watched as his fingers nimbly flowed down the keys, his eyes closed in concentration.

Their chess trophy sat on the piano lid. Had he just come to return it?

"Are you going to enter, Bella?"

He didn't open his eyes. She walked over and sat next to him on the short bench, their legs touching. She swallowed. She didn't dare hope.

"One of your favorites, is it not?" he asked.

"Yes."

"You always liked the more lively, uplifting tunes, while I preferred the dirges."

"No. I like anything that you play that shows your emotion. And that's nearly everything you play. It is the only time you let yourself go."

She thought of how he looked while making love and added, "Almost the only time."

His fingers stopped their motion and lifted off the keys. He opened his eyes to look at her.

"I have behaved very badly, haven't I, Bella?" he asked in a low tone, almost a whisper.

"I understand why you have done so."

"Ah, but understanding does not mean I haven't behaved badly."

"No," she whispered.

"And understanding is different from forgiveness."

"I forgive you."

His fingers touched her chin and finished untying her bonnet, lifting it and pulling it from her head.

"What do you forgive me for, Bella?"

"For lying to me."

"Yes." He pulled a pin from her hair.

"For hurting me."

"Yes." He freed another.

"For making me think you didn't love me."

His fingers traced her cheeks, her forehead, her chin. His fingers were soft, gentle, reverent. Her eyes slid shut and she felt him press his lips lightly to the lids.

"You won't need to forgive me again. I promise you."

A tear slid down her cheek and he kissed it.

"Don't cry, Bella."

She opened her eyes and saw the gentle look in his. His lips touched hers. Tears mingled with a gentle knot of unfolding passion as Marcus's unspoken declarations moved through her.

He pulled back and framed her face with both hands. "I'm taking the chance that my health will make us both miserable. That my illness will make you resent me and make me resent myself. That any children we have will be cursed with the same—having to watch us suffer, having to suffer themselves."

He shuddered. "And I am willing to do all within my power to make sure none of those things happen. To make us both happy instead. To love any children as a product of the two of us.

I will do anything to make sure that any children we have will not be cursed. That even if something happens to one of us, the other will see that bit, that spark, in a child, so as to not leave them behind."

"Oh, Marcus. I will never do that to our children."

"I know you won't. I *know*. But the doubts take time to calm, and until then, these things I pledge."

"And I pledge the same. We will beat this. Together. You know we will."

He closed his eyes and pressed a kiss to her forehead. "It is scary the things that I would do to be with you, Bella. To spend one more day with you. So yes, I have to believe we will."

Tears threatened to pour down her face, so she motioned to the settee in the corner. "I believe you promised to ravish me on the settee once, and never quite followed through."

He smiled, and for the first time, the shadows softened in his eyes.

"I'll need to remedy that posthaste."

His hands were gentle and reverent, and she returned the gestures with all the love she had. And when they finally came together, it was the most wonderful feeling—better than anything before, layered with love and understanding and hope.

And when she fell over the edge with him deliberately pulsing inside her, his eyes claiming her, needing her, she thought she would never feel more whole, more loved.

The completion that she so desperately desired flowed through her and produced another set of convulsions, the euphoria almost too much to bear.

He was looking at her as if she were the only person in the world.

She felt a tear escape.

"Don't cry, Bella. It seems that I am destined to make you cry."

"Tears of happiness, Marcus, tears of happiness. Don't push me away again."

He kissed her softly. "I won't. I promise I won't."

"I love you, Marcus."

"I know, Bella. I love you too. I will never stop."